JENEVEH PROJECT

QUENTIN COPE

COPYRIGHT & DISCLAIMER

The moral right of Quentin Cope to be identified as the author of this work has been assessed in accordance with the Copyright, Design and Patents Act, 1988.

This book is a work of fiction. However, some real events and places may have been referred to or been described and unless otherwise noted, the author and the publisher make no explicit guarantees as to the accuracy of the information contained in this book and in some cases, names of people and places may have been altered to protect their privacy. Any other resemblance to actual persons, living or dead, events or locales is entirely coincidental.

No part of this book may be reproduced, stored in a retrieval system, or transmitted by any means without the written permission of the author.

IMAGES: morguefile.com

Copyright © 2012 Quentin Cope

www.quentincope.co.uk

All rights reserved.
ISBN-10:1478347228
ISBN-13:978-1478347224

Also available in E-Book format

SURVIVAL
Keep it short and keep, it sweet,
Before thy maker thou doth meet

OTHER BOOKS BY QUENTIN COPE

Fiction
Nostradamus: The Last Christmas
The Unicorn Conspiracy
The Ludlum Prediction
The Doksany Legacy
Rosalind
Deliver By Moonlight

Non-Fiction
The Writers Useful Compendium
501 Writers Useful Phrases
501 '*MORE*' Writers Useful Phrases
501 Writers One-Liners
101 Fiction Writing Tips

Biography (Joint Authorship)
Tony Collins – Football Master Spy

CONTENTS

Ch 01	*An unwelcome intrusion ...*	1
Ch 02	*The Iranian Problem*	11
Ch 03	*A Daring Plan*	23
Ch 04	*The Gamble*	31
Ch 05	*The Plan*	41
Ch 06	*Abu Musa*	51
Ch 07	*The Decision*	73
Ch 08	*A Contract with the Devil*	85
Ch 09	*The London Conspiracy*	97
Ch 10	*Hong Kong*	115
Ch 11	*The Withdrawal*	131
Ch 12	*A Trip to Iraq*	141
Ch 13	*A Friend In Need ...*	159
Ch 14	*A Murder Most Foul*	169
Ch 15	*The Saboteur*	187
Ch 16	*An Unexpected Visitor*	197
Ch 17	*The Langley Decision*	211
Ch 18	*A Fatal Error*	223
Ch 19	*An Uncomfortable Matter*	239
Ch 20	*The Mysterious Enemy*	265
Ch 21	*Silent Surveillance*	285
Ch 22	*The Troublesome Turncoat*	295
Ch 23	*The Attack*	307
Ch 24	*Mission Accomplished?*	317
Ch 25	*The Disaster Unfolds*	329
Ch 26	*On The Run*	343
Ch 27	*A Near Miss*	357
Ch 28	*The Escape*	367
	Epilogue	379

Chapter One
An Unwelcome Intrusion ...

The powerful black 6-Series BMW sped through the tight Oxfordshire country lanes of England; the two men inside dressed immaculately: pin-striped black and grey three-piece suits, crisp white shirts and polished black shoes matching the expensive, finely worked hide of their attaché cases. They knew the address they were looking for and headed directly for the picture postcard, 16th Century red brick and thatch cottage - where they halted.

'Great spot,' said the driver.

The other, turning to leave the vehicle looked up at the house and simply said:

'Swinton!'

The taller one, lean, fit-looking with a straight-backed military bearing, knocked on the door to the cottage. It opened almost immediately. A blank faced but attractive, well presented thirty-something woman, barely concealed her irritation at being disturbed at home on such a rare, warm peaceful July Sunday morning.

'Yes?' she questioned

'We are looking for a Mr John Swinton?' queried the tall one.

'Would I be correct in assuming you may be Mrs Swinton?' he continued.

'I am ... and you are?' came the sharp reply.

'It's a business matter, Mrs Swinton'

Chapter One – An Unwelcome Intrusion ...

'It's Sunday.' She insisted.

'I offer my apologies ... but I'm afraid the matter is quite urgent.'

She studied them, their immaculate appearance dismissing any untoward suspicions, and sighed.

'Well, if you must!

'He's working,' she added, coolly ... showing them into a room at the rear of the property, obviously serving as a well used and generally untidy office.

A minute or two later, John Swinton entered, frowning ... quickly taking in the size and style of the two men standing before him.

'Who the hell are you?' he offered harshly.

'Its business,' stated the taller man.

'Important business, Mr Swinton' emphasized the other.

'I don't know you do I? What's so important that you have to arrive here on a Sunday with no call and no appointment ... err ... I'm afraid you will have to ...?'

'We represent certain commercial parties in the Middle East, with whom you have had dealings' interrupted the shorter one, who glanced pointedly at Swinton's wife, giving out a small, barely perceptible smile.

'I'm afraid there are matters we need to discuss – private matters sir'

All color began to drain from Swinton's tanned face.

'Sorry Charlotte, I know it's Sunday but ....'

Her irritation showed visibly as she turned away muttering to herself - and with a slam of the door - she was gone.

'Sorry about that' Swinton breathed 'You'd better sit down'

The tall man smiled, but his eyes remained cold and distant.

'No need' he said ominously 'this won't take long!'

Swinton felt a wave of physical sickness coming over him. He knew, in his heart of hearts that something like this was coming. The one hundred thousand pounds borrowed from Contec Financial Services had an interest tag of twenty thousand pounds. The final payment was due on the first of the month. It was now the tenth.

'Look, I — '

'Sit down at your nice desk, Mr Swinton,' ordered the shorter one.

Swinton hesitated.

'*Now*, please.'

Swinton obeyed … fear clearly etched on his face.

The tall one placed his black hide attaché case on the beautifully finished, leather-topped oak desk, flicked the catches open, spun it around and lifted the lid. Swinton saw the contents and recoiled immediately turning completely ashen. The case contained a shining steel axe with a polished wooden handle and a piece of A4 size paper, folded in two. The tall stranger took out the paper, placed it carefully on the desk in front of the transfixed businessman, let him see the axe for a further few seconds, shut the case firmly, locked it then swung it back by his side all in one fluid and possibly well practiced movement.

Panic welled up inside as John Swinton cautiously opened and quickly scanned the unfolded document in front of him.

'This is impossible!' he blurted.

The shorter one leaned over him and murmured.

Chapter One – An Unwelcome Intrusion ...

'I think you need to find a way to *make it possible* my friend!' and with that they left him without another word, let themselves out and drove unhurriedly away.

Swinton sat rooted to his executive chair with the cold sweat of fear dripping onto the unfolded paper in front of him. He stared at the figures and dates neatly typed on the otherwise plain sheet of paper, the murmured threat still warm at his ear:

"Make it possible"

"But how!"

He exhaled a long sigh of frustration, hearing his breath, uneven and shallow as he read the printed figure of £20,000 at the top of the sheet and the dates running down the left hand side until the fifteenth of the month; a figure of £1,000 written against each date. After the fifteenth, there was just a large handwritten question mark, and if he could find no answer to his dilemma - a question mark that now hung over his fate like the gleaming silver steel axe!

As the executive class BMW headed south down the M1 motorway towards London, a call was being made from the car phone; the connection unusually swift to the Persian Gulf State of Abu Nar. The shorter one laughed gruffly at something the man in Abu Nar had said; then without further word, replaced the handset in the cradle between the front seats and glanced at the driver. A smile passed between them.

"All done' the short one confirmed.

The two men had met their contact in Abu Nar some ten years previously when they were both serving as part of the British SAS. The three men, with similar values and some parallel experiences became three adventurers for a short while, spending most of their early time together getting rat faced in bars, legal and illegal, spread throughout the Arabian Peninsula. Their 'man in Abu Nar' was now heading up an International business empire. He had done well. In fact, he had done *very* well and they worked for him on a regular basis. This particular job was now done, a welcome donation would shortly be made to two offshore bank accounts and they could now get back to the more familiar skyline of London.

Declan Doyle stepped out of his silver grey Mercedes with the words from his favourite Queen track ringing in his ears.
Is this the real life?
Is this just fantasy?
He pushed the car door shut, making his way toward the rear entrance of his office building. He was smiling. Sometimes for Doyle it seemed his life in the tiny Gulf state of Abu Nar in 1987 really was fantasy.

This miniature Sheikdom was part of a collection of small tribal states located on the South side of what was known to America as the Persian Gulf, but to just about everyone else – the Arabian Gulf. All the Gulf States were up to their knees in oil and since the dramatic increase in crude prices in the early seventies, were now up to their navels in money. This was hard cash money; the kind that not only changed lives, but whole damn nations.

Declan was in fact living the day to day dream that the Gulf Sheiks had freely provided. He was 40 years old, physically fit and a multi millionaire in dollar terms. His oilfield engineering and supply company,

Chapter One – An Unwelcome Intrusion ...

Associated Oilfield, was an International operation and his Gulf business group, Contec, was turning over five million US dollars a month ... and climbing. He paid little or no tax to anyone and his companies produced profits that many others of similar size could only dream of.

It was six thirty in the morning and on this hazy July day the temperature was already twenty eight degrees. It was going to be hot ... perhaps in more ways than one.

Declan entered his office past a 'telex' machine with rolls of printed messages strewn over the floor as they had spilled out of the holding tray overnight. The telex machine was his reliable lifeline – his means of talking to every corner of the planet, twenty four hours a day.

He was hungry for a dollar. It was dog eat dog in his world. He was a tough man in his business life and equally rigid in his private life. With a name like 'Declan Doyle' many people who met him for the first time expected to hear a rhythmic southern Irish accent. He wasn't necessarily proud of being English, far from it, but he hated to be stereotyped as an Irishman, just because of his name.

Declan had a pretty busy day planned and to start he gathered up the first telex roll and began to cut it up into messages. As he finished slicing off the last one, the phone rang. He instinctively glanced up at his office wall clock. It was a little past a quarter to seven. He allowed the phone to ring for a second or two. Declan always felt he had a sixth sense in business and this time the 'sense' told him not to answer. Perhaps he should have listened.

It stopped ringing.

Declan's eyes refocused on the handset for a further

second or two. He began to turn away.

It rang again and this time he answered immediately.

It had begun.

The voice on the other end of the phone was acknowledged with a curt

'Yes Paddy, what can I do for you?'

Paddy Doherty, or to use his correct title, Colonel Brian Patrick Doherty - Retired, who actually *was* an Irishman, through and through, was the last person he expected to be receiving a call from at that hour.

'Well now young Declan' the Irishman replied 'How are things with you this bright and shiny ......'

Declan cut him short.

'Paddy, whatever it is you want, just spit it out. I don't have the energy for blarney and bullshit at this time in the morning'

Paddy was a shady, confusing and some considered sinister figure who at one time was a military training advisor to Sheik Omar, the ruler of Abu Nar. No one really knew what he did now, but he was under the sponsorship of the Defence Minister and Crown Prince of this bustling oil rich state. He was overweight and over age for most things now but Declan had always been a bit wary of him. Paddy was not prepared to ignore the undisguised rude manner of Declan's reply and now his tone stiffened.

'We need to meet *Mr Doyle* and we need to meet today' Paddy continued purposely in a lower, firmer tone, nearly spitting the words *Mr Doyle* in to the mouthpiece.

'I am a very busy man *Mr Doherty*, so tell me what it's about'.

Chapter One – An Unwelcome Intrusion ...

'The subject of our meeting cannot be discussed over the phone and you are to tell no one about it' Paddy replied quickly.

'I do not attend *meetings* that don't appear to have a subject - and unless you can find one that is interesting enough, I will be putting this phone down in approximately ten seconds' came the curt reply.

'I would advise you to attend this one Declan as someone, such as your lucky self, could, with my assistance and good offices, come out of it ...' he paused for obvious effect '... several million dollars better off!"

It was a simple statement.

It was a great hook for a man like Declan Doyle.

He considered what had just been said for a second or two.

'You will have to do better than that Paddy'

Declan was now very interested indeed, but felt that playing the conversation a little cautiously with the overblown Irishman, wouldn't go amiss. It didn't work.

'I will meet you in the lay-by at the ten mile point on the road to Hattami Fort at eleven o'clock ... and be alone!'

The surprisingly confident tones of the well connected ex-colonel forced Declan to ponder the situation. Was there really a potential pot of gold waiting for him half way down the desert road to Hattami? He would no doubt find out at eleven o'clock that day.

He put the phone down without another word. He knew he would be there. Paddy may not be so sure; so let him stew a little.

Declan settled back into his chair as he began to dissect the short conversation that had just ended and savour the question of what he could possibly do with *several million dollars* more'.

~~~~~~~~
~~~~

Chapter Two
The Iranian Problem

Two miles away, in a small block built villa, nestled between a clump of mature date palms and a patch of waste land, Paddy Doherty carefully put down the telephone handset. He was smiling to himself. It was a smile of satisfaction. He knew Declan Doyle, the Englishman with an Irish name, would be at the arranged meeting; he would not be able to resist. Paddy was sitting in a room he liked to call his 'office' He was waiting for a minute or two to calm down after his conversation with Doyle. He didn't like the man and sometimes it showed. The two had crossed swords before on a couple of occasions. Paddy had come out bruised from both of these verbal altercations. He was not generally a vindictive man, but to his way of thinking, there was something that didn't ring true about a man who was named Declan Doyle and totally denied he was Irish.

He picked up the handset again and rang a number at the American Consulate in Dubai. The call was immediately connected and Paddy spoke for a second or two.

There was no sound from the other end, no greeting, no recognition and no goodbye. Once Paddy had spoken, the line was disconnected. Paddy felt a little flushed as he slammed down the phone.

'Rude bastard' he shouted out loud.

Paddy could shout as loud as he wanted, but it would

Chapter Two – The Iranian Problem

make no difference. His blood pressure was up and he had started to sweat again. He was too old for all this crap, and now he would ponder for a while the length of spoon he would need to safely sup with the particular set of devils squeezing his 'nuts' right now!

~~~~~~

It was damned hot. Declan sat in his car in the lay-by a few miles down the road from the fifteenth century mud fort at Hattami. It was three minutes to eleven by his wrist watch and one minute earlier by his car clock. The outside air temperature was rising past 35 degrees and humidity close to 90 percent. The car air conditioner, as good as Mercedes make them, was struggling to keep up. Paddy's old and slightly weather-beaten, Volvo appeared in the distance.

He was on time.

Slumping unsteadily into the passenger seat of Declan's car, Paddy had a not unexpected sweat on and wiped his brow several times with a grubby, grey coloured cotton handkerchief before offering a greeting. There was not much 'bonhomie' between the two men and despite the climbing outside air temperature, the atmosphere inside the Mercedes was somewhat icy. There was little or no eye contact as the discussion began.

Paddy started by recounting the continuing situation with the Gulf War between the Iraqis and Iranians. Paddy was well informed, as he should be. Declan had long considered him as the possible eyes and ears of a hidden away intelligence operation, probably buried in the bowels of some nondescript Victorian building in

London's Whitehall. Declan was of the opinion that a really good war was also *really* good for business and certainly on the South side of the Gulf, that was very much the case.

'The war is not going well for Iran' Paddy continued.

'The world's largest offshore oil terminal at Kharg Island has been literally bombed to bits since 1982 by the Iraqis and despite constant rebuilding, as soon as production restarts, the bloody Iraqis bomb it again - and they are remarkably good at it too' he added.

'But surely they have a good outlet from land based oil fields in the North' replied Declan.

Paddy paused for a second, annoyed at the interruption, and then went on to explain that production in the North had been badly hit being so near to Iraqi borders and the single low capacity pipeline down to the coast at Bandar Abbas was just about all that was left.

'The big problem is that all the loading facilities are built for large or very large crude oil tankers and since the recent acquisition by Saddam of the infamous Exocet anti-ship missile *and* the means to deliver it - the export of oil in any reasonable quantity has more or less ceased'

Declan knew the efficiency of the French made Exocet, as did the British Navy from their painful experience during the Falklands conflict. Even in the hands of an idiot, the Exocet was a formidable weapon.

'They are in the shit Declan and if they are going to survive, something needs to be done'. Declan remained silent. This could not be taken as a sign of encouragement from the continuingly perspiring ex-colonel sitting next to him. Words now spilled from

Chapter Two – The Iranian Problem

Paddy's mouth, his damp forehead constantly attended to with a quick and nervous dabbing movement of the grubby handkerchief.

From what Declan knew of him, this obvious show of nervousness was untypical of the man.

'Oil output in Iran is now down to around 600,000 barrels a day and falling. They can produce oil Declan ... as much bloody oil as they need ... but they can't get it out! To put the matter simply, if this carries on, they will very shortly run out of money. If they run out of money, they will lose the war. If they lose the war, that territory hungry bloody madman, Saddam Hussein, will walk into Iran ... and with yet another blind eye turned by the so called super powers, immediately turn his attention to the Arab states on the South side of the Gulf!'

He paused for a second to let the real meaning of the words sink in.

'Think about it my friend. That means *here*, right *here!* How long do you think your miniscule little empire would last with an Iraqi jack boot kicking your office windows in every bloody weekend?' He leaned back; more confident now ... and continued.

'This whole damned thing is running away from the Yanks. They simply can't control Saddam and the British are actually shitting themselves. The Russians of course, are watching the whole situation very, very carefully, but they have their hands full in Afghanistan and the Chinese, as ever, remain inscrutable'

Paddy leaned back into the passenger seat, mopped his brow yet again and wiped a now obvious trail of saliva from the corner of his mouth. Declan was paying full attention as he asked coolly.

'So what do you need from me Paddy?'
'You mean officially?'
'Yes'
'Well, I'll tell you ... officially. The Abu Nar Defence Minister would like to know how crude exports can be increased by Iran, possibly using the already substantial Iranian owned coastal tanker fleet. The question is simple and the answer may be complicated, but whatever *it* is, *it* has to happen now - not in six months, not in twelve months - it has to happen *now* !'

Paddy slapped a dampened thigh excitedly with an open hand to emphasize the word 'now'. He was trembling noticeably, dripping beads of sweat on to the grubby, creased trousers of his standard dress for literally all occasions - a regulation military cut, light-brown safari suit. He instinctively reached toward the air-conditioning control.

It was fully up.

Even Declan was becoming a little unsettled now. He had never seen Paddy in such an agitated state. Declan weighed up the situation for about thirty seconds and then asked cautiously.

'When you say the Defence Minister of Abu *Nar wants to know*, who I assume you actually work for; I suspect that you actually mean Hossein Mousavi, the Iranian Prime Minister ... *wants to know*?'

Paddy nodded his head in nervous agreement.

'So let me ask you this. If I did come up with a solution to the problem, who would actually be paying me?'

There followed a slightly pregnant pause as Paddy screwed up his face and with a long, outward sigh, reluctantly raised a bowed head to now look Declan straight in the eye. The words tumbled out quickly.

Chapter Two – The Iranian Problem

'This project will be run by the IRGC. They will be responsible for payment and, as far as you are concerned, all other aspects of the job'

It was now Declan's turn to wipe a dampened brow as he attempted to quickly digest and place in reasonable order the words that Paddy had just delivered to him. He was less than happy ... and it showed. The IRGC were better known as the Iranian Revolutionary Guard, a powerful and ruthless organisation of right wing religious stalwarts who were well funded, well trained and known to have strong and convincingly unhealthy connections with just about every major terrorist group in the world.

'Your paymaster will be Mohsen Raza' Paddy added hastily in a barely perceptible murmur.

At this, Declan's face flushed involuntarily. The consequences of doing any kind of business with the much feared head of the 'Rev Guard,' one Mohsen Raza could be dire indeed. This was a most dangerous individual, labelled with an International reputation. Even the Israelis were wary of him. If anything went wrong with Raza in charge - heads would roll and that would be in the most literal of senses. Declan felt it was perhaps time to start backing away.

'Look Paddy, to be frank with you, this all sounds a bit *not my sort of thing...*'

He was cut off by the desperate looking Irishman who waved an admonishing finger, raising the tone of his voice to a near teeth grinding screech.

'Now you look here Declan ... you son-of-a-bitch, you damn well need to come up with something - for your own benefit – not for mine! I am advising you that whatever the outcome, you have to at least look as if you've tried to come up with a reasonable solution. There is a lot at stake here. My Sheik is not a happy man and if you simply turn down a request to even *look* at what could be done, then you may find renewing all of your very comfortable trade licence arrangements in Abu Nar much more difficult in the future. If Iran falls over my friend, we will all be fucked. This request has come to my man directly from Mohsen Raza himself!' As Paddy spoke, Declan's overriding thought was that whatever needed to be done, or in fact could actually be done - it would not be cheap.

He turned his business hat on.

'But why me Paddy, why not put your proposition to some of the big boys like Hall Burton or McDaniels?'

'Raza cannot work with organisations that are infiltrated at every level by the CIA' he paused, choosing his words carefully. '… and the US State Department is not about to allow any American company to do anything to assist the Iranians. In fact, you must well know that they are up to their arse in intelligence backing for Iraq right now. No sir. This has to be handled by someone who has no reputation to lose, is not connected to any *spook* organisations and has the distinct possibility of pulling it *off* … whatever *it* may turn out to be!'

There were one or two convincing arguments in there somewhere, Declan thought, and although the *'no reputation to lose'* reasoning hurt a little, he shrugged it off mentally and began to think more positively about the possibility of some large sums of money exchanging hands.

'OK Paddy, I'll have a look at it but I will need a lot of researched information ….'

Chapter Two – The Iranian Problem

Paddy interrupted immediately, excitedly telling Declan he had a load of maps, charts, production figures, pipeline profiles and pumping station capacities in his car and he jumped out to retrieve them. They were all stamped by the National Iranian Oil Company, and filled the back seat of Declan's Mercedes. As he firmly closed the door, Paddy turned abruptly. He had found some new levels of courage from somewhere. The voice, however, was still shaky.

'You have five days to come up with something and if one word of this is breathed to a living soul...'

The threat was violently cut short as Declan grabbed the Irishman by the lapels of the sweat stained and near shapeless safari suit jacket and pushed him hard against the rear door of the car. Patience had finally deserted him.

'Let me assure you of one simple thing Paddy. If the job can be done, I can do it. Whether I would *want* to do it for your particular client is another subject. If this job is to be done, it will be impossible to keep it a secret ... and before you start threatening me, you should remember that I have long arms too. If anything goes sideways here, that I feel has your scheming little cloak and dagger hand anywhere near it, someone will be paying your extended family in Ireland a visit.'

The squarely delivered statement appeared to have the right effect. Paddy's face had taken on a noticeable pallor and his hands, protectively clasped over Declan's wrists trembled uncontrollably.

Without further word, Declan released his hold on the jacket as Paddy, with a stumbling, awkward gait, moved quickly to his car and drove off in a haze of rising, choking sand dust - with not even a glance back in Declan's direction. The sun at its near midday height was in his eyes as the voluminous cloud gradually settled and eventually dissipated.

There was a momentary flash on the low mountain top marking the boundary of the Hattami Valley to his left. It could have been anything. A reflection from an old tin can dropped by an uncaring ex-pat weekend explorer, a flash from the glass of a cheap watch owned by a local herdsman, or even an unintended reflection from the coated front lens of some powerful Bausch & Lomb military binoculars. He caught the location and instinctively turned back in the general direction to see if it would happen again. It didn't and as he was now in a hurry to get back to his office he attached no significance to it.

As things were about to turn out, this was Declan Doyle's first mistake.

~~~~~~

The drive back to the Sabeen Road office took about fifteen minutes. Declan's mind was in full compute mode all the way. He knew the facilities at Kharg Island. He had done work there. The actual job was worth a few million much needed dollars at the time, but was also a job he wanted to forget. He had … up until now.

~~~~~~

Back in his office, Declan continued to ponder the situation surrounding the unusual and possibly unhealthy opportunity that had just been put in front of

Chapter Two – The Iranian Problem

him. The inherent risks were that whatever he managed to come up with, the whole execution process would have to be played out in the front line of a major war.

'Could he keep it all under control?' he asked himself several times. This was a very big question indeed. He knew he had the balls but did he have the ability?

As he continued to think carefully through the probable pitfalls, he reasoned that in fact it was the political element that was more worrying than any of the yet unknown practical issues. The success or failure of a project such as this, could have a lasting effect on the future of the whole of the Gulf region. From the outset, it appeared to be an onerous responsibility.

For the Americans to let Saddam Hussein loose on Iran - had been a mistake. On the other hand, Ayatollah Khomeini was regarded by most western politicians as a dangerous right wing Islamist. He had already shown the Americans that nothing would be kept sacred to dull the aims and aspirations of the Islamic revolution. He had ordered the holding of a considerable number of American diplomatic staff hostage in Tehran towards the end of nineteen seventy nine, which prompted the highly embarrassing and failed hostage rescue attempt, along with the eventual 'exchange for arms' deal that ultimately brought the hostages back home.

Greed or ambition, depending upon a particular point of view, was fighting common sense.

Greed would become the eventual victor.

What Declan didn't know, whilst making his decision, was that the conversation he had just had with Col Paddy Doherty would in fact change the whole course of his life and the lives of many others around him. To him, business was simply a game and the riskier the business the better the game. Declan had made the decision.

He would definitely go for it ...

As far as he was concerned - the game was on.

~~~~~~~~
~~~~

Chapter Three
A Daring Plan

Declan arrived at the gates of the Abu Nar Oilfield Supply Centre at exactly five minutes to six o'clock. The early morning temperature was a comfortable twenty three degrees and humidity well down from the average summer highs of ninety percent plus. After his meeting the day previously with Paddy, Declan had made phone calls, some of which carried on well into the night. However, for the few hours he had left, he slept soundly and was up at five, showered, sorted and ready to go.

One of his first calls had been to Byron Hamilton, the owner of the Abu Nar Oilfield Supply Centre, perfectly located down on the creek side. Eight work boats were tied up, loading and unloading equipment with one small three legged jack-up rig tucked in at the end of the quay side under repairs of some kind. It was a busy place. The man who owned it was even busier and that was why Declan had arranged to meet him at six o'clock this very morning.

Declan entered Byron's office. The ashtray, perched precariously on the edge of his desk, was already full and the yellow fingered Canadian had another cigarette

Chapter Three – A Daring Plan

on the go. The smoke filled room felt claustrophobic and noisy with a window mounted 'wall banger' air-conditioning unit that had seen much better days, thrashing away behind him. Byron had been in Abu Nar a long time; longer than Declan. He was a hard headed old Oilfield hand who had fallen on his feet. He worked hard and didn't know it any other way. He also had contacts with just about everybody in the oil business worth knowing - and one or two that weren't.

The first cup of coffee arrived and Declan began the conversation. It took about an hour to explain the whole situation as it had been described to him, with a few viewpoints of his own thrown in where necessary. Byron interrupted rarely and when he did it was just to clarify the odd point here and there. Declan could make out the tell tale signs of growing interest with Byron's normally bland expression turning more sanguine as the story unwound. By the time he got to what he considered to be the end, Byron had become perceptibly energised.

'Well Declan, you may already know that we are doing a lot of work at the moment on Sirri Island for the NIOC. The situation right now on Sirri is unclear. The Iraqis attacked in some force again only recently. The small refinery is out of action, all main power sources are just about shot to ribbons and that boat you see loading there -' Byron pointed out of the slightly grimy window towards the quay ' - is full of the largest generators we could find just to keep the construction facilities going. 'So what's the overall situation … from your viewpoint?'

'It's not good my friend. The Abadan Refinery went years ago. The Petrochem Plant at Bandar e Khomeini is only half complete and on hold. Kharg Island is now completely out and so the tanker shuttle to Sirri has stopped'

Byron leant back in the creaky timber and green faux leather desk chair, spinning a plastic pen between his fingers.

'So, the whole story so far seems feasible?'

Byron thought carefully before replying.

'I would say they are pretty desperate. The Iranians are running out of money. The monkeys are taking over the damned zoo. We will not accept any form of payment from the NIOC now except for irrevocable International Letters of Credit, confirmed on an International Bank *outside* of Iran'.

'Well, can we have a look at all the possible options?'

Another welcome cup of coffee arrived and Byron, who had been scribbling notes regularly on a lined A4 pad for the past hour, moved to the wall behind his desk, where hung an exceptionally large, laminated colour map of the Gulf. He began to think out loud, for Declan's benefit, about what options could actually be available to a struggling Ayatollah Khomeini. The

Chapter Three – A Daring Plan

biggest enemy as far as he was concerned, was not the Iraqi's but simply 'time' itself. The map that Byron was studying showed most of the known or working Gulf oilfields, including the major Iranian onshore and offshore operations.

Kharg Island, located about sixteen miles from the Geneveh shore line, was where the collected oil product linked up for export on massive ocean going tankers. Longer than the Empire State Building is tall ... and displacing over half a million tons, this type of vessel provided a massive target for a modern air delivered missile. The only way the Iranians could get oil out by sea was to use their own uninsured fleet of coastal tankers in a risk laden attempt to ferry oil, in smaller quantities, to the terminal on Sirri Island near the Straits of Hormuz. Unless a replacement for the loading terminal at Kharg could be found, the consequences for the NIOC were dire.

The modern way to solve the problem would be to put a Buoy Mooring System somewhere. This literally was a ballasted steel buoy, only a few metres wide, two thirds submerged, floating in the sea and moored using a series of steel cables attached to the sea-bed. This was known as a Single Point Mooring or SPM. The technology had come a long way in the past few years but the problem was that a pipeline had to be laid from the shore to the SPM to provide an oil supply. This involved a substantially sized pipe laying vessel or barge to be employed with the pipe being 'pulled' from the vessel and laid to an accurate line underwater. This was also a very large and not very athletic target for Saddam's newly acquired Exocets. The head scratching continued. More coffee came. Silence ruled for several minutes.

Declan's brain was operating in quiet overdrive as he leant back in to the fake Chesterfield with eyes closed in some level of contemplation, blanking out all the industrial sounds surrounding him. He was picturing the whole process of the pipe being laid, the pipe appearing out of the water and disappearing up the beach to the pumping station. As clear as day, looking up the beach, he could see the men working on the final welds; looking out to sea, the lay barge on the distant horizon and in between, on the surface, nothing, no sign that a pipe was being laid at all, absolutely nothing.

That was it

Declan's eyes sprang wide open as he pushed himself up from his uncomfortable seat.

'Instead of pulling a pipe from a barge, why the hell don't we pull it from the beach' he exclaimed.

He turned to face the old oilfield hand, expecting a reaction of some sort from Byron.

There was none.

Declan persisted.

'If we can pull a pipe from the beach into the water,

Chapter Three – A Daring Plan

there will be no real target for the Iraqi's to hit. There will be *no* lay barge. Don't you see Byron for god's sake - there will be no *bloody* lay barge. This is the way forward my friend, an SPM, a single point mooring! We can surely get the Iranians to provide some sensible protection onshore so we have just got to come up with a way of feeding the pipe out to sea from a manufacturing facility based *on* shore…not *off* shore!'.

Byron's leathery, tanned and craggy features appeared to crack perceptibly as he began to absorb the seemingly inspired uttering's of an elated Declan. Slowly but surely the gentle change of expression morphed in to a full smile.

He spoke.

'I don't think that pulling a pipe to an SPM from land to sea has ever been done before Declan - however, that doesn't mean it can't be done' Byron added quickly.

'But, can *we* do it Byron?' questioned an agitated Declan.

'We will have to find out … and the only way to do that is to make a few phone calls. I know of an operation in Singapore that could possibly handle the engineering, but the big question will be time'.

Byron fell back into his chair and reached for the telephone. 'Now bugger off Doyle and leave it to me' he said irritably. 'I will get back to you later today' adding in a firm voice … 'and do *not* ring me … I will ring *you*' Declan's step was substantially lighter as he strode purposely out of Byron's office and back to his car. He knew if anyone could come up with the right solution, this man could.

The Abu Nar entrepreneur now felt somewhat more confident than he had when he arrived at the Oilfield Supply Centre that morning. It was eleven thirty and bloody hot. The meeting had finished earlier than he had expected so there was time for a quick call in at the office before thinking about a liquid lunch.

~~~~~~~~
~~~~

Chapter Four
The Gamble

The lunch venue was chosen as the Country Club for one sensible reason … Declan was the Chairman.

Penny was waiting for him. With all that had been going on, Declan had not seen her for a few days. Their 'association' was not necessarily unusual and one that suited both parties - or so Declan told himself. He did not want a 'live in' relationship; he was too busy making money. Abu Nar also had some strict rules about non-married couples living together and no way was Declan marrying anyone right now. Penny did not want a permanent situation either - or so she said. Penny regarded marriage as a conversation between two consenting adults that would eventually be allowed to get out of hand. She was several years younger than Declan and officially she worked for one of his companies which supplied her with an income, a flat to live in, a car to drive and a residence visa to make her existence legal. However, she occupied her time, and harvested significant amounts of well earned money working for a real estate business in Dubai. Penny was, in all respects, Declan's 'girl'. It was a 'suitable arrangement'

Declan glanced at his watch. He wanted to get out of

Chapter Four – The Gamble

there before the heavy drinking gang assembled, as they did every Thursday lunch time. Even worse, would be an invasion by this week's tribe of opportunity hungry 'Brit' salesmen searching him out to make all their dreams come true. They were generally a pain in the backside, often very, very insistent and regularly solicited a rude response to an inappropriate approach.

Declan had decided he would arrange to meet Penny later that evening for dinner at his villa. Penny noted that Declan was in a pensive mood and commented on it.

'What's up Declan?

'Sorry?' he questioned.

'What's up with you today? You seem very far away. Is it something I've done?' she queried.

'No ... no, it's nothing you've done, it's just that I have a lot on at work right now and a few hard decisions have to be made'

'But I thought everything was going so well! ...' Declan cut her short and reached for her hand across the table.

'Everything is fine Penny. What about meeting up later at my place? I'll cook you some dinner - and I promise, you will get my *full* attention'

Her smile was a knowing one as she took his hand and caressed it very gently. Penny was not a beautiful woman. She was much better than that. She was a handsome woman and one of her smiles could light up a complete room or have men young and old succumb to her charms in a second. She got up from her chair, moved over to Declan and kissed him gently on the cheek.

'I look forward to that' she whispered and then glided her way across the room turning a few heads at the bar as she went. As he was driving away from the Country Club, Declan received a call on his car phone from Byron. Dinner would have to be cancelled and after he put the phone down, he rang Penny's number, leaving a message.

She would be pissed off.

He had agreed to meet with Byron in his compound at seven o'clock that evening. Declan had tried to extract more information about what Byron had come up with to no avail. He would have to wait until the evening.

~~~~~~

When Declan arrived at Byron's residence it was exactly seven o'clock. As he approached the large steel double gates to the walled compound, a uniformed guard swung one aside and let Declan's car through with a salute and a smile. The villa he was heading for was located at the far side of the compound.

Byron's head houseboy met him at the door and showed him in to a spacious, beautifully furnished split

Chapter Four – The Gamble

level lounge area. The unpretentious Canadian would have preferred a grubby old trailer caravan sat next to a drilling rig somewhere out in the desert where he could listen to the comforting hum of a Cat Diesel generator all night. Unfortunately, his sponsor, Sheik Khalid did not see it that way and therefore Byron had been forced to learn the ways of socialising, accepting his status in the local community and the living of the Abu Nar dream.

A large glass of iced lager was waiting for him on a kidney shaped coffee table placed between two comfortable looking cushioned chairs. Declan occupied one and as he sat down, Byron appeared.

Byron was not one for small talk and appeared eager to move straight to the moment where they had broken off their last discussion.

'Firstly, let me confirm that pulling a large pipeline from land to sea has not really been done before' he stated.

'Some years ago in Sarawak an attempt had been made to pull an eighteen inch diameter pipe two miles to a damaged well head. The contractor had used winches in combination with a head frame and pulley blocks to pull the pipe out to sea … but it didn't go well and was eventually abandoned'.

Byron went on to tell a visibly disappointed Declan that he had been in contact with the engineering people of Ocean Marine in Singapore. They had studied the

Sarawak project carefully and felt they had rooted out the problems. Declan's features took on a brighter look.

'However' Byron continued '… to provide any useful capacity to an oil loading station, the undersea pipe line would need to be at least twenty four inches in diameter' Byron's normal calmness was edging away. He moved in closer to Declan in order to make his point.

'Listen Declan … I think this damned job can be done' the tone of his voice was rising steadily in excitement.

'Instead of trying to drag an ever increasing dead weight across a relatively abrasive surface such as a sand and gravel beach, the way to go would be to lift the whole damn thing and push it'.

Byron took in Declan's studious expression for a second or two, expecting a reaction.

There was just a glimmer and with that Byron took some form of encouragement and carried on.

'The way to do that' he announced, pausing for effect

'… is to use tracked pipe layers'

Declan was left computing hard in an attempt to fit together the odd elements of the jig saw being formed by Byron's revealing words. The biggest standard pipe layers that Declan knew of were Caterpillar D9 models. They were not easy to get hold off. 'On initial estimates, we will need about six big Cat's on the lift and two in reserve. The whole process is simple' Byron was nearly

Chapter Four – The Gamble

shouting now. 'OK … OK Byron – just bring it down a little' Declan requested with a forgiving smile.

'How the hell do we weld possibly miles of 24 inch pipe together and then lift it without it breaking?.

'This is the genius of the plan Declan' Byron continued excitedly.

'A steel bed will be constructed to lay three six metre pipes together. This will be fitted with two sets of powered rollers. One set will rotate the pipes as they are being welded. The second set will transport the pipe forward when joined … to lay in the cradles of the D9 tractors. The pipes will be completely supported throughout this delicate welding and movement process. A portable X-Ray unit will run on tracks, scanning the welds before the pipe is moved and as each section is added, the pipe layers will simply track forward in line at the side of a pre-dug trench. In the trench, the pipe will be supported on more passive steel cradles, again fitted with rollers - until it hits the water line'

Byron was now alight with enthusiasm leaving Declan still trying to catch up, to actually picture the whole process in his mind.

Byron had stopped talking and the required image was gradually firming up for Declan.

'You need to tell me more Byron'

'The trench and the Cat's can all be provided with a good enough camouflage cover, they would be damned hard to spot from the air. As the pipe hits the water, a plate will be welded on each end to form an airtight tube. That tube will be filled with compressed air just enough to maintain buoyancy and float the seaward end of the pipe in the water - halfway between the sea-bed and the surface'. Declan's eyes were now half closed as he pictured the scene. It was dawning on him. This was possible, this could be done.

As if to confirm this as yet unspoken conclusion, Byron shouted.

'Come on Declan, wake up for god's sake - this *can* be done'

Declan's eyes were now wide open as the big question came rummaging to the surface.

'But can it be done in a sensible *time* scale Byron? Can it be done in *time*?

'It can be done, with a tight programme, in a few months and the engineering can start as soon as some money is released in to the system Declan' Byron replied confidently and added

'But my big question is – Can you *handle* it? ... and more importantly, can you damn well *finance* it?'

The two men locked eyes in a searching gaze for a few silent seconds. The atmosphere was expectedly tense. They were both looking for the same, possibly elusive assurance in each other; an assurance that could be translated in to unquestionable *trust*. Not actual trust in the plan, not trust in the people who would have to

Chapter Four – The Gamble

work the plan, but simple, unswerving trust in each other.

Without averting an eye Declan replied quietly but firmly

'Yes'.

After a further few lingering seconds, Byron looked away. He seemed satisfied. He moved over to a large flight bag sitting by a window and re-sited it next to the glass topped coffee table. It was now time to get in to some detail.

Declan mused for a short while over what had just been discussed. It appeared the job could be *could* be done. It could also be done within a matter of months and the engineering *could* start as soon as some money was released by the Iranian paymasters. It was Declan's turn now - and he had a hundred questions for Byron as the two men talked animatedly through the best part of the remainder of the night.

A sleep deprived Declan Doyle threw himself in to bed at just before four o'clock the following morning. There were a couple of non-complimentary messages on his house phone answering machine from a very annoyed Penny and one from his right hand man, Andy about having to 'get rid' of one of his ex-pat engineers, currently languishing in the Dahfra police cells. Several beers too many at the Rugby Club bar the previous evening, were identified as the cause. He would be on a plane first thing that very morning. Declan's head was buzzing but he knew he needed sleep. The next few days were going to be busy and stressful. Byron would cost up the operation from trap to line and produce an initial project plan for Monday ... just three full days, and over a European weekend as well. To lubricate the wheels and show a suitable sign of commitment to Byron, Declan would transfer fifty thousand US Dollars to the Oilfields account later that day.

'There are no 'week ends' in the oil business' Byron confirmed confidently with his promise, leaving Declan feeling somewhat assured and as a result was sound asleep in less than ten minutes.

Over the following three days, Declan and Byron were pushed in to working sixteen to eighteen hour shifts as were most of the stretched, tired and sometimes grumpy staff in Declan's office and the Oilfield Supply Centre. The task of putting such a massive project together in such a short period of time was daunting, but one by one, the hundreds of files, messages, estimates and project programmes were being gradually condensed in to one single, bulky project file and further down in to a condensed outline consisting of just four closely typed sheets of A4 paper.

Everyone involved had been sworn to secrecy knowing that any slight rumour at this stage would probably end up with some of them following the same

Chapter Four – The Gamble

route as the errant and hung over engineer who had left Abu Nar on a one way ticket early on Friday morning.

Declan made the call to Paddy Doherty late on Sunday afternoon making arrangements to meet the following day. Again, Paddy insisted on some sort of 'neutral' venue. He was totally obsessed with his 'cloak and dagger' security tactics and finally Declan grudgingly agreed to meet in a room that Paddy would book at the Ras Al Khaimah International Hotel. Despite its impressive title, the whole property was a dump and Declan was not particularly looking forward to his meeting ... set for eleven o'clock in the morning.

~~~~~~~~
~~~~

Chapter Five
The Plan

The drive to Ras Al Khaimah was uneventful. In response to Declan's enquiry at the hotel desk, a brightly mannered and well spoken Indian receptionist advised him that a Mr Doherty was already waiting for him in room one zero four. As the room was only on the first floor, Declan used the stairway, quickly located the room and knocked the door a couple of times. Paddy had a pint of chilled beer in one hand as Declan entered the room and indicated with the other towards a large ice bucket nurturing three more unopened cans.

Paddy had got it right so far.

The window mounted air conditioning unit was making a hell of a racket but was in fact blowing some discernible amount of recycled, but gratefully received, cooling air. Declan lowered himself in to one of the three thinly upholstered chairs gathered around the low table.

Paddy sat opposite Declan, remaining disturbingly quiet after the initial polite greetings had been dispensed with. He took out a grubby looking handkerchief, wiping his brow with it before focusing back on his guest. There was little point in messing about with too many niceties, so Declan got stuck in.

Chapter Five – The Plan

He had with him a large file containing substantial detail about the project ... and the four sheets of A4 paper that simply, but effectively, outlined the plan.

Paddy may have been many things, but he was no engineer. All he wanted to know was 'could it be done? what would it cost? how long would it take?' Declan handed Paddy the four sheets of paper and whilst he was eagerly reading through them, Declan began to describe what was on offer.

The plan, Declan explained, was to put a single point mooring facility known simply as an SPM in the straits between Kharg Island and Geneveh, five miles out from the Geneveh shoreline in about one hundred and twenty feet of water. The completed facility would be able to load small coastal tankers at a rate of 4,000 tonnes or approx 25,000 barrels of heavy crude oil an hour. If an attack of any kind was imminent, the tanker could get under way immediately providing a less vulnerable target than a stationary VLCC hooked up to a quay side facility.

In theory, the SPM would be able to load over half a million barrels a day, which would nearly double the current but severely declining 600,000 barrels per day achieved the previous month. Even at the current price of nearly eighteen US dollars a barrel, an extra nine million dollars a day would provide the lifeline that Mr Mousavi and the hard pressed Iranians desperately needed. Paddy was on his second read of the papers spread out in front of him. Was he actually taking on board anything that Declan was saying to him? Declan carried on.

'That's the plan Paddy, but there are one or two small problems to master'

Paddy looked up from the papers apprehensively. He had heard the word 'problems' and was now all ears.

'The first *problem*, which isn't a real difficulty, is that the SPM has to be connected somehow to the shore by a pipeline. The pipe will need to be twenty four inches in diameter and it can't be laid from a barge'.

There was a Hollywood pause. Paddy remained silent; his damp, creased brow and raised eyebrows underlining a curious, questioning look.

'Using a lay barge some one hundred and twenty feet long, displacing around eighteen thousand tons and hanging on the end of a twenty four inch steel pipe, would present a unique and more or less stationary target for Saddam's newly acquired Exocet missiles'

There was another telling pause as Declan took a breath. The bad news was next!

'The only way to connect the SPM is to pull a pipe from the shore – and that's the real problem – it's never been done before'

Paddy's face immediately took on a painful expression, perspiration breaking out again like a hot shower. The urge was there to say something, but what?

Chapter Five – The Plan

He tasked himself to remain controlled and silent.

Declan continued.

'The thing that connects the pipe from the shoreline to the SPM is called a pipeline end manifold or PLEM. This will be a complex and expensive structure for this particular application and will be especially designed and manufactured as a one off.'

Again, although he felt prompted to say something, Paddy remained taciturn as he proceeded to open his second can of beer.

'This highly crucial element of the whole project will be about eighty metres long, thirty metres wide and cost around thirty five million dollars.'

'Jesus Christ…' Paddy breathed quietly.

'To install the massive manifold section, the whole unit would have to be on the surface for around twenty four hours as it's positioned and lowered in to over one hundred feet of water. Once it's on the sea floor, it could be considered safe'.

There was a long pause now as Paddy took time to gulp down some of the cool beer straight from the can. He finally spoke.

'Could be?'

'Could be'

'So what you're telling me is that your hair brained scheme consists of two key elements. One has never been done before and the other, most crucial element, will be sitting on the surface for at least twenty four hours enabling the bloody Iraqis to carry out target practice until they actually blow it to shit – that's really what your telling me then!'

Paddy took another nervous swig of his beer. 'What kind of guarantees are on the table Declan, because as it stands … and I am *no* engineer, the plan you propose seems to be fairly unworkable?'

'Well Paddy, it's all we have and as far as I am concerned, I'm pretty convinced it will work. If I didn't think that – I wouldn't be here' he stated with a firm edge to his voice.

Paddy paced the room with beer can in one hand and grubby handkerchief in the other. Declan thought, yet again, the man seemed very, very nervous. Surely his head couldn't be on the block for this one, he was simply the messenger – wasn't he?

Was there something else was going on here?

Declan spoke again, choosing his words carefully.

'The vessels and equipment required for the job will be insured by the contractors who will provide on-site services, as will the men who will work in the relevant danger zones. However, the manifold can only be insured under a conflict zone contract for a listed total loss, such as an attack by an established enemy or loss at sea during towing. I have to tell you that the possible claim window is very narrow and the premium is horrifically high, but we have actually found a company who will insure it on a total loss basis. Just about

Chapter Five – The Plan

everyone else in the marine insurance business has declined to quote' Paddy sat down, still clutching his can of half consumed beer 'For God's sake ... it gets even worse' he muttered, more to himself than offering some form of useful comment. Then he posed the expected question.

'What kind of protection will the Iranians have to come up with?'

'This is crucial Paddy. They will have to provide twenty four hour air cover, have some good ground to air missile capability ... and a fast patrol boat presence. Our insurance for the PLEM will depend on it and men's lives will very much rely on it; so it had better be damned good!'

'What about the landline section, the part that will join up with the forty two inch main line at Geneveh' Paddy poked at the paper in his hand.

'Doesn't this feed the whole bloody facility?'

'This is a fairly straightforward operation' Declan explained '... of cutting a trench in good ground and is only a couple of miles long. I have no real worries about this part of the work'.

Paddy appeared a little calmer. He knew it was time for the big question.

'OK, how much and how long?'

Declan waited for a second or two before replying – trying to gauge the situation. He was still slightly put off by Paddy's nervousness and his right brain, the one in which a small alarm bell was ringing, told him he should add a few million – just in case. The Englishman now had Paddy's full attention.

When Declan finally spoke, he revealed the cost of $120 million and a timescale of eighteen weeks construction, with four weeks for engineering and design.

'You are bloody well joking' Paddy breathed.

'That's a hell of a lot of fucking money my friend' he paused '- and to be frank with you, I think it's way out of budget for our friends across the water' He was very irritated - and it showed.

Other than the now frustrating racket from the air conditioner, there rested a tensioned silence in the room. Declan could see that Paddy struggled with the whole concept and therefore waited for the inevitable.

Then it started.

Paddy erupted in to 'too many unknowns, too much risk, too long a time, too expensive', just about 'too much' of everything. Declan let him rant for a few minutes and then calmly began to gather up the file and loose papers.

The meeting was over.

Declan got up from his chair and finished the remainder of his now warm beer in one long swallow. He turned to the still seated, still angrily mumbling ex British Army Colonel, fixed his eyes on him and stated,

Chapter Five – The Plan

without emotion ... 'There are no options here Paddy. This is a take it or leave it proposal and it's not open to negotiation. I've spent over fifty thousand dollars on it so far – and I'm not spending a penny more – until I see some damned cash on the table!'

Paddy could take the offer to his paymasters or not. It was of little or no consequence to him. It was a gamble. He headed for the hotel room door. Paddy was now literally dripping as he stopped the Englishman with his hand on the door knob. He grabbed the papers, pushed past Declan and left the room - without another word.

The red faced, sweaty and uncomfortable looking Irishman took the shaky elevator to the lobby. Sitting with his back to the elevator doors, in one of the low chairs scattered around the lobby seating area, sat a tanned but fair skinned, tall and well proportioned man in a grey short sleeved shirt and charcoal trousers. He had what would normally be taken for an American military haircut; crew cut flat on the top and nearly shaven on the back and sides. As the lift door opened the man turned his head. Paddy exited the elevator and for a brief second, their eyes met. Paddy nodded quickly in some form of recognition, turned away and headed for the main hotel exit door. His blood pressure was rising steadily and his heart felt as if it were beating so fast, it could be considered to be out of control.

On the drive back to Abu Nar, Declan quickly ran

over in his mind the pros and cons of what was now set in motion and he hoped to god that he had got it right. In truth, he was not totally convinced that pulling such a large pipe from the beach was to be without its problems. This was the absolute frontier of oilfield engineering technology. It would be risky enough under normal circumstances and a wise man might say totally impossible being carried out on the front line of a major International war. However, the key motivation for Declan at that particular moment was the thought of the clear twenty million or so dollars of profit that could be banked and even a few million more - with a little bit of luck and some very tight project management.

He was of course a little uneasy about the kind of people he was dealing with and there remained a consistent niggle at the back of his mind with regard to the strange and sometimes unsettling behaviour of Paddy Doherty. He put the Irishman's nervousness down to the possibility that he was playing the role of 'man in the middle' and could be the only one not making any real money out of it all. As for the Iranians, he had dealt with worse in his life and to be honest with himself, he enjoyed *'the game'*.

He savoured the moment as he pulled up outside his office - confident he knew the risks and the associated consequences.

Chapter Five – The Plan

Little did he know that some dark forces were very much aware of Declan's meeting in Ras Al Khaimah that day and the kind of *'games'* they played could sometimes have some much more terminal outcomes.

~~~~~~~~
~~~~

Chapter Six
Abu Musa

The call came two days later. 'Be at Abu Musa Island on Thursday morning, to meet with parties interested in your Geneveh proposal'

It was a short call from Doherty who curtly delivered the single, simple sentence and without waiting for a reply, put the phone down. Abu Musa Island was about forty eight miles north of Abu Nar stuck out in the Arabian Gulf with disputed title between the Iranians and the Gulf states. This was not going to be easy. To get there provided two equally difficult choices, by air or by sea.

There were no commercial flights and no ferries from the south side of the Gulf to the island … and never had been. Declan, however, had his own, much cherished forty two foot motor sailing boat and a Cherokee single engine aeroplane. The boat would be the easiest choice. However, it would take some time there and back. Trips to Abu Musa from any of the Gulf States were not encouraged and when he got back, questions would be asked.

The aeroplane was a better, quicker alternative but there would be problems in filing a flight plan. Call sign Golf Bravo Echo Hotel Yankee was a well equipped

Chapter Six— Abu Musa

flying machine fitted with long range fuel tanks and full instrumentation. Declan used the plane a lot to 'clutch' around the Gulf.

The decision was made and so was a phone call to Paddy. Declan explained that if he was to be in Abu Musa the next day he would need some sort of 'no questions asked' flight permissions and Paddy would have to get them from his friend Sheik Ahmed, Minister of Defence. Declan waited for the tag line as Paddy huffed and puffed in expounding how difficult it was to do something like that and at such short notice ... etc ...etc ...

Declan cut him off in mid moan by asking the uncomplicated question

'How much Paddy?'

'Well Declan, as you know these things are simply not easy to organise and ... umm ... can be quite expensive. I will have to pay out at the airport ... then there is the minister's office ... all the ...' Declan cut him short once again. He did not want to listen to any more of this crap.

A figure was agreed to be provided to Paddy ... in cash. It was a lot of money for such a small favour.

Information that the flight was fixed came later that day with a stipulation that Declan would route in and out of Abu Nar via Ras Al Khaimah. Abu Musa was not to be mentioned, at all, to anyone and no questions would be asked by air traffic control in Dubai, Sharjah or Ras Al Khaimah. Flying through RAK was no big deal and only added ten minutes each way to his journey. He was eager to get going.

~~~~~~

Early next day, Declan was past the General Aviation gate at Abu Nar air port and heading towards his aeroplane sitting on the apron outside the general aviation hanger. Weather looked good and within ten minutes he was up and away from runway three zero and turning right to Ras Al Khaimah. He made a radio call to the RAK tower, receiving clearance to land. It was a good touch-down … on rarely used, metre thick, shimmering hot tarmac. Declan taxied over to the control tower as instructed. As he approached, Tom Whitby, the air traffic controller, radioed permission to take off and added whimsically

'Watch out for other traffic'.

Declan hit the rudder bar to turn Hotel Yankee back on to the runway, pushed the throttle hard forward and was airborne within seconds. With flaps up and a short spiral to five thousand feet, the gleaming white Cherokee, with a bright red stripe and oversize company logo, headed toward Abu Musa Island. Declan calculated he would be there in twenty minutes. He had not flown to Abu Musa before and remained wary of his possible reception. As the tiny Island came

Chapter Six— Abu Musa

in to view, Declan dropped the sturdy little aeroplane down to one thousand feet and made a pass over what could be considered a runway. It was a simple, levelled sand strip about half a mile long with some faded markings at each end. There was not much sign of life. The sand strip looked OK from the air, but sand strips were notorious for hiding potholes and pockets of soft material. A decision had to be made. Declan checked the wind and chose which direction to make his approach. With full flap and flying just above stall speed, he lowered Hotel Yankee gently to the deck.

Although the air conditioning was operating on full blast, Declan was clammy with concentration. The ride was as expected; uneven and uncomfortable, but he did not want to risk touching the brakes on this sort of surface, so he let the speed drop off until the aeroplane rolled to an eventual stop, about twenty metres from the end. He looked around to see if there was any where to go to find some shade and noticed a small timber hut about a hundred yards away to his left. He kicked the rudder bar and revved the engine to turn the plane 180 degrees ready for takeoff.

With everything switched off, Declan jumped out of the Cherokee, taking two large box files with him full of documents now titled 'The Geneveh Project' and headed towards the hut. He was already dripping in the sauna like climate. It was unbearably hot and oppressively humid as he looked back behind him, the shimmering heat haze dancing off the runway only adding to the eeriness of this unusually quiet and airless scene. He was nervous in these surroundings and clutched the aircraft keys in his right trouser pocket tightly. He checked his watch. It was a little before ten o'clock and after a minute or two a white ghostly shape appeared through the watery shimmer that was the far end of the runway; a shape that gradually morphed in to the outline of a Nissan Patrol double cab truck. It was heading toward him at some speed, leaving a trail of billowing sand and dust behind.

The vehicle braked hard as it stopped literally feet away from where Declan was standing. The rear cab door swung open and a bearded, dishevelled looking individual leapt out brandishing an AK 47. He grabbed Declan by the shoulder and pushed him roughly in to the back of the Nissan, which took off again and sped the few remaining yards to the hut. Declan found himself wedged tight between two armed tribesmen both of whom smelt strongly of stale sweat and cumin spice. They looked like tough Pashtu and both stared, unblinkingly, straight ahead. In the front was a driver in some sort of military uniform and a passenger wearing a crisp white dish-dash.

The vehicle pulled up and a long agonising moment passed before the passenger turned and introduced himself. He spoke in perfect English.

'Good morning Mr Doyle. My name is Mohsen Raza

Chapter Six– Abu Musa

and I am your one and only contact with my country in relation to this interesting project we are here to discuss today'

So, this was it. The man with alert and intelligent steel grey eyes now turned towards him was the much feared head of the Iranian IRGC, but known to Declan and the rest of the world as the 'Rev Guard'.

He was beautifully presented and manicured with a neatly trimmed jet black beard and matching close cut hair. He appeared to be surprisingly young. Declan expected someone in his late forties or early fifties, but even upon close inspection, this man could be no more than around thirty or so. The hand offered by way of polite greeting was long fingered and artistic with trimmed and healthy looking shiny nails. The near hypnotic dark grey eyes held a piercing depth to them. He spoke his exceptionally good English with only a very slight and nearly undetectable American accent. The only jewellery on display was a very expensive looking gold Rolex watch which was somehow unexpected to be seen hanging from the arm of the man ruling a bunch of supposedly highly disciplined, but nevertheless, vehemently religious fanatics.

Everyone got out of the truck and entered the hut, Declan being firmly guided, not quite pushed, but firmly directed by one of the armed guards. They were in a radio facility of some kind and the atmosphere was surprisingly cool. The walls were all covered with racked radio equipment humming and buzzing away in the background. In the cleared centre of the room sat a bare, well used, steel table surrounded by four uncomfortable looking folding chairs.

Mohsen Raza indicated to Declan that he should sit at one and his host lowered himself in to one opposite.

The guards all stood around the perimeter of the room. There was no conversation between them but Declan noted they were bright looking and alert and did not take their eyes off him for one second. He hoped he would quickly get used to the smell. At a sign from Mohsen, the driver produced a thermos flask along with some small ceramic cups and set them on the table. The Iranian poured the sickly sweet tea into two of the cups and gave one to Declan. Although the presence of Mohsen Raza was intimidating, Declan knew that the head of the IRGC needed him much more than Declan needed Mohsen Raza, so his reasoning was that two great minds, in one small room, with a common purpose could possibly result in some profit for someone, somewhere. So this was to be the actual beginning.

The perfectly groomed individual in front of him spoke first.

'Well Mr Doyle, it appears that you have an interesting project to show me'

The words were transmitted clearly in an even, unintimidating tone. There was no preamble, no

Chapter Six– Abu Musa

explanation as to who Mohsen Raza was, how he represented who he actually represented ... in fact no information whatsoever.

So, as there were to be no pleasantries here today, Declan decided to get stuck right in. Without a word of reply, he opened up the file and withdrew maps, diagrams, technical drawings, flow diagrams and budgets and distributed them as best he could on the surface of the steel table. Mohsen lit a cigarette and began to study the information laid out before him.

'As you will be aware by now Mr Mohsen, our proposal to get oil exports going again from the existing facilities feeding Kharg Island, is to place a tanker loading buoy, or SPM, in the water about five miles from the shoreline between Geneveh on the mainland and Kharg Island itself'

He spoke carefully and clearly. There was no discernible reaction from Raza who was studying a detailed map of the area around the proposed site. Declan continued.

'The process of installing the SPM is quite straight forward and the installation of the required land line up to Geneveh appears to present few problems' He paused, Mohsen Raza was still head down amongst the information provided on the table.

'However, there are two areas of the construction phase that could be considered – delicate' Raza raised his head and spoke sharply. His eyes had lost their initial friendliness. 'What do you mean by *delicate* Mr Doyle?'

'Well, in simple terms, we will need to pull a twenty four inch pipe *off* the beach – and this has not been done successfully before' The piercing, unblinking stare underlined a menacing look ... full of authority, as Declan took a deep breath and continued.

' – and the bit that connects everything together, the manifold or PLEM, sitting on the sea bed, will be a major target for about twenty four hours whilst it's being floated in to place'

Mohsen was a well educated, university graduate, who had a good grasp of a wide variety of subjects, but he was no oilfield engineer. He stubbed out his cigarette in a jagged edge tin that had been placed on the table by one of the guards.

'Tell me about pulling the pipe' came the quick response, the penetrating gaze still firmly fixed. Declan was feeling decidedly uncomfortable, but hoped upon hope that it didn't show.

'We have confidence in a process that uses heavy duty pipe layers to actually lift and push the pipe as each section is added. The dead load will be dramatically reduced by making the pipe a big buoyant tube as it lays, totally submerged, in the water'.

Declan searched for a second or two through the project file and pulled out a three dimensional drawing showing how the whole process would work. He placed

Chapter Six– Abu Musa

it on the table in front of Mohsen Raza who studied it wordlessly for several minutes.

The Iranian lit another cigarette. Declan was dying for one, but daren't ask. The inquisitor then posed one or two quite sensible questions to Declan. He had obviously been well briefed by oilfield engineers, probably from the NIOC. Mohsen Raza did not look up from the table, but appeared satisfied with the answers being provided as he pulled out a large drawing of the pipeline manifold from underneath several closely typed budget papers.

'Now tell me about the … er … what you call it … PLEM?'

Declan's answer was straightforward.

'This item is crucial to the whole project. As you can see, it is a complex construction - is very expensive to manufacture and will need to be placed exactly on its spot on the sea bed. To do this the whole unit will need to be floated in to a surveyed position on the surface and then gradually de-ballasted so that it sinks in a carefully controlled manner. I have to be honest with you, all the time the PLEM is on the surface …' he paused '… it is a very large target!' 'How long could that be? Mohsen enquired, looking up pointedly once again from the mass of information spread out on the table. 'Up to twenty four hours' stated Declan firmly.

At a sign from Mohsen, more tea was poured, one cigarette was extinguished and another one lit.

'So, Mr Doyle, what guarantees are you offering ... *if*, of course ... *if* we apply some credence to this slightly left of centre scheme of yours?'

'Well, Mr Mohsen, what kind of *protection* are *you* offering to the project?' Declan replied quickly.

The Commander of the Iranian Rev Guard paused for a second.

'I will tell you now that we could provide air cover with the highly efficient American 'Hawk' ground to air missiles. We have obtained these as a result of a series of discussions with one of our friends in the American CIA. The fact that we hold such sophisticated weaponry is not common knowledge, but I have a feeling it may be in the public domain shortly. You may not be aware Mr Doyle that the Zionist enemy has two satellites dedicated to twenty four seven surveillance of my country. Whatever the Israelis know, the Americans know. Whatever the Americans know, the Iraqis know ... so there you have it'

He smiled gently as he imparted this important information to Declan who further discovered that this 'gift of arms' was related to the failure of the American hostages rescue operation in Iran named 'Operation Eagle Claw'. Somewhere in the middle of it all stood the rumoured management of one mysterious figure known as Colonel Oliver Gresham. Raza continued.

Chapter Six – Abu Musa

'We also have four squadrons of upgraded F4 Phantom aircraft that can operate from Kharg on one side of the straits and at a new airstrip we could provide at Dalaki, a few miles inland on the Geneveh side…'

'What about the marine element?' Declan interjected

'We have some well equipped fast torpedo boats that could patrol the entrance to the straits and they are also equipped with anti-aircraft heavy calibre machine guns. However, have no fear. Saddam's hyenas do not have the courage to come that far south in surface vessels.

The biggest single risk is an air attack from Exocet missiles. The Iraqis now have the means of delivery and we know they have the training and political will to use them in the expectation of shortening this bloody war'

Both men were now left thoughtful and silent. Mohsen Raza eventually stood up and began to pace the room, moving continuously, as he discussed the detail of the proposed military involvement in the project. After ten minutes or so, Raza turned unexpectedly on Declan and asked sharply

'You do of course have some insurance plan for this large floating target, just in case….'

The sentence trailed off uncompleted, but Declan got the message. He felt the colour rising in his face as he replied.

'Insurance for all aspects of the job will be provided by the individual contractors employed directly by my company, Associated Oilfield – except for the subsea manifold - the PLEM. This is a most difficult element to insure, but we do have one positive response from a specialist underwriter based in Hong Kong. It's bloody expensive – but it's all we have'.

The head of the IRGC sat down, another cigarette on the go. He leaned in across the table toward Declan until the two faces were only inches apart.

'Well, let us all hope that in thinking the unthinkable, your underwriter will pay up and this *delicate piece of engineering* , as you so succinctly put it, is replaced and replaced quickly before either yourself or your insurance agent plan any long holidays!'

A shiver moved gradually up Declan's spine. Raza knew his chilling words had had the right effect. He leaned back in to his chair again, seemingly dismissing Declan's presence. The Englishman's eyes were drawn toward the jagged edged tin can that served as an ash tray. It was now overflowing, but no one in the room made an effort to empty it. As if to read Declan's mind, Mohsen gestured loosely toward the tin and one of the guards rushed over to obey a command from the second most powerful man in Iran.

The ashtray was once again empty and now perhaps the bargaining would begin.

As the battered tin receptacle returned, Declan checked the time. It was past one thirty. Mohsen picked up a single sheet of paper from the pile in front of him,

Chapter Six– Abu Musa

lifted his head and locked sight with the seemingly unflustered and unblinking European sitting in front of him. He couldn't quite make up his mind whether or not this confident, perhaps over confident businessman, was somehow playing a complex game with an unfathomable outcome or was in fact a genuine entrepreneur and technical innovator simply out to make some money. Could he actually produce 'the goods' from the slightly scary plan that he had spent the last three hours explaining, justifying and sometimes even questioning himself?

Either way, he was playing a dangerous game and within the next few minutes Mohsen knew he would have to make up his mind about trusting this outwardly straightforward but possibly devious Englishman with an Irish name, who had a healthy reputation for 'getting things done' but with an often less healthy reputation for fairness and honesty. The alternative was to simply cast him aside. Mohsen Raza looked down at the set of papers in his hand headed 'Budget'.

'You will of course realize Mr Doyle, that the project value as written down here is totally unrealistic'

Mohsen spoke evenly and convincingly with a focus that beheld a certain shrewdness now directed toward Declan, reading body language, searching for a sign or reaction betraying weakness. It was like a bolt from the blue. Declan coloured slightly, but that was all.

Mohsen continued.

'How on earth do think that my hard pressed government can come up with one hundred and twenty million dollars, *in cash* for a project of this size. It is totally unrealistic my friend – and to be frank with you our budget is nowhere near this amount'

He began to laugh out loud. Declan steeled himself; showing no emotion. 'Stay calm' he told himself. He had trained well. Inside, his stomach was churning, his brain racing. He had made sure that the profits he was looking for were well disguised.

Through the uncontrolled and genuine outburst of laughter, Mohsen Raza was studying the Englishman keenly. He was a trained interrogator and many who had had the misfortune to be a subject of scrutiny by this man in the past had not lived long enough to tell the tale.

Declan replied firmly.

'What you have in *your* budget Mr Raza does not concern me. This is *my* budget for a job that *you* need doing. Now, unless you want to go through the budget justification documents in detail, which I think extends to around one hundred and fifty pages of calculations, the summary sheet you have in your hand is what it will cost you to get this job done'.

The mood of the negotiations changed immediately.

The head of the Iranian Rev Guard was forced yet again to weigh up the metal of the man and -

Chapter Six— Abu Musa

considering the circumstances - what appeared on the face of it to be a strong, possibly even courageous resolve. He remained uncommitted and silent for well over a minute. He was angry inside. He then got up from the table, his irritation ill concealed and began to once again pace the small room. There was a look of concern on the face of each of the two body guards. The driver moved toward Mohsen and whispered something in Farsi. Whatever was said was dismissed with a slight wave of the hand.

The tone of Mohsen's voice was now elevated and tetchy.

'I have had one of our senior NIOC engineers look at your proposal overnight and he informs me that the mechanics, materials and services for a project such as this should be less than half of the ridiculous sum you have here'.

'Well, that may have been true ten years ago. Unfortunately, this technology was not available ten years ago and no one was pricing these works to take place in the front line of a major bloody war. Every single contractor that I have approached has encountered horrific insurance problems, workboat lease values have doubled along with the bonuses required by the men who will have to actually do the work. No sir, Mr Mohsen, this is the price – and if you can't afford it – then this meeting has just ended'

As soon as the last sentence had spilled from his

mouth, Declan knew it was a mistake, a sense of panic now welling up inside. The head of the IRGC lit another cigarette, his face an inexpressive mask as he sat back down at what had now become the negotiating table. The guards and the driver appeared to be at some higher level of attentiveness. Tension in the room was building. Declan was beginning to show small but obvious signs of stress. In fact the idea was forming in his mind that he ought to be considering some sort of plan to get the hell out of there. His forehead glistened with common signs of stress as he continued to fiddle unconsciously with his pen. This did not go unnoticed by Raza who now appeared to be more under control as he proceeded to verbalize carefully and calmly.

'Tell me about the payment programme you have outlined Mr Doyle'

'Well, I have lots of up-front payments to make before the project can be considered activated, so I will need forty million up front in to the AOS Midland Bank account in Jersey. A further forty million will need to be transferred to a nominated bank in Abu Nar when the PLEM and SPM are attached to the towing tugs and the last forty million transferred to the bank in Abu Nar when the tugs pass through the Straits of Hormuz. You will have to be responsible for the security of the tugs and the tow from the Straits of Hormuz to the positioning site'.

Declan's uninterrupted reply was noticeably shaky.

Chapter Six– Abu Musa

Wiping his brow with the back of his hand, he continued. 'Payments must be considered to be pre-completion and not post-completion of works as I am afraid the credit rating of your government will not support third party finance on a project of this size'

Just for fun he added '… and any other size for that matter!'

Mohsen Raza stubbed out what would be his final cigarette in the half full, battered tin ashtray and wordlessly indicated to the driver hovering in the background to collect up all the documents strewn across the steel table and put them back into the two charcoal coloured box files.

The table was eventually cleared … except for the half full stinking tin ashtray.

The atmosphere had, by now, become decidedly chilly. Mohsen Raza leaned across to Declan. He was so close, their noses were nearly touching. A bead of sweat dropped from Declan's eyebrow on to the table with a near audible 'splat' in the awkward silence. He felt sure that everyone in the room had heard it.

'I hope you are not playing me for a fool Mr Doyle because the consequences of doing so would be most painful to your person'

The two men's eyes locked together; mesmeric and unblinking.

'I know all about you Declan Doyle and some of what I know, is not nice. So if we continue in any sort of relationship together, you will need to remember one simple thing' He paused for a second or two, searching the dark brown dilating pupils of the impassive Englishman. He then leant even further forward, his voice a mere whisper in Declan's ear.

'There is an ancient Persian proverb Mr Doyle … that in English goes like this.

'He who wants a rose must respect the thorn.'

Mohsen Raza leant back into his chair and spoke again – his words managed, enunciated to the letter, quietly delivered and controlled.

'I am that thorn Mr Doyle … Do not *fuck* with me'

Declan was visibly taken aback. The depth of the delivery appeared to have the right effect and somehow he didn't expect to hear this particularly western expletive, from this particularly non-western individual. Mohsen Raza banged the table firmly with his right hand in a final exploding emphasis to what he considered to be the very terminal words of this negotiation.

He quickly raised himself from the table.

The meeting was over.

One of the guards immediately came alive and rushed to open the door as his respected leader moved toward it. The driver was carrying the two box files.

Raza turned sharply to face Declan, who was still seated – blank faced.

Chapter Six— Abu Musa

'You will receive a telex advising you of our decision whether or not to proceed with this project' he paused thoughtfully 'before midnight today. If we do proceed, the project time you have indicated of eighteen weeks is too long and will be shortened to sixteen weeks, including the tow from Singapore - *without* compensation. You will need to produce a suitable insurance certificate for the *delicate* item as part of the contract documents. All other instructions will be contained in any further documentation you will receive from my office' he paused yet again '... and *only* from my office'.

No handshakes, no further discussion, no lift back to the aircraft, no problem. The meeting was over, the job had been done. Everything was now in the hands of somebody's god – somewhere - but which one was looking down favourably on the miniscule island of Abu Musa today?

The Iranians left in a vortex of asphyxiating sand dust, a quantity of which pursued Declan through the open door of the now empty, timber radio hut. He sat there for a second or two, gathering his troubled thoughts.

Had he cracked it?

He wasn't sure

One thing *was* obvious though after today's confrontation; if the telex *did* arrive and Declan *did* accept this rather unusual contract, there would be no going back. As he reviewed the situation in his mind for the final time, his thoughts terminated on the day's events so far. On the bright side, he figured he had actually survived his first meeting with the infamous head of the Iranian Revolutionary Guard. On the dark side, he had tasted the humour of the man ... first hand! Declan was still decidedly shaky as he exited the hut and made his way back to Hotel Yankee ... the adrenalin still flowing.

Within five minutes the little Cherokee was in the air, flaps up, climbing to three thousand feet and heading back toward Ras Al Khaimah. The landing was near perfect on the massive dark billiard table expanse that was runway 'one-two'. Declan dutifully taxied up to the apron beneath the control tower, switched off the engine and jumped out to stretch his legs. He kept the door to the aircraft open and the radio on, waiting for someone in the tower to give him permission to take off again to Abu Nar.

Some long minutes passed.

He was now becoming impatient and gazed up in a mood of restrained frustration at the darkened overhanging observation windows of the tower.

What was taking so damned long?

Declan was unable to make out the outline of a tall, lean and fit looking man behind the blackened glass,

Chapter Six– Abu Musa

studying him with interest through military field glasses. The dark figure checked his watch and made a note of the time. It was exactly three o'clock in the afternoon.

Colonel Oliver Gresham, Middle East Director of Covert Operations for the CIA, didn't look too happy.

~~~~~~~~
~~~

Chapter Seven
The Decision

By four o'clock, Declan was back in his company building in Abu Nar. As he entered the outer office, which had been temporarily converted in to a project engineering department, a rush of people came at him all looking determinedly for five minutes of his time. In sharp response to his hustling staff came a meaningful 'not today gentlemen' as he closed his personal office door firmly shut.

He rang Esther, his private secretary for a cup of coffee and leaned back in his chair feeling quite exhausted. The coffee came and now it was time for a quick review of where he stood.

Project value on the table agreed at $120 million – good.

Project time reduced to sixteen weeks - leaving only twelve weeks on site – not good.

Insurance for the PLEM manifold now totally down to Declan – do-able.

If the Iranians pay $40 million up front, $20 million will go straight in to Declan's Jersey bank account – very good.

If the job get's screwed up in any way whatsoever, Declan will have literally no place to hide – very bad.

Chapter Seven – The Decision

Now he would simply have to wait.

It was six thirty in the morning when Declan arrived at his office again the following day. As he normally did, he went to make an entrance through the rear of the building. It was a modern, commercial construction with various showrooms on the ground floor and offices and engineering design facilities on the first and second floor. He unlocked the outer and inner glazed double doors and made his way briskly up the stairs. Half way up he suddenly stopped. Something was wrong. Instinctively Declan ducked down low, now stopped in his tracks listening for any unusual or unexpected sounds. After waiting for nearly a minute, he proceeded carefully up the remainder of the stairway and at the top, turned right in to the corridor leading to his outer office. The once glazed entrance was smashed completely and a pile of shattered glass fragments lay scattered on the floor. Declan pulled himself up again - and listened. There was no sound of movement inside and so he moved forward with care.

The main outer office area was a mess. He quickly made a visual check of the room, eyes focused on the Telex machine sitting just outside his office door. The door was closed and didn't look as if it had been forced. There was no paper roll in the machine and no expected reels of messages in the receiving tray.

He picked his way carefully through the many manila files strewn across the floor. This was a professional job. He quickly checked the rest of the offices. There was no immediate sign of vandalism anywhere in the building and therefore it could be assumed that just a detailed inspection of files, along with the theft of the telex receipts was the end game.

Declan tried his office door. It was unsecured and had been simply levered off the door jamb. He looked carefully around the timber panelled room, observing every object and its place. There were signs that someone had been moving around in the office. He checked the side draws in the oak desk pedestals. They had all been forced open. However, the front panels appeared not to have been investigated. These panels were designed to look simply like a solid, unhinged cover for the draw backs but did in fact conceal a copy Telex ribbon punch secreted in one side and a video recorder in the other. Obscured behind the timber wall panel joints in each corner of the office were fitted miniature sound activated video surveillance cameras. It was today's technology. Everything that took place in that office was recorded twenty four hours a day. Only he, Esther and Andy Peters knew about this slightly unusual business practice, but it had saved his skin on many occasions and provided a sometimes illegal but welcome business advantage on others. Declan played the evening tape back on the twenty two inch TV set that was a permanent fixture at the side of his desk.

It was as expected, very dark and very quite. A murky

Chapter Seven – The Decision

figure could be made out moving around Declan's office. The concealed Telex punch machine was connected to the main office Telex system and it simply made a punch tape copy of everything that came through the system. If the tape was taken out and run through a mechanical reader, the Telex machine would print out every message that had been copied to the tape. Declan took it and fed it through the reader in the main office, placing a new paper roll in the machine, pressing the 'read' and 'print' buttons and leaving the whole apparatus to do its work.

He returned to his office to chew over what had happened. There were a few of his competitors, as well as the oilfield 'big boys' who no doubt had a 'sniff' about Geneveh and wanted to know what was going on. The Iraqi's would very likely have more than a casual interest, and then of course there were all the 'spooks' and weirdo's of the International Intelligence community. He couldn't rule anything or anyone out and would have to be much more diligent with security if this horrifyingly risky project ever got off the ground.

Deep down, he suspected the devious hand of Paddy Doherty here somewhere and would consider whether or not to confront him later. Right now, the priority was to find out if a contract had been received overnight from the Iranians; what if anything could be missing, what this team of professionals were after and more importantly, what intelligence they may have actually gathered during their visit? Andy was the first to arrive at just after twenty past seven. His office was on the other side of the building but he noticed the mess in the corridor and came straight to see Declan.

'Morning Declan'

'Morning Andy'

'So what happened?'

'Well, you tell me Andy. I came in this morning and saw what you see. It appears that someone wants to get to know us better'

He smiled. Andy was not amused.

'Is this related to the Geneveh job?' he questioned bluntly.

'It may well be Andy, but unless we have a contract with someone, such a careful nocturnal inspection of our premises could possibly be considered ... premature!'

'Well have we got a contract with the Iranians?' Andy questioned; frustration showing in the clipped response.

'The Telex machine will tell all my friend' stated Declan reassuringly, rising from his desk 'So - let's go and see'

The roll was nearly exhausted as they both approached the stuttering printer. Fifty feet of paper lay curled up on the floor. Declan pulled a chunk from the continuous reel and threw it across to Andy.

'Scan that for something from my new Iranian best friends and I'll tackle this lot'

Chapter Seven – The Decision

With a lack of unnecessary conversation, Declan and Andy scanned the hundreds of messages in typed capitals. Andy found it.

'Cut it off Andy ...' shouted Declan '... then let's have a look at it in my office'

It was over 2000 words long. It was a contract. There were no niceties and acceptance was required by eighteen hundred hours that day by return Telex. The first $40 million would be in the AOS Jersey account by electronic transfer at noon the following day and Raza's name was all over it. This would not go down well with 'the troops'!

Declan had carried out an initial scan of the whole document and was now re-reading it in more detail. Andy had finished his read, leaving him staring blankly at the copy in front of him.

'What the on earth is this Declan?'

Andy was agitated

'Are you trying to get us all killed?'

He took a deep breath.

'All those poor bloody guys out there' he pointed to the outer office '... who have *incidentally* worked their *nuts* off for you during the past few days, are under the impression that this project is for the NIOC ... *not* the bloody Rev Guard'

Declan looked up from his reading. 'Did I ever say that?' came the sharp reply.

'The National Iranian Oil Company are the

beneficiaries of the project, but they are not the ones who are paying us. That's all'.

'What do you mean ... *that's all*! Simply being in the same room as that murderous bastard Raza is bad enough - but doing business with him directly - actually relying on him, as an individual to get paid over a hundred million dollars is probably as near to committing commercial suicide as I can describe it'

Andy was clearly upset and Declan was visibly angry that someone such as him was questioning his business acumen. He was a man who demanded complete loyalty from his staff and that was something he had never questioned in Andy. He had expected him to be 'over the moon' at the prospect of earning over a hundred million dollars, not sitting in front of him 'bleating'.

There was a strained silence for nearly a minute, both men searching for the right words to defuse what could become a 'rock and a hard place' situation. Declan spoke first. The words ... carefully chosen, but not one's that Andy really wanted to hear.

'Andy, there are going to be two ways to run this job. One of them is *with* you' he paused '... and the other is *without* you'

The atmosphere in the warm Ash panelled office turned perceptibly tense. Andy opened his mouth to speak but Declan cut him off. 'Before you say something you may regret, you need to consider both your position and mine'.

Chapter Seven – The Decision

Andy's face was flushed. He was infuriated. Declan knew that Andy, his right hand man, most trusted employee and perhaps his closest friend, could get a job anywhere in the Gulf. A well connected European in Abu Nar, in nineteen eighty seven, was a priceless asset and Declan did not want to lose him.

'My position is simple. I have to grow my business and there is not much that I won't do to make that happen. This is the job that could *make us* Andy and when I say 'us' you know that you will always get your fair share of anything that this company eventually becomes.'

Andy stood - clenching his fists tightly, the serpent on his shoulder urging him to burst in. However, the years of working with Declan had taught him the most valuable lesson in any form of communications is when to say nothing. This was one of those times.

Declan continued.

'I know I am definitely supping with the devil at this particular table, but this is a once in a lifetime opportunity and we have to make it work. Byron and his team are confident they can do it, even in the reduced timescale. Our guys are confident we can manage the project and we literally have all the people and expertise we need sitting here right now. Remember, 'you do what you are' Andy - and you are employed by me until I stop paying your damn wages!'

Andy could contain himself no longer. He knew his

immediate future and a hundred and fifty thousand dollar salary could be at stake here.

'This man is a proven murderer, a leader of mindless fanatics, a financier to just about every extreme terrorist operation in the world and simply one you should not be doing business with. This bloody 'so called' *contract*, is not worth the paper it's written on. Why on earth are you not insisting that you work for the NIOC under *proper* contractual terms and conditions? Why are we not having an appropriate negotiating period, not just a three or four hour meeting with a lunatic on a useless stretch of sand stuck out in the middle of the Arabian Gulf?'

'Andy, there are three very good and very simple reasons that will take twenty seconds to explain.

If the NIOC was running this job, we would not even see the front door let alone be asked to provide a price.

If the NIOC was running this job, outfits like McDaniels, Hall Burton, Schlumberger, Technip and Global would be all over it and we would be lucky to even get a smell - let alone a sensible sub-contract.

If the NIOC was running this job, $40 million would not be in my Jersey bank account by midnight tomorrow'.

Andy looked up quickly, studying the man in front of him, searching for something, but for what, he didn't know. Much was spinning round in his head. He had supported him in everything he had done so far and a

Chapter Seven – The Decision

lot of it had been very near the mark legally and he knew it, but was this just a 'bridge too far'? He remained silent. It was no use arguing with Declan Doyle. Once he had made up his mind, you either jumped aboard a train already travelling at speed or you were left behind at the station. It had been an exciting few years so far and he wanted it to continue. Money was not and never had been the total issue with Andy Peters although he had not been short of it since hanging his hat on the rack that had 'Contec Group' written beneath it.

'So Andy, I think you need to make up your mind'

Andy wasn't expecting that.

'Let me know if you wish to remain part of this company – or not, by lunchtime. I simply can't piss about after that, I have too much to do and….' Andy was already on a sharp intake of breath as he cut him off.

'No need to wait until lunchtime. I *am* on board but I do ask you to take care what you do and how you do it, with a promise to tell me *everything* as it happens' he paused ' … and I do mean *everything*'

The dark cloud hanging over a very special relationship was finally lifted. A knowing smile passed between the two men, a smile that could have became laughter as Andy moved forward, confidently, placing the contract copy on Declan's desk.

'I'll call a full staff meeting for eight fifteen and you

had better come up with a damn good reason as to why this whole office looks as if a bomb has hit it' The door closed carefully and Andy was gone.

Declan sat back in his chair, visibly relieved that calling Andy's bluff had worked, as he didn't have a clue who he could possibly consider to replace him.

It was eight o'clock – and a Friday; an official and religious day of no work in Abu Nar. However, a majority of staff were arriving at the office and connecting with the photo copied handwritten note distributed by Andy telling them not to touch any disrupted files or opened draws. There would be a meeting addressed by 'the boss' at eight fifteen. Declan left his office, nodded towards Andy standing by the glassless frame of the main office door. Declan sat on a desk and addressed the seventy odd staff assembled in the room. Andy remained by the door.

'I have called this short meeting to tell you what seems to have happened over night. As you can see, we have suffered a break in of some sort. We are not clear as to what actually happened but I need you all to carefully locate and check every one of your files. If you think anything is missing, please tell Andy. If you feel that something may have been removed from a file and then perhaps replaced, please let Andy know. Make a list on a piece of paper of any draws that have been opened, forcibly or otherwise and give it to Andy. For

Chapter Seven – The Decision

the guys in the drawing office, please check all your printed drawing stocks and drawing issue sheets.

Someone at the back of the assembly called out

'What happened Declan?'

'To be frank with you, I don't know. However, we will *not* be calling the police and not one word of this disruption to our business is to be breathed to a living soul outside of this office. The job you have all been burning midnight oil to bring together is coming to a conclusion and as the location and type of work involved is a bit sensitive, it may be that someone wanted to find out some more. It was a professional job so perhaps they got what they came for. Whatever has happened here, we must not take our eye off the ball. Let's get this place cleaned up and then get back to work'.

A semi-satisfied murmur circulated through the room as Declan returned to his office. The assembled engineers, technicians and managers had been working eighteen hour days for the past week and they were understandably grumpy. He picked up the phone and left a message for Andy to meet with him in his office at nine thirty. It was going to be another long day.

~~~~~~~~
~~~~

Chapter Eight
A Contract with the Devil

At nine thirty exactly, on that hectic and slightly depressing Friday morning, Andy arrived in Declan's office. His boss already had a massive blank 'programme of works' planning sheet on his desk and a set of coloured pencils. He was busy scribbling activities down the left hand side of the sheet.

'Come in Andy and order us some coffee please. I won't be a minute'.

The coffee came and the meeting began.

'OK Andy there are two things that need to be done immediately. Get hold of Tom Wickes at Cox and Gibson, our solicitors and tell him you need to meet with him, at his office, at ten thirty today. No if's, no buts, we all know its Friday. Just tell him to make himself available. The meeting is to be private between you two and is not to be diarised within his office. If there is any problem whatsoever, you tell him to ring me'.

Andy made a note on his ever present yellow lined legal pad.

'Next, ring Bill at ABR Findlays Bank and tell him you need to see him at twelve o'clock. Again, we all know its Friday ... but no lunches, no bullshit, just you and him in his office at twelve' Andy made another

Chapter Eight – A Contract with the Devil

note. 'Anything else?' 'Not immediately. I need you to pin down this contract before the end of today. We have until midnight to reply to the Iranians and we need contract terms and conditions checked, operational legalities agreed and most importantly of all, suitable finance in place. Once we press the button on this, things will move very, very quickly and I hope to God we have everybody in place to stay on top of it'.

The words and delivery were concise. Declan was on fire. Andy smiled quietly to himself; the devil help anyone who didn't agree with Declan Doyle on this particular day.

They spent the next ten minutes deciding the 'tack' to take with the solicitors and the bank. If ABR stuttered or hesitated in any way, shape or form, Andy was to leave immediately and get hold of Mohammed, head of the National Bank of Abu Nar where the word 'hesitation' was not in their dictionary.

'Don't mess about with them Andy. Tell them what we need and tell them we want a written agreement by four o'clock this afternoon'

Declan's job was to meet with Byron at ten thirty and sort out a programme of works and a set of supplier payment schedules. He had spoken to Byron after his staff meeting and Byron was dropping everything to get the job off the ground. Both Andy and Declan were buzzing. The game was definitely on.

Byron pumped Declan's hand as he entered the

gloomy office by the quayside. 'Sit down Decs' said Byron in an excited voice.

Declan hated the shortening of his name and grit his teeth as he sat back in the uninviting Chesterfield.

'You won't be so bloody bright when you hear that those bastards have ripped two whole weeks out of the job Byron'. Declan was smiling.

'I don't give a shit about two weeks. It will be tight, but we have handled bigger, tighter jobs than this before and I'm sure we can get the programme right'.

'Yes, but not in the middle of a damned *war* Byron!'

A knowing glance passed between the two men. A reply was not necessary.

The inevitable coffee was put on order and the review began.

The two men commenced to root through the detail, moving around schedules here, cutting a day or two from a manufacturing programme there and scribbling in coloured blocks on the new programme of works in order to make the whole project fit the revised time schedules. There were one or two 'not a cat's chance in hell' moments but gradually the massive schedule began to fill with blocks of colour; the whole programming task becoming easier with the ending of one particular process automatically kick starting another.

Andy's meeting with Tom Wickes of Cox and Gibson, Solicitors, did not take place at ten thirty as planned.

Chapter Eight – A Contract with the Devil

Andy was left sitting in the reception area outside Wickes's office for nearly a quarter of an hour.

'Not even a bloody cup of tea' he muttered irritably to himself.

As it was Friday, the offices were operating in minimum staff mode.

Andy was not happy.

Eventually a tall, lean, well groomed and pinstripe be-suited figure beckoned Andy into the cool confines of his well appointed office. Tom Wickes appeared *not* to be a fool from the outside, but he was a lawyer. Andy didn't like Tom Wickes and sometimes it showed. Today was one of those days.

As Andy sat himself down on a comfortable corner sofa unit, in the company of the senior partner of the Abu Nar office of Cox and Gibson, Tom offered a hand of greeting which was purposely ignored.

'Let's get down to it Tom' stated Andy firmly.

'I have a contract document here' he produced a photocopy of the contract sent by the head of the IRGC. 'I want you to go through it in detail and have a contractual report ready for Declan by four o'clock this afternoon'. Tom Wickes took the several sheets of photocopy paper from Andy and started to quickly scan them. A slight but cynical looking smile began to invade his normally professionally blank appearance. He replied to Andy's firmly delivered statement in a well practiced, condescending and generally superior tone. Andy unflatteringly considered him a man of insolent charm; a result of too many 'ass-roasting' sessions at some minor public school or other.

'I am afraid this is not possible Andy'

He delivered the words quietly and precisely.

'This is a complex piece of work and I will need to literally shut this office and get everyone that I have in our contracts department' he paused '… and just about every other department as well, to provide you with an advice document by four o'clock. Oh - and by the way - in case you hadn't noticed, it's Friday'

That was it. The fuse had been lit. Andy jumped up from the sofa and lunged toward the grand glass topped desk behind which Tom Wickes was barricaded.

'If you hadn't kept me waiting for fifteen *fucking* minutes this morning, you would have had fifteen more *fucking* minutes to do it in' screamed Andy. The senior partner of Cox and Gibson was so shocked he recoiled backward and nearly fell out of his designer executive office chair'.

'Excuse me … please … I …' Tom spluttered. Andy cut him off.

'This is not a *fucking* request. You have Declan's numbers on your phone. Dial one of them and tell him you can't do it'. Cox and Gibson owed their very lucrative existence in Abu Nar more or less entirely to Declan. When their business permit was being blocked

Chapter Eight – A Contract with the Devil

by Gulf Arab owned legal firms in the early seventies, Declan took up the cudgel, became the Cox and Gibson's sponsor and still was to this day. They had made millions out of this arrangement and were not about to screw around with Declan Doyle.

Andy turned on his heel and headed for the door. Without turning, he shouted back.

'Four o'clock … in my office!'

Next stop … ABR Findlays Bank.

~~~~~~

Bill Turner was a likeable man and as Andy entered the impressive marbled edifice of an entrance hall to the ABR Findlays Bank Building, Bill was waiting for him - hand outstretched and lift door locked open. Bill was a worker. He had built the ABR bank in Abu Nar from an 'also ran' to one of the most respected International banks trading in the Gulf. Bill and Andy got on well and socialized together often.

'Hi Andy' Bill shouted across the echoing hall. The two friends were smiling as they shook hands.

'Something interesting Andy?'

'Very' came the encouraging reply.

'Shall we go for a quick lunch round at the Astoria?'

'No Bill, this is heavy stuff and Declan is in full flight'

Bill Turner was initially curious and now he was completely intrigued. He had come up with some rather unorthodox finance packages for Mr Doyle over the years and ABR was the Contec Group's main banker. There had been days however, when various particular proposals put forward by Declan Doyle were so left field, they had been beyond even the spiriting influence of Bill Turner. Maybe this would be one of those days. Once seated in Bill's spacious office on the twenty first floor of the glass curtained ABR building, Andy began.

He produced another copy of the contract, a project specification filling a complete box file and a four page précis of the whole proposal.

'First read the contract Bill and then have a look at the condensed version of the project'

Without further word, the Gulf CEO of ABR Findlays jumped to the task. The inevitable coffee arrived, Arabic and English. It took fifteen minutes for Bill Turner to digest the meat of what was before him. He had an excellent, sharp and analytical mind; an attribute rare in bankers, most of whom would admit they couldn't even *read* a balance sheet let alone write one.

'Ok, let's have a look at what I think is here' he stated enthusiastically. This was big bucks, bigger than Declan had ever hung his hat out for before, especially all in one go. The CEO of ABR knew he would have to be cautious. 'It looks as if Declan is doing a deal with the Iranians to place some sort of tanker loading facility in the straits off Geneveh. The time scale is capped at

Chapter Eight – A Contract with the Devil

three months on site, the financial penalties for non-performance are horrific, but the profit margins seem to be about standard for this type of work, even without a war going on right in front of you'

'You may be interested in this piece of paper, which of course you have never seen and is the ... er ... shall we say secondary and of course, confidential budget with a revised projected profit and loss account'

Bill took the paper, scanned it, then read it again carefully.

'Good god Andy, there's nearly $35 million of extra profit in here' Bill exclaimed.

'Abso-fucking-lutley William! This is what we think we can do the job for and as you can see from the contract documents, the Iranians have accepted it, although you will understand - they have not had sight of this particular budget paper or, at least we hope so' Andy added thoughtfully - a thought relating to the break in and the possibility that this document, or something like it, was what the intruder was after. He made a mental note to discuss it with Declan later.

'So, what do you want from me?'

'We need a facility separate from Contec. We want to open an account for AOS that will exclusively service this project. We will need a rolling credit of $20 million'

'It's a hell of a lot of money Andy and it may be outside of my influence, but I will get on to Australia right now and see what buttons need to be pressed'

'I'm afraid it's more urgent that that Bill. My instructions are that if I cannot leave this office today with a guarantee that this facility will be in place by midnight - then I am to go and see Abdula Mostafa or Mohammed at the National Bank of Abu Nar.

He paused.

'I need you to pull out all the stops on this one my old friend. This crazy job is complicated enough without having idiots managing the financials'

'The big question Andy is the obvious one - and I have to ask it. Do you think he can handle a job like this? Deep, deep down Andy, forget all the loyalty shit - do you really think he can handle it?'

'Well Bill, you know the man probably as well as I do and you also know that, in his book, the word 'impossible' is merely an opinion!'

Both men smiled in unison. The answer was a good one and they both knew it.

'Give me a minute Andy' Bill got up from his desk and left the room. He came back about ten minutes later.

'Here's the deal. Who will be operating the account?'

'As usual, it will be me, Tony the Group Chief Accountant and of course Declan himself'

'OK. My authority without consultation is limited to $15 million. So what I propose is that we open two accounts for AOS with a credit line of $10 million each. That means I will not have exceeded my credit limit on

Chapter Eight – A Contract with the Devil

each account, but we will have to work both accounts together to make sure funds move smoothly between them. The accounts will of course be revealed to my senior directors, at some stage. I will naturally receive a major bollocking and if necessary, I will be knocking on your door for a job'

Both Andy and Bill smiled once again as the conversation paused.

'If you can accept that - then I can have the documents called up within the next few hours for Declan to sign. You will have to make sure he understands about the two accounts though as there will be two lots of papers to be dealt with.

'No problem Bill - you are an absolute bloody star. Declan will be well pleased - and I'm off to tell him now. Thanks my friend'

With that, Andy headed towards the door.

'... and don't forget that we are both on the first tee tomorrow at six o'clock' he shouted back

'I'll be waiting for you - as usual Andy' came the laughing reply as Bill Turner sank back in his chair.

'What on earth have I let myself in for' he pondered as he once again settled down to look in detail at the contract with the name Mohsen Raza printed at the bottom of the last page. Bill Turner knew he had put his backside completely on the line for Mr Doyle. 'This could be a rocky ride' He muttered as he picked up the phone to call in his senior managers to the office.

~~~~~~

The next two weeks were hectic. Contract Reference 112/406, or 'The Geneveh Project' as the venture had now firmly been labelled, was in full swing. All other projects at the Contec offices had taken a back seat as Declan became totally consumed in getting everything in place to start works on site, on time and to schedule. He had often preached to his managers that success was related not to' what you know' but to 'who you know' and he had always encouraged his staff to 'get to know people'; entertain, play golf, go sailing, join clubs and just simply sell themselves out in the market place.

'Everyone you meet in a place like Abu Nar could do you some good, somewhere down the line!' he told them – regularly. His marketing philosophy of 'get them pissed and bribe them' was well known in the Gulf States, half of Houston and most good pubs and Hotels in London.

Now was payback time.

~~~~~~~~~
~~~~

Chapter Nine
The London Conspiracy

It was time for Eric Saunders to join the controlled chaos of exiting a tediously full Gulf Air flight at London Heathrow's Terminal Four. He hated flying. He hated it even more since the new austerity measures imposed by London had taken effect just a few months previously. Not for Eric any more the guilty pleasures of First Class travel, the accompanying caviar and Bellini pancakes, champagne cocktails and perfectly presented roast beef. It looked as if those days were permanently over. Life in Her Majesties Secret Intelligence Service was not as it used to be.

During the long walk to the Immigration desk he resigned himself to being pushed and elbowed by a plethora of Asian workers taking a break from their arduous duties in the heat sodden island of sand known as Bahrain. Whilst avoiding elbows from the side one would rarely be able to avoid elbows from the rear, inflicted by the blacked out Bahraini women, only dark flashing eyes showing to a curious world, who could simply not wait to get into a taxi and head at some speed directly for Harrods.

Eric hung back. His bruised body could take no more. As the milling crowd in front of him diminished, he

Chapter Nine – The London Conspiracy

picked up his pace. Arriving at the Immigration desk, he flashed his passport and glided through. He had no baggage to collect. This trip to UK was a short one. He had everything he needed in a compact, cleverly designed and cabin friendly tan leather case. He would be staying at his club, 'Boodle's' on St James Street whilst he was here, as he did every time he was in London.

'Back in the scrum again' was the thought attached to the reality.

As he left the baggage hall he was met by a wall of Asian 'greeters' with what looked like an average of ten excited and animated individuals to every passenger. They were packed solid, blocking every possible exit from between the straining stainless steel barriers.

'Oh Shit!' he muttered to himself as he barged a way through. The next big hurdle would be a taxi. He was right. With fifty or sixty Arabs all waving frantically at the taxi rank and prepared to pay treble to get to Harrods first, Eric knew he stood no chance and went back in to the terminal in search of a phone.

He had a number to ring in such a situation. It was a private hire company used by the 'Service' on regular occasions. Ten minutes later, a shiny black Jaguar appeared. Eric Saunders slipped in to the back seat and gave out the address.

'Century House, please … One hundred Westminster Bridge Road'

'Right you are sir' replied the casually dressed, quietly spoken driver and the car pulled smoothly away for the early afternoon drive in to the heart of London. The weather was crap as usual, but this did not bother Eric. He loved London. It was his city. This was where all his chums were. This was where all his contacts were. He didn't really know what the hell he was doing wasting his life away stuck out on a shitty, stinking little island inhabited by a bunch of highly strung, over pompous, squabbling Arabs.

As he relaxed back in to the comfortable grey hide leather seats of the Jaguar on the smooth ride in to the City, he had some time to think. In fact, what the hell was he really doing with his life, running back and forth at the beck and call of his boss on the C2 Desk at Century House?

He had nothing against his controller; in fact they got on well together. They both went to Trinity, Cambridge and both studied politics. They both came from good 'old money' families and both had somehow made working for the Secret Intelligence Service a career. However, Eric had been passed over for promotion now on two occasions. The last time was only six months previously and he remembered the non-comforting words of the head of the service well - very well indeed! 'You need to be a little more alert old chap. You need to choose your friends more carefully and we

Chapter Nine – The London Conspiracy

cannot afford any more situations like the Lebanese ... er ...'

The head of the SIS was left searching for words.

'You know what I mean old chap, that lady nearly did for you and we must have no more of it. Can't you get married or something?'

As he left C's office that day, he did actually question what was really going on in his life. He wasn't married and had never felt the urge to. He was not gay, although he did have some near misses at Cambridge. He had convinced himself he was just waiting for the right 'girl' to come along. Eric Saunders OBE was forty three years old and not in the best of condition. He ate too much and drank far too much and he did like the company of women, but not all the time. Great to eat with, great to drink with, great to screw with ... but that was where it ended for him.

The Lebanese affair, that was very close to being his complete undoing, had started at a Bahrain British Embassy 'do' in the expansive gardens of the embassy compound on Government Avenue. These were regular events, laid on by the senior embassy staff still living in the eighteenth century, for reasons of 'showing the flag' and 'entertaining the locals'. Eric did not go to these kind of functions very often, but on this particular day, he had nothing else planned and his absence from many other events had been noticed by the

Ambassador, stimulating some severely negative comment from his boss on the C2 desk.

Her name was Jamila Haddad. Jamila in Arabic meant 'beautiful' and she definitely *fell* in to that category - in bucket loads. It was one of the first things he told her - and that evening she also *fell* into his bed. Her job was described by her as a secretary to the manager of a well known Lebanese food import company, based in Beirut, with an office and well established track record in Bahrain. The Lebanese Civil War was in, what the intelligence community called, the 'Fourth Phase'. The PLO had been thrown out and it looked as if this now more or less partitioned country, could be brought back together again with a little determination shown by behind the scenes negotiators.

Although the Lebanon was strictly out of Eric's sphere of operations, he was copied in on all negotiations that the British were involved with and these of course were regarded as Top Secret.

The long and short of it was that the beautiful Jamila was not all that she appeared to be and in fact was a senior intelligence operator for the PLO. She was not on anyone's radar and even the CIA seemed to have little or no history on her. When the Israelis did a snatch job in to Gaza one fateful evening late in eighty five, they not only got their man but a bunch of very revealing documents, some of which contained Eric's 'scratchings' in the margins. Jamila had been busy and

Chapter Nine – The London Conspiracy

disappeared off the face of the earth the day after the raid.

The 'Service' is a fairly straight forward operation in hierarchical terms. There were the 'Aristocrats' or 'Cats' for short, who came from privileged backgrounds, went to a public school and on to Cambridge or Oxford, where they were recruited in to the 'Service'. The process was simple, although most of the recruiting came by way of the numerous college clubs and pubs of Cambridge and the near surrounds populated mainly by ersatz political mercenaries and a sprinkling of the real thing. Despite the far reaching consequences of the nefarious activities of the 'Cambridge Five' in nineteen sixty three, Cambridge was always regarded as recruiting 'fertile ground' for the Secret Intelligence Service.

Eric Saunders was one of those who eagerly took up the challenge. His real identity was The Right Honourable Algenon Eric Heathcote-Saunders OBE, known by family members simply as 'Algy', a term he hated with a vengeance. His father had died when he was seventeen, his elder brother had been killed in the war and his younger married brother, married sister and mother all lived quite happily within the ninety four rooms that made up the East Sussex family pile, Flimwell Manor.

He paid all the bills from the substantial family estate; paid allowances to his brother and sister and looked after his mother with dutiful care. The one thousand three hundred acre estate employed thirty staff and whenever he was in England, he would visit, which was always a cause of great joy to his family. Eric did not use his full title and never had, although his father disapproved when he was alive. He preferred the straight forward nomenclature he had adopted of Eric Saunders and that was how he had made his way through life - so far.

There were two other 'types' that were easily recognisable within the Service and they were the 'Gung Ho's' or 'Gungs' for short and they had made their way in to the fold via the military, mostly Army and Navy. All the rest were individuals that actually did all the work. They were recruited from just about anywhere to provide all the mechanics of running this massive organisation. They were called the 'Technicians' or 'Technos' for short. The current head of the Service was a 'Gung' and so tended to favour all the other 'Gungs' down below. However, the real power within the Service *was* and always had been, with the 'Cats' who were all his 'chums'. As expected, they had mostly rallied round when Eric had slipped off the rocky road to save him from the very greatest humiliation of being expelled from the Service.

So, instead of just serving a normal twelve month rotation posting to Bahrain, he was now to stay there until his masters saw fit to re-habilitate him back in to the real world of espionage and the simmering political

Chapter Nine – The London Conspiracy

hot-bed that was still the cold war. Eric was pondering his situation in some detail as the Jaguar carved its way through the heavy traffic of the metropolis in the direction of Lambeth. He had been called to London to discuss some Irish chap who was seemingly causing a bit of a stir in Abu Nar. Anything to do with the Irish rang the odd alarm bell in Eric's mind, especially since the degrading outcome of the Littlejohn incident in 1972. It nearly finished the Service, or MI6 as it was known publicly, and was probably responsible for the age of austerity that had crept up to blanket his employer ever since. It was rumoured amongst the 'Cats' that MI5 was up to its neck in it all, but nothing had been proven and since that day MI5 had found the most favour with the Intelligence community's political masters.

The black Jaguar pulled up in front of the anonymous concrete and glass portico of the Devereux designed, Century House building, on Westminster Bridge Road. The twenty floors of an architecturally nondescript construction had been allocated to the SIS in nineteen sixty. They moved in during sixty four and more than twenty years on, the whole place was now in near overload. Eric exited the purring vehicle, thanked the driver, signed a sort of driver's duty sheet and extricated his tan leather travelling case from the boot of the car. He pulled his newly acquired building pass out of his jacket pocket and hung it round his neck. He had only used it once before. The thick plastic card that held his photograph and a number of unintelligible codes was imprinted with some sort of magnetic strip that magically opened doors and made lifts work. The 'Technos' had been at it again.

The card allowed the movements of the wearer to be monitored at all times whilst inside the building and recorded on some state of the art computer programme. Computers and Word Processors were beyond Eric's normal span of interest, but over the last few years, the whole place had been littered with them, resulting in just about one on every desk, in every office. Eric was a non-believer and preferred pen, paper and a simple 'slide in the pocket' calculator for all of his computing needs. He was a Dinosaur and freely admitted it.

The lift he was standing in front of made a 'dinging' noise and a light flashed above it as the doors slid open noiselessly. He moved forward followed by three or four others and hit the button for the tenth floor. Seconds later he was out of the lift and walking the labyrinth of dull grey carpeted corridors in search of room ten thirty three which was the office of the C2 Middle East Desk Controller. He slid his security card over a wall mounted reader and the door magically clicked open. The well equipped secretarial station, complete with computer and printer, potted plants and

Chapter Nine – The London Conspiracy

a coffee machine was manned by Sybil. She was best described as a nice lady of maturing years who had been with the Service for a long time.

Sybil looked up as her visitor entered. She was smiling happily as she got up from her seat and moved toward Eric, kissing him gently but affectionately on each cheek.

'How lovely to see you again Eric, darling!'

'Great to see you again too Sybil - how have you been these past few weeks?'

'Oh fine. Except for all the normal trouble and strife that goes on around here, I'm really in good shape. Will you be going down to Flimwell on this trip?'

It was a question she already knew the answer to as Eric always went to Sussex when his visited the UK.

'Yes, absolutely Sybil, in fact I'm driving down tomorrow for a couple of days - and if you could arrange a car for me, that would be really appreciated'

'Of course Eric, please give my regards to your mother … and you know who is waiting to see you'

Sybil, with a wry smile, pointed toward the inner office that housed the controller of the C2 desk, Christopher StJohn Briars. Christopher always liked to be called 'Christopher' and the 'Saint John' always had to be pronounced 'Sin-gen'. He was a 'Cat' and had been a year below Eric at Eton. He had joined the Service two years later than Eric and was now two seniority grades above him. This reasonably meteoric elevation in civil service rank made little difference to their personal relationship, a relationship that both men considered to be a good one. Neither needed the money that automatically came with the job. Both were career agents of the Service, purely because they had never ever contemplated doing anything else.

The door to Christopher's office was ajar and a deep voice with a cut glass accent could be heard shouting 'Come on in *Algy* old boy' followed by laughter from both the Controller's office and Sybil. Using 'Algy' was a wind up that had been in place for all the years they had known one another and made Eric smile childishly as he kissed Sybil one more time on the cheek and entered Christopher's office.

'Coffee Sybil!' Christopher shouted as Eric attempted to secure some level of comfort in the black leather and chrome armless chair waiting for him in front of his controller's desk.

'So, my dear friend, how are things in the bright, beautiful and sunny climes of the Arabian Gulf?'

'Absolute crap Christopher ... and you know it' Eric replied as a further dry smile passed between them. They had only met face to face about a month previously when Eric Saunders had been summoned to the UK for one of the regular field agent's briefings about events in the Gulf War and some disturbing updates on Russian activities in Afghanistan. The two men took several minutes to catch up on the recent

Chapter Nine – The London Conspiracy

activities, including promotions and some demotions of mutual friends and when the second pot of coffee came, it was taken as a cue to get down to more serious business.

'As you know, the reason I have called you here Eric is for you to tell me what you know of the activities of this Declan Doyle character in Abu Nar'

'To be totally frank Christopher, I don't really know a lot. I have spoken to our man Paddy Doherty who tells me he has nothing concrete except that Doyle is trying to put together some sort of oil shipping scheme based out of Kharg Island … for the Iranians of course. However, as we well know, Paddy is not the most reliable source we've ever had and would sell his own mother for the right price. He may actually know more than he's letting on. It's all in my regular reports somewhere'

'Is it worth oiling the wheels a little with some hard cash do you think?' Asked Christopher.

'Well, for all I know these two bloody Irishmen might be cooking up some story or other, just to get the result you are suggesting'

Christopher looked hard at his friend for a few seconds before replying.

'Perhaps you didn't know Eric, but there is only one Irishman involved here, the other used to be one of ours' 'Yes, I know. Paddy used to be a 'Gung' who had a reputation for being a bit sly and probably untrustworthy. When we eased him out, there was a fairly substantial sigh of relief in some quarters'

'No. I mean Doyle. He used to be one of ours'

'What?' exclaimed Saunders who was slightly taken aback.

'He was a 'Techno'. Ex RAF reconnaissance, trained further at Bletchley Park. He was into communications, microwaves and all that sort of stuff, and seemingly good at it too. He had a cover with a major UK telecommunications company. We sent him in to Nigeria in sixty eight during the Biafra affair. The rebels were taking out the government communications installations we had only installed a few years previously. Doyle was sent in as a civilian expert to try and keep communications in that god forsaken hole running. He had been involved with the initial project and knew his way round the country and the system. No body guards, no SAS, just a low profile approach that he insisted on. No one on either side was supposed to know of his connection to us.

Unfortunately circumstances overtook him when rebel troops raided across the river Niger to Okwe and dragged him back to Onitsha. The bridge had been blown from the first day of the war and no one from the government side had the stomach to mount a raid to get him back. As far as they were concerned, he was a European Mercenary and it didn't help that he was captured with a band of Belgians who were being paid

Chapter Nine – The London Conspiracy

by the Government to protect the district leader.

They beat the shit out of him for several months before we knew where he was. He eventually got out, putting a few to bed in the process, but he was really pissed off. He accused us of all sorts of things, some of which were probably true knowing the politics of the situation; oil supplies and all that. It was a messy affair and any connection between Doyle and the Service has been scraped'. Eric leaned back a little further into the creaking, sparsely upholstered chair as he considered what had just been said. Being 'scraped', as far as Saunders knew, meant that every single piece of data linking an individual to the Service had been erased. This person did not exist and had never existed as far as MI6 or MI5 were concerned. But that obviously didn't apply to individuals of a certain rank, or with particular influence, as Christopher seemed to know all about the man. Eric was a little confused and somewhat annoyed. He needed to know the history of every character of interest residing, or even passing through his 'patch' and in this case he now knew he had been kept completely in the dark.

'So Christopher - if this 'ex-Techno' has been scraped, why are you telling me all this?'

'Because, I want you to understand the level of the man Eric - he is not even Irish - his English family roots go back eons. He hates any reference to an Irish connection and that probably accounts for him and that drunken idiot Paddy Doherty, not getting on very well'.

'He has no file then?' It was a question.

'No Eric, he has no file. All you need to know about him is what I've just told you'

Saunders fiddled with his tie for a moment. Christopher knew it was a sign of irritation. Eric looked up after purposely clasping his hands together.

'Then the next natural question my dear friend must be … what's the interest here? Do we care about some sort of half assed project to help the Iranians get a few more barrels out of the Gulf? From where I'm sitting, they'll need a bloody lot more than a few gallons of oil to get them out of the shit they are in right now. Surely this farcical war cannot go on much longer with the Yanks backing the Iraqis and the Russians, so screwed up, they have a full time job keeping 'Glasnost' alive, troops in Afghanistan fed and watered, and the fires still burning at home before planning to get into world war three over a bunch of Muslim fanatics!'

'We care my dear Eric, because we are the Secret Intelligence Service and it is our job to know what is going on in the big wide world. You are our man in the area and we want to be aware of the mechanics and the politics of any situation that involves British Nationals – and - as you have so *succinctly* put it - a bunch of Muslim fanatics!'

Eric Saunders got up from his incommodious seat and helped himself to another coffee. He remained

Chapter Nine – The London Conspiracy

standing. 'Now Eric, I want you to get to work on this Doyle business. We do not want to interfere in any way - right now - but as you well know, policy is often liable to change and we want to be prepared. What is extremely important is for us to be comfortable in some sort of assurance that the CIA know no more about what is going on than we do. That's really all my old friend - so I want you to have a nose around'

'Look Christopher - I know he's been scraped, but do we have any more background on this Doyle character at all?'

'That's why I wanted you here. There are still some 'Technos' downstairs who knew him. Sybil has a list. I also want you to have a chat with Percy Wainwright on the C4 Western desk and Charles Bickerstaff on the C6 Africa desk. He's been pretty active in both those areas in the past few years and by searching out various shall we say 'not quite kosher' opportunities, has managed to accumulate a substantially larger amount of cash than he ever would have working for us'

He paused with a comical but pained looking expression and both men grinned knowingly at the reference to 'cash' and 'the service'!

'Build up a file and take it back with you. Get hold of Paddy and squeeze him a bit more. Have our commercial contacts in Abu Nar step up to the plate a bit. Let's simply find out what the hell is going on'.

'All right Christopher, leave it to me. I'll have

something more detailed back to you within the next couple of weeks'

'Good man' Christopher shook Eric's hand. It was a sign that their short meeting was over.

'Are you going down to Sussex now?

'Yes, I think Sybil is conjuring up a car for me. I'm staying at my club tonight, do you fancy dinner – and you must bring Janice of course?'

'I most certainly do and Janice has kept today free hoping to see you … so no need to 'ring home for permission'. Both men laughed out loud. Janice was Christopher's wife and she adored Eric.

'So - around seven thirty then at - let me see - what about the Mon Plaisir in Covent Garden or - maybe the Wellington Club in Knightsbridge?'

'I think the Wellington old chap. Janice absolutely loves the little band there; simply couldn't be better for both of us. See you in the upstairs bar at seven thirty or as near as I can get Janice to be ready … and no talking shop!'

A further smile passed between the two friends and work colleagues as Eric left the office.

~~~~~~~~
~~~~

Chapter Ten
Hong Kong

It was the end of a long, hot early August day in downtown Kowloon for Tony Swales, Managing Director of Far East Maritime Insurance Group (FEMI). It was seven o'clock on that Tuesday evening August fourth. He didn't know it yet, but it was to be a date he would remember for some time – for all the wrong reasons He wanted to go home. The last two weeks had been a bit hectic in arranging and laying off risk on an insurance deal with a company called Associated Oilfield Services Inc. His company had been forced to underwrite much more than would be normal in the kind of deal being negotiated and shit or bust, he was in for a third. Declan Doyle, the CEO of AOS had put some pressure on him relating to a fairly hefty lump of cash money he had needed to call on three years previously. Tony Swales had now repaid that debt and so, in some ways, he was relieved to be at the end of it all. Declan Doyle was not the kind of person you wanted to owe favours to. Tony was looking forward to going home to see his much loved four year old son and have dinner with his astoundingly beautiful wife An Ni. The trip from his office in the heart of Kowloon business district to his home in Clearwater Bay was only

Chapter Ten – Hong Kong

about eight miles but would take more than half an hour to push through the early evening traffic. Sitting in the armchair comfort of a 500SEL Mercedes did take away a little of the pain and to have a fantastic house at Bay Villas, with views up to Silverstrand, was an absolute privilege that few could afford.

Tony Swales loved his house, loved his family, loved his job and today, with Declan Doyle off his back for ever, he was totally enjoying life. The phone call to An Ni was a quick one just to let her know that he was leaving the office. He was focused on getting to the underground car park, and as he exited the elevator doors. A voice called out

'Good Night Mr Swales'

'Good night Chui' Tony replied without looking back to the security desk. Tien Chui, night security manager for the building, lifted up the telephone, dialled a number and spoke quickly in Cantonese.

'Hou' OK

He checked his watch. It was four minutes past seven o'clock. Now someone other than Tien Chui and An Ni knew that Tony Swales had left the building. Within a minute the CEO of FEMI was feeling secure, enveloped within the hand stitched cream hide leather interior of his stretched S Class Mercedes.

Time to go home!

The traffic was intense as it always appeared to be at that time and yet again Tony reminded himself that he should leave the office either a little earlier or a little later than seven o'clock. After fifteen minutes he was on the Clearwater Bay Road and with traffic easing making good progress. For some strange reason, tonight, more than many other ... he simply wanted to get home.

~~~~~~

An Ni was spinning out noodles from a solid block of dough ready for dinner. It was an art rather than a skill and she was often cajoled into showing off her 'art' by enthusiastic guests at the frequent dinner parties held at number six Bay Villas. She glanced up at the kitchen wall clock. It was five minutes or so past seven. She knew that Tony was on his way. A fresh lobster weighing in at over a kilo was under preparation; chillies and herbs had been chopped and a bottle of crisp Chardonnay was cooling in an ice bucket.

Four year old Jonothan was sleeping in his bedroom. An Ni and Cho Li the nanny, had worked hard to tire him out during the afternoon. Then, Cho Li had caught a taxi to visit her sister who worked for a family in Sai Kung, a fifteen minute ride away.

Life was good for the Swales family. An Ni was as happy as she could remember and she was as in love with her fantastic husband today as she was when they first met on the Star Ferry travelling from Hong Kong

Chapter Ten – Hong Kong

Island to Kowloon some seven years previously.

Things, however, were about to change.

She didn't take any notice of the front door bell at first, but when it was sounded repeatedly impatiently, An Ni remembered that Cho Li was out.

She finished the noodles and completed laying them out on a cloth to dry for a few minutes. Moving quickly to the sink, she washed and dried her hands hurriedly, making her way to the front door. Her mind was literally elsewhere as she glanced at the video image of the visitor on the reception hall display. It was a man who must have been quite tall. He was European, dressed in a suit and tie, carrying a small briefcase.

An Ni opened one side of the heavy, panelled hardwood double doors. She was smiling, as she just about always was and enquired of the stranger …

'Can I help you?'

'Good evening, I am so sorry to disturb you at this time, but are you Mrs Swales, married to Mr Tony Swales?'

'Yes, I am' she replied confidently, still projecting her most engaging smile. She had a second or two to take in the athletic build of the stranger at her door; the military style crew cut hair and the tanned square, chiselled features of the man.

The blow came from nowhere.

An Ni blacked out immediately.

Mr Blue and Mr Green were dressed in black overalls

zipped to the neck, black cotton balaclavas, black leather gloves and black canvas shoes with pattern-less soles. Around each belted waist hung a Beretta 9mm pistol filled with fifteen rounds, half a dozen sets of black plastic cable tie handcuffs, a double edged hunting knife, a large pair of wire cutters and a set of screwdrivers.

Mr Blue and Mr Green were not dressed to party.

Mr Blue had entered the house through the rear. He had quickly and silently surveyed all the rooms noting the small boy sleeping soundly in a ground floor bedroom. He had closed the door to it quietly, heading for the kitchen. He followed the female occupant of the kitchen to the front door as she answered the insistent bell. As soon as she replied positively to Col Oliver Gresham's question, he struck from behind.

The single blow would put her out for a while. He caught her as she fell, looking to the Colonel for instruction. The well dressed man at the door moved his head to indicate the main living room, pulling a plan of the property from his pocket as he moved inside. Mr Green, who had been waiting outside, was tasked with lookout duties to the front of the house. All three men were in contact through miniature UHF radios.

Oliver Gresham checked communications once again with each of his team before closing the front door and following Mr Blue in to the generous living area. Except for the radio check, there had been no conversation.

Chapter Ten – Hong Kong

Gresham collected a dining chair from an adjacent room. Mr Blue took a roll of black 'Gaffa' tape from his overall and taped the now hand cuffed An Ni to the chair.

She was still dozy and had not fully come round. The taped mouth ensured that An Ni remained silent.

They waited.

The Colonel checked his watch. It was twenty five minutes to eight. The UHF radio crackled and a voice came whispering over the ether.

'Green. Car coming' pause 'It's a big Merc … It's our man!'

Mr Green sank back into the shadows as the black Mercedes 500 SEL cruised in to the driveway. The car stopped outside the three-bay garage and out jumped Tony Swales, happy to be home; happy to get out of the murderous, relentless traffic of Hong Kong and be rested in the beauty and tranquillity of Clearwater Bay. He pulled his key from his jacket pocket and pushed it in to the front door lock. It wouldn't turn. The door was unlocked. That was unusual. When An Ni was in the house, the front door was always locked.

He paused for a second, instinctively looking around him. The door pushed open. He paused again listening for sounds. There were none. This again was unusual.

There was no more time for thought as Mr Green grabbed the hesitant home comer, pulled one arm tight behind his back and lowered him to the floor in one practised movement. Three seconds later, with little or no sound, Tony Swales was handcuffed and his mouth taped. He didn't really know what had hit him. What he did know was that whoever his visitor or visitors were, they seemed to know what they were doing. He needed to take care.

Some seconds later he was picked up off the floor in a single easy motion by Mr Green and moved in to the living room. As the door was pushed open, he saw An Ni tied and taped to the chair. Her eyes were wide, pleading, questioning … fearful! She made no noise through the restraining black tape covering her mouth.

Tony sank toward the floor as he took in every detail of the scene into which he had been pushed stumbling and mumbling by his captors. Where was Jon, his four year old son?

'Keep him on his feet Mr Green' came the sharp instruction from the tall, fit looking be-suited individual who had a slow, considered southern American accent and appeared to be in charge. Tony received a sharp tug holding him completely upright. What the hell was happening, who were these fucking people, where was his son?

The man in charge spoke again.

'Now Mr Swales, this will hopefully not take long and with your co-operation, could end up being a painless experience. That however, is up to you'.

The sentence was delivered in monotone with no

Chapter Ten – Hong Kong

emphasis, no emotion; very matter of fact and accompanied by a menacing look, full of alarming authority.

'You may be concerned about your son who is actually sleeping in the bedroom across the connecting corridor. The door has been closed and hopefully he should remain asleep for the short time it will take us to conclude our business!'

Tony could feel the colour draining from him as he took in every syllable of what he was being told. A cold hand was closing around his heart, a kind of fear where time physically stands still. An Ni was now in tears and looked completely desperate. He felt so bloody helpless.

'Just to make sure we do not waste any time and that you realize the seriousness of your situation …' Gresham turned to the overall clad figure standing behind An Ni

'Hit her' he breathed.

Mr Blue stood in front of the helpless female figure bound and taped to the dining chair, drew back an arm and hit her in the face with so much force, the chair and An Ni tipped over.

Tony Swales let out an involuntary, high pitched cry of frustration mixed with anger, instinctively attempting to move forward resulting in a sharp pain pulsing through his right shoulder. His arms were pulled right up his back, so high, that he thought for one second his shoulder had been dislocated. He was in severe pain.

As Mr Blue pulled the chair and An Ni upright again she was near the point of complete breakdown, making horrible gurgling noises, unable to escape as screams of pain, or words of damnation were impossible to deliver due to the ever clinging black 'gaffa' tape. The man in charge did not flinch; satisfaction reflected in the glacial, commanding and hostile eyes.

'So you see Mr Swales, we are here for one thing and one thing only' he paused to slow the delivery and emphasis of his remaining words '…… and we will not be leaving without it. Do you wish to co-operate or not? Please nod or shake your head'

Tony Swales was searching feverishly for any sign of what this well planned invasion of his home and sadistic violation of his family was all about in the depths of the cold impassive gaze that now locked the prisoner and his captor together. There was none. The narrow stare reflected a mood of chilling detachment.

He nodded his head. Mr Green leant over his hostage from behind and ripped off the tape. Tony Swales took in a large gulping breath. He was about to utter an obscenity, but thought better of it. His face tightened in to a mask of bitter hatred. These guys were hard-cased professionals and if things didn't go exactly the way they wanted, someone was going to get badly hurt. Whatever this was all about, his family came first. He turned back to the shattered figure of An Ni still bound and slumped in the chair in front of him. Her swollen,

Chapter Ten – Hong Kong

pleading eyes were streaming with tears, her face bright red and a dark and ugly bruise had begun to appear on the left side around the cheek bone. To see his beautiful, adoring An Ni in this horrific situation, with himself simply a helpless observer, the emotion completely overcame him and he began to weep uncontrollably.

Tony Swales received a sharp, stinging slap in the face from Mr Green as he stood in the living room of his home, a home invaded and despoiled by ruthless strangers; strangers who wanted him to …

'Listen up Swales' shouted Gresham 'Listen up and hunker down as this could be your lucky day' The irony was not wasted on Mr Blue and Mr Green who both let out a quiet and muffled chuckle from beneath the cotton balaclavas.

'You have an arrangement with a company called Associated Oilfield Services to insure, under war zone risk, a large piece of offshore equipment. Am I correct?'

Tears streaming down his face, Tony Swales nodded silently in reply.

'Mr Declan Doyle has agreed to pay you a premium of $12 million for this service. Am I correct?'

There was a short pause as Tony formed the words carefully in his mind.

'The actual amount is twelve million, one hundred and sixteen thousand four hundred and fifty five US dollars' he whispered. 'Good' The American Colonel pulled out the house map from his pocket along with a pen and wrote the exact number down.

'Now let's get down to business' he continued.

'How much are you holding and how much is laid off?'

'We are holding thirty three per cent' muttered a completely defeated Tony Swales'

'I am surprised Mr Swales. Can your company afford to hold one third of close to a gross fifty or sixty million dollar risk?' There was no time for a considered reply.

'I think not Mr Swales. So here is a new risk for you to weigh up. Whatever Mr Doyle has over you to take on such a gamble will have nowhere near the consequences of failure that not co-operating with me will have. If you think he is a mean asshole, wait until you get to know me better. I have the power to make the sun set on your world ... *permanently*! Do I make myself *clear* Mr Swales?'

Tony Swales was now visibly and un-controllably trembling. An Ni was still slumped, bound and taped in the chair, motionless. He knew she was in pain. He remained silent. Was his son OK? Were these bastards telling the truth about his son? Was he sleeping, unharmed in his ground floor bedroom? He muttered the barely audible words 'My son ...'

'Later Mr Swales – when we have finished our business' Gresham spoke in a low and menacing tone.

Chapter Ten – Hong Kong

He pulled out a slip of paper from his pocket with a telephone number written on it. He walked over to the telephone situated on a small glass topped side table located next to a three seat cream leather settee. He motioned to Mr Green who moved in to action by pulling the cutters from his belt and breaking open the plastic handcuffs. Although his hostage appeared submissive, he knew in his game that appearances could be deceptive. He was watching him carefully.

'Come and sit here' It was a command not a request.

Mr Green pushed Tony in the direction of the sofa. He sat down as ordered, rubbing his sore wrists.

'Now listen carefully. In a moment or two, I am going to ring the number on this piece of paper' He showed it to Tony Swales. 'Do you recognise it?' he queried. Tony nodded his head. 'When Mr Doyle answers, you will not offer any pleasantries, you will tell him that you have withdrawn from your contract to insure the manifold structure of the Geneveh Project. You will not engage in any discussion on the matter, you will simply tell him that all required documentation will be telexed to his office tomorrow. You will then put down the receiver. Tomorrow, you will make sure that all of the cancellation documents are issued, as promised and any existing signed original copies of the insurance certificate are returned to you and destroyed.' He paused for a second whilst Swales took it all in.

'Do you understand what I am telling you Mr Swales?'

Gresham barked. Without waiting for a reply he continued.

'Once you have done this, our business will be completed. We will leave you and your wife and son in peace'.

'Who the hell are you' hissed the now completely defeated, subjugated and humiliated insurance broker.

'That is none of your concern except to say that Mr Doyle is dabbling in something that he shouldn't and the consequences of his actions could well undermine the policies and ambitions of whole nations. You have no options my friend and shortly, Mr Doyle will have none either. Do you now understand what you have to do?

'Yes'

Gresham checked his watch. It would be afternoon, about one o'clock in Abu Nar. Swales rang the number. Declan Doyle answered. The conversation was short and went as Gresham had instructed. He replaced the handset, his face was grim.

At a sign from the Colonel, Mr Blue took out his belted knife and with one simple action cut the tape securing An Ni to the upright chair. She fell forward. Mr Blue severed the plastic handcuffs, lifted up her head and carefully pulled at the tape across her mouth. She whimpered as he did so.

Her dampened eyes were closed. She looked frighteningly lifeless except for the near silent weeping.

Chapter Ten – Hong Kong

Tony's heart was breaking just looking at her. He felt totally exhausted. The adrenalin effects were seeping away and the swelling, unwanted emotions of total defeat and humiliation, in not being able to defend everything he held dear, had now kicked in.

'Check the boy' the American Colonel said to Mr Green who quickly and silently moved out of the room. He turned his head sharply. 'Don't move Mr Swales' he barked. Mr Green was back in seconds.

'The boy is OK and still sleeping' he stated quietly.

'We are leaving now Mr Swales' Gresham whispered in the ear of his deflated and subjugated victim as he bent over him, now laying awkwardly, draped across the leather sofa.

'The usual rules apply. Do not attempt to follow us, do not contact the authorities and do not have any more conversations with Declan Doyle. I am a man that has access to much information and if you break any of these rules' he paused 'I will know – and I will be back. Any further visits from me will be most *regrettable* and not quite so friendly'

The heated, tobacco laden breath of his tormentor engulfed the senses of the traumatised insurance broker as he lay still, the word 'regrettable' ringing in his ears – and then, as they came, they were gone – silently.

At the sound of the front door clicking shut, An Ni jumped up from her chair and ran in to the ground floor bedroom where her four year old son Jonothan was still sleeping soundly. She silently crawled in to the bed beside him, clasped him close and closed her eyes. Her boy was safe.

Tony Swales lifted heavy eyelids and focused on the telephone beside him. He lifted the handset and placed it by the phone. No more calls today. In a daze, he walked in to the ground floor bedroom and lay on the floor next to the bed where his wife and son were sleeping.

They were safe.

He began to sob quietly as he picked up the faint noise of the private Telex machine starting up in his study located at the end of the ground floor east wing.

Tap..tap..tap…tap…

~~~~~~~~
~~~~

Chapter Eleven
The Withdrawal

Declan Doyle stared at the telephone handset in total disbelief. Had he actually just had that conversation with Tony Swales? He was silent for a moment, his mind in turmoil. What the hell was going on? What on earth could have happened to make Tony renege on his already confirmed deal to insure the PLEM manifold? As he repeat-dialled Tony Swales house number he shouted 'Esther!' His secretary came running in to the office wearing a worried and questioning look.

'Esther, get a telex out to Tony Swales right now at his private number and his office number. Tell him to ring me. I don't care what time of day or night … but *ring* me he must. Then get on to every contact we have in his office we have a home number for and ring them. Don't take any shit. Tell them to get hold of that asshole Swales and tell him to *ring* me'

Esther moved quickly to get on the case, unsure of what response she would get, but when her boss was in a mood like this, the best thing to do was not question anything but just get on with it. Declan sat silently in his office, fuming, with eyes tight shut in an attempt to focus on what was happening. After a minute or two, he opened them, picked up the phone and dialled two.

Chapter Eleven – The Withdrawal

'Andy - get in here!'

Andy knocked and entered the high ceilinged, ash panelled office and sat down in front of Declan's desk, waiting for a sign of recognition.

'Andy - we are in the shit - big time'

'Tell me about it' came the quick reply.

'That tosspot Swales has just cancelled the insurance on the PLEM'

'He's what?' shouted Andy

'He's damn well *cancelled* it …'

'But …' the reply tailed off in to nothing as Andy began to quickly calculate the consequences to the Geneveh Project.

Declan spoke quietly.

'Have the original insurance documents been lodged with the bank?'

'They came through by courier yesterday and I took them down there this morning'

'Get on to the bank and tell them you need them back for an hour or two as you forgot to copy them for our files or some such crap … but get those documents back!'

'What are you going to do' Andy asked curiously.

'I'm going to forge them'

'You're going to do what!' Andy exclaimed.

'If the bank gets even a small sniff that we have no insurance, they will have to pull the plug on the whole damned deal. We are too far down the road Andy and that mad bastard in Iran is going to cut my bloody throat if we cancel the deal now. So, the first priority is to sort the bank out'

Andy was completely taken aback. He had known Declan do some hair brained, close to the edge things in his time, but this was criminality on a big scale. He was agitated but remained silent, making notes on his yellow legal pad. It was no use arguing with the man when he was like this.

'Collect them from the bank and then take them down to Argawal at Xerox and get them copied in colour. Make sure they are aligned absolutely square and match the paper for weight, colour and if possible a water mark, as near as you possibly can. Use some whiteout to take out any staple marks. The copies must look as close to the original as possible. Then bring them back here. When you get back, contact Mr Shetty of Aqbal Engineering, the guy who makes our steel quality stamps and tell him to get his arse round here'.

'Is that all?' Andy queried.

'That's all' Declan replied sharply. He looked up. Andy was still sitting there. He didn't look happy.

'Andy, desperate situations require desperate measures. Do you remember the 'letter of comfort' stroke we pulled on the ABR Bank three years back?

Andy nodded resignedly.

'Where would we be now if we hadn't pulled that one off? Just trust me on this one Andy and get on with it'.

Chapter Eleven – The Withdrawal

Mr Shetty sat in Declan's office next to Andy Peters as the task was being explained to him. Resting on Declan's desk was a cast iron hand press for the company seal. The metal seal block had been removed. Mr Shetty was studying a square of paper that appeared to have been cut out of a document. The square contained a grey imprint of what looked like a seal for a business called Far East Maritime Company. Declan spoke.

'I want you to make me a seal block exactly as the one I'm holding in my hand but engraved with information you see on the imprint' Mr Shetty looked up and then turned with a questioning glance in Andy's direction.

'And when do you want this seal?' was the crucial question.

'In two hours' came the firm reply.

Mr Shetty remained nonplussed. He knew that anything wanted in two hours would carry a big price tag.

'And how much are you prepared to pay for this seal ... the seal you want in two hours Mr Doyle?

'Five thousand Dirhams Mr Shetty - in cash - in two hours time' stated Declan.

Mr Shetty left smiling.

'So what's going on' asked Andy politely.

'Well, once we have the seal, we will take the copied insurance certificate and confirmation documents and impress them with the seal right over the point where the originals were pressed. FEMC will want all original documents back and we will give them to them to stop any further fuss. The copies, you will take back to the bank this evening. If you are casual about it, they won't even look at them. My bet is they will just shove them in the project file and that will be that'.

'Are you that confident?' asked Andy.

'They are all *your* bloody mates in there; I'm relying on you to pull it off'

Declan allowed himself the luxury of a smile. It was infectious and caught by Andy for a brief second as he made his way out of the office.

Declan checked the clock in his car. It was a few minutes before seven. Andy had phoned only ten minutes earlier to confirm that the documents had been accepted by the bank and as Declan had envisaged, there was only a cursory scan to check the letterhead and a quick feel of the impressed seal. Then, they were simply dropped in to the AOS project folder. The job was done and Andy was on his way to have a drink with Peter McKewan, the ABR Securities department manager. It would be a late night for him, Declan thought.

He pulled up in the Abu Nar Country Club car park. It was full. He carefully manoeuvred the big Mercedes in to the reserved parking space marked 'Chairman'.

He needed a drink.

Chapter Eleven – The Withdrawal

As he walked through the bar, several hands went up in greeting but he had no intention of stopping. He headed for the office of the General Manager, tapped the door and entered. Geoffrey Bowes-Stewart was engrossed in drawing up staff rotas. He looked up as Declan sat himself down on a comfortable sofa in one corner of the amply proportioned clean and tidy office. He picked up the internal phone and ordered a beer from the main bar. After a few seconds, he threw the red biro on to the desk top and stated to no one in particular.

'Sod it, I think I'll have one too' He picked up the phone again and ordered a large brandy.

'So, what's happening Declan?' enquired Geoffrey.

'More to the point, what's happening with you?' asked Declan.

'It couldn't be better I'm pleased to say. Takings are up again this month and staff sickness is down nearly ten percent against the same time last year'

Geoffrey was grinning from ear to ear. Declan smiled, his spirits lifted. He cherished the company of this man. In his short tenure as General Manager, Geoffrey had become a reasonably close friend.

The drinks arrived and Rajan, the Head Barman, shook hands and greeted Declan before he left.

'Cheers' was the joint toast as the conversation continued. 'If you don't mind me saying, you look a bit knackered old chap'

'To tell you the truth, I've had a hell of a day of it Geoffrey'

'Want to talk about it?'

Declan paused thoughtfully. He needed to unload to someone and Geoffrey had proven to be totally trustworthy in the past.

'Do you remember about a month after you arrived here, I brought a guy up for what turned out to be a very long lunch and in fact I think it was the first time we got pissed together'

Geoffrey thought for a second or two.

'Was it that guy from Hong Kong? Wasn't he some kind of insurance broker or something …?'

Declan interrupted 'That's the man, absolutely spot on. His name is Tony Swales and he's screwed me over – big time'

He sipped at his ice cold beer, proceeding to reveal the bones of the Geneveh Project, including the part that the delicate positioning of the PLEM manifold would play. Finally he revealed the role the Iraqis would be expected to play in trying to destroy it and the part that Tony Swales had now refused to play in providing some total loss insurance.

Another set of drinks came.

'Well, if you now have no insurance on the job, aren't the banks going to be a bit wobbly?'

It was a sensible and perceptive observation. Geoffrey Bowes-Stewart was no fool and purely due to the fact

Chapter Eleven – The Withdrawal

he had a double barrelled name, some people made the mistake of taking him for one. Declan flushed slightly as he replied quickly

'I think I've managed to solve that little problem'. There was a further thoughtful silence for a few seconds as beer and brandy was downed. Geoffrey rested his glass and more to himself rather than a continuance of the conversation, muttered quietly

'It's a pity the bloody Iraqis couldn't simply stop the war for a day or so for you to sink the underwater thingamygig ... then you wouldn't have a problem' He picked up the phone to order a refill.

'Do you fancy some dinner Declan?'

Declan's thought processes were slowly untangling. Something halted the clearing mental haze with a jolt.

'Say that again' Declan demanded.

'Do you fancy some dinner?'

'No, not that, the thing about the Iraqis' he said excitedly.

'I just *said* that ... if the Iraqis could stop the war for a day or two, all your bloody problems would be solved'.

Declan leapt up.

'Jesus Christ, I could kiss you' He shouted as he made his way to the office door.

'Dinner?' questioned Geoffrey.

'No Geoffrey.

The only link to food I am concentrating on now is 'bacon' and how you might just have saved mine'

He turned as he reached the door placing a finger to his lips.

'Geoffrey. Not a word about this conversation. I'm leaving now and a big, bloody great *thank you*'.

'For what?' came the confused response.

'When it's all over ... I'll tell you'

Then he was gone.

As Declan made his way back to the car, he could hear his phone ringing. It stopped before he could open the door. He checked the number. It was Penny.

'Oh shit' He shouted out loud as he started the dusted, grey Mercedes. He was not where he should have been. The message light was blinking and he had a feeling the message waiting for him would not be a polite one.

~~~~~~

The next morning Declan was seated in his office. It was Wednesday - and six thirty in the morning. The night had been a long one. Penny had issued a 'final warning'. Declan had consumed one or two whiskey's too many.

He was on his second cup of coffee - and on the phone.

'I am waiting to speak to someone who can put me through to General Hamad Sadique' he shouted down the handset.

Chapter Eleven – The Withdrawal

The line to Basra was terrible but he had now had three goes at it and was determined to speak to Hamad at this attempt.

'... and don't cut me off ... please.' he added somewhat desperately. Another five minutes went by. A hollow sounding voice came out of the crackling handset.

'Salam alekum'

'Alekum salam' Declan replied

'Shu ak barak' how are you?

'Zein, tammam' I am well

'A Hamad hunaa?

'Yes, Hamad is here' came the quick response - in perfect English.

'I think it would be better if we spoke English rather than Arabic my friend ... as I feel my English may be slightly ahead of your much appreciated efforts with my mother tongue!'

The person at the other end of the line paused waiting for confirmation.

'That is very considerate of you'

'What is it you want and who are you?'

The tone could be considered a little crisp and the continuous breakup of the line made communications difficult.

'My name is Declan Doyle and I am trying to speak with General Hamad Sadique. I met the General last year at the UK Derby horse race in the company of a good friend of mine, Mr Lewis. He gave me this number and said that any time I was in Iraq, to give him a call'

There was silence. General Hamad Sadique was number two in the Iraqi Air Force. He had made it very clear over large quantities of ice cold Bollinger, consumed in the luxurious surroundings of a balconied private box at Epsom, that he was very much 'up' for such a decedent western lifestyle and any help that could be provided to move his life in such a general direction, would be gratefully received. In other words – he was bent.

The thoughtful silence was eventually broken.

'I will tell General Sadique that you wish to speak with him. Please give me your number' Declan did so with a promise from the echoing, crackling and distant voice that Hamad would ring him back within the hour.

The hour turned out to be exactly five minutes. The phone rang. The line was perfect and the greeting effuse.

'Salam alekum my dear friend Doyle. How great to hear from you. How kind of you to call me. What a big honourable pleasure. What a ...'

Declan cut him off.

'Alekum salam Hamad. I am so pleased you found the time in your very busy schedule to ring me back'

'No problem, no problem my dear friend ... if there is anything I can do for you ... asking is all you need'

Chapter Eleven – The Withdrawal

'I would like to fly up to Iraq and see you Hamad. I would also very much like to have a private and *confidential* discussion with you. No minutes, and no recordings ... and I would like to see you, face to face at such a meeting ... as soon as possible' Declan spoke carefully and slowly to make sure he was understood. There was a pensive silence from the other end. Then General Sadique, number two in the Iraqi Air Force, spoke in a less profuse and possibly more controlled manner.

'I can see you tomorrow Mr Doyle. I will be working from my office at Basra Airport. If I remember correctly, you have your own aeroplane, Yes?'

'Yes' replied Declan.

'Good' continued the General 'I will leave landing clearance at the airport. When you arrive, taxi to end of runway three-two and someone will be waiting for you. By the way, what aircraft you have now and what is call sign and ... err ... flying time?'

'I have a PA28-235 call sign Golf Bravo Echo Hotel Yankee'

'This is good Declan - I will be at Basra airport from around ten o'clock. Radio in to Basra tower if you have delay and let them know when you pass to north of Bahrain'

'Thank you General, you are most kind'

'It is nothing my dear friend. Let us hope that whatever you need from me I can provide and that our meeting will be bearing of much fruit. Until tomorrow Mr Doyle'

'Until tomorrow then' echoed Declan. The line went dead as he held the handset thoughtfully for a few seconds before replacing it.

Was the game possibly on – again?

~~~~~~~~
~~~~

Chapter Twelve
A Trip to Iraq

It was Thursday morning, five o'clock when Declan left the Metrological office at Abu Nar Airport. He clambered in to the left hand seat of the gleaming red and white Cherokee. The 'Met' report was good for the whole day and with checks done, a kick of the rudder bar and a push on the throttle, Hotel Yankee was out on the taxiway.

The trip to Basra was faultless and nearly four hours later, Declan was logging ten miles out from the airfield with the tower offering clearance for a straight in approach. Within minutes he was rolling toward the end of the runway following an instruction to turn right and head for a dull grey military Mazda truck parked on a wide apron to the side of which was a block built communications building. Declan positioned the aeroplane ready for an exit back on to the runway and was greeted by a smiling Iraqi who extended a hand to help him jump to the ground.

'Salam alekum' the uniformed figure shouted.

'Alekum salam' Declan replied cheerily as he was ushered politely in to the building where the instantly recognisable figure of General Hamad Sadique was

Chapter Twelve – A Trip to Iraq

seated at a large table in one corner of the room. He got up immediately and walked over to greet his visitor. The two men sat down at the table, next to one another. The expected Arabic coffee appeared, and then they were alone.

Hamad Sadique looked resplendent in his crisp, well tailored Air Force uniform as he poured the steaming hot coffee.

'I hope you had a good trip Declan' he said. '… and before we start we need to make arrangements to fill up your aeroplane for the return journey'

Declan pulled out his International Aviation Fuel Card to present to Hamad who waved it away.

'There is no need for that Mr Doyle … you are my guest and a few gallons of fuel for me is nothing'

'That is very much appreciated my friend' Declan replied gratefully. It was surprisingly cool inside the building and Declan felt very relaxed. The Iraqis were a friendly and hospitable nation of people, so much different to their arrogant and generally rude neighbours in the tiny but oil rich next door state of Kuwait. So - how to begin this delicate conversation?

'Well my dear General, how is the war going?' Declan kicked off.

Hamad Sadique looked up in surprise, lit a cigarette, taking time to absorb what could be construed as a slightly flippant opening remark made by the optimistic looking Englishman. He didn't think that the European millionaire sitting in front of him had travelled six hundred miles simply to ask how the war was going. 'Well ...' He paused '... to tell you truth my dear, it has been what your chess player's call a bit of stalemate at this moment'

Hamad was studying his visitor carefully in an attempt to get to the depths of this confident individual, one he had only met once before, over a year ago, at a horse race in the UK.

'But I am pleased to just come back from France where my pilots finish training on latest Mirage F1E. This has Exocet capability and we now have ... er ... how you say ... *fully operational* squadron based at Al Taqqadum ... outside Baghdad'

Hamad played along with whatever game the Englishman thought he was orchestrating and talked animatedly for well over half an hour with interjections here and there from Declan, the odd question, the odd smile, the odd 'congratulations'.

'But of course you must know all this my friend Doyle' he added thoughtfully as he stubbed out his fourth cigarette. This was perhaps a warning. Declan needed to chose his words carefully.

'I do naturally have a continuing interest in what is happening in the Gulf generally and specifically what is happening in the sad conflict between two great and ancient nations. But of course, it is always better to get it *straight from the horse's mouth*'. He smiled engagingly.

Chapter Twelve – A Trip to Iraq

The General frowned 'Are you calling me a horse?' he interjected.

'No … no … no … my friend, this is just an old English saying meaning that we are getting information from the highest and most trustworthy source'

The General smiled.

'Ah' he said knowingly 'You bloody English and your sayings … so now let us use another popular saying that has something to do with bulls … and shit!'

The General had stopped smiling – and so had the eyes. Declan knew he had to tread carefully with a man who had a reputation for volatility, although so far he appeared relaxed and confident and had an amusing way of telling a tale. Another coffee hit the bottom of the small ceramic cups and both men drank quickly. Declan decided to go for broke. He leaned forward across the table as he spoke.

'I have a small project under way in the straits between Kharg Island and Geneveh'.

No reaction.

'I need some help to ensure that the project get's finished on time and with the minimum of fuss and disruption'

'So what does that have to do with me?'

'We have taken as many precautions as we can to protect the project site but there is one very small part that needs to be more or less guaranteed to work … or …' 'I will finish that for you Mr Doyle … or that maniac Raza will cut your balls off' Hamad laughed out loud

'We know all about your project for the Iranians Mr Doyle ... and who is controlling it. You know of course, the man you are dealing with is a complete lunatic, has sent hundreds of thousands of good Muslims to their deaths on our Southern front, using tactics more related to World War One trench warfare than those used by modern, highly mobile armoured groups' He sighed 'Such a waste of so many young lives'

'The man I am dealing with may be a lunatic, but he threw you out of the Al Faw peninsular last year and although it took over 30,000 troops to do it, he is still there - I believe'. The General's face darkened.

'What is it you want Mr Doyle? ... Let us stop this talk of war and start a more sensible conversation about ... money!'

That was it, the door was open, Declan mused. Now we can get down to the nitty-gritty.

'My reason for being here is very simple Hamad. I want, on a certain day, your agreement that will ensure my project is not attacked in any way by your forces' There followed a calculated silence and a poker players blank reaction from the smartly uniformed General sitting in front of him.

Declan continued warily.

'We have a very large item that needs to be towed in

Chapter Twelve – A Trip to Iraq

to place, positioned over a substantial period of hours and then sunk to the sea bed. Once this operation is completed, you can do as you wish' Declan sucked in a controlled deep breath, a nervous sign that did not go un-noticed.

'So, what are you asking - that I ground the whole Iraqi Air Force?'

'Well - no, not really, just to make sure that no one fly's near the site on a particular day or at a particular time.

'How long you need this 'no fly' arrangement to stay in place Mr Doyle?'

'Well ...' Declan replied thoughtfully 'If the positioning goes well, it could simply be a matter of a few hours. If not ...' He paused. He was beginning to feel slightly uncomfortable '... it could be say - twenty four hours'

'As I told you earlier Mr Doyle, we now have Exocet missiles and the planes to deliver them - *effectively*. My pilots are good - and well trained. Anyone of them who would destroy your project - my dear Declan - would become a National hero - and our esteemed leader Saddam Hussein would bestow some very great honours on them!' Hamad studied the Englishman's face in an effort to gauge the temper of the moment. The slight shimmer on the forehead told him something but there were no other real giveaways. The intelligent eyes were clear and focused. Hamad Sadique had Declan Doyle's full attention. 'Do you know what the penalty is for attempting to bribe senior military officials here in Iraq - *in wartime*?'

The words were purposely loud and emphatic and as Declan heard them - his heart sank.

'For God's sake' he thought desperately 'I may have screwed up big time here'

Nervous perspiration ran down a cheek as his brain leapt into top gear. Was this just a situation of impasse or the start of a fairly long term in the notorious Abu Ghraib prison? A myriad of thoughts were surging through his mind as he attempted to wrap his considerable reasoning powers around what appeared to be a very dangerous situation. He let his eyes drop and in any other set of circumstances, this could have been taken as a sign of defeat.

Suddenly, the uniformed figure in front of him leapt up from his chair, his face darkened, his fists clenched - and then - nearly fell down again in fits of laughter. For a few lingering seconds, Declan was confused until the realisation finally hit him. The General was taking the piss.

He let out a long sigh of relief as the Iraqi general moved round the table to pat him vigorously on the back. He returned to his seat as a rarely seen child like grin reflected Declan's embarrassment. His shoulders sank as he relaxed back in to his chair. Hamad spoke again. 'What you are asking is well within my granting

Chapter Twelve – A Trip to Iraq

Declan – I can make sure that your project is safe from attack by my planes any day you name' He was still smiling '... but how much is this very special service worth my friend? This will be the very big question for you'

A reply came quickly, perhaps too quickly.

'I had in mind a figure of fifty thousand crisp, new United States dollars General' Declan replied calmly, knowing that the man negotiating in front of him would want double that amount.

'You will need to add one hundred thousand to that figure my dear' came the considered reply. Both men were again scrutinising one another carefully across the wide polished timber table. It was Declan's turn to now play hardball.

'I simply do not have that amount available General. I have had to cut the price down substantially to keep out competition and I will be lucky to break even'

Declan swallowed hard hoping that his tightened expression had not given anything away. The General was not impressed.

'How much are they paying you for this job? ... and think carefully before you reply Declan as at some stage, I am sure I will be able to find out ... and it will be much better to be honest with me now!'

He was still smiling but there was now a perceptible edge of menace to his voice, the eyes alert and searching. Declan thought through the situation for a long moment. 'The whole job has been valued at one hundred and twenty million with everything being double or treble cost due to the war ... especially the cost of men on site and vessel rates for support craft. I will be lucky to make a couple of million if the job goes well and could possibly *lose* a couple of million if the job goes badly'

He paused for a second studying the General's body language for an indicator of any description. There was none.

'One hundred and fifty thousand dollars Mr Doyle ... up front ... in a nominated bank account in Dubai ... within five days from today' The reply was firm, the face expressionless. Declan was between a rock and a hard place, but pride was now taking over. He knew it shouldn't ... he knew he could afford a hundred and fifty thousand easily out of the insurance premium he would no longer have to pay. Pride was the brother of greed today, and Declan was out to win.

'One hundred and twenty five thousand dollars General - up front - in a nominated bank account in Dubai tomorrow morning at nine o'clock'

Hamad Sadique remained thoughtful for what seemed an inordinately long time. It was in fact less than a minute.

'To accept that figure, you will need to throw in a box for me and my complete family at Royal Ascot next year ... as well'. He was serious. Declan smiled

Chapter Twelve – A Trip to Iraq

inwardly. They both knew that this little 'extra' would add another ten thousand dollars to Declan's bill and require a few favours from his friend Mr Lewis again. What an asshole. He held out his hand wordlessly. It was accepted by General Hamad Sadique, number two in the esteemed Iraqi Air Force - and now - the deal was done.

Declan breathed a sigh of relief as the two men shook hands. Some necessary small talk followed mainly relating to horse racing, which appeared to be a bit of a passion with the General and if not the horses themselves, certainly the gambling and mixing with the 'upper classes' of British society. Declan felt he now had the measure of the man and with no more deals to be done, it was time to go.

As Declan fired up Hotel Yankee, completed his checks and steered the little aeroplane out on to the runway, the general remained in the building. Who knows who may have been watching?

Priority clearance to take off came over the radio from Basra tower and within a minute or two the little red and white aeroplane was in the air again and heading back to Abu Nar, hopefully in time for a well deserved dinner for two at the Yacht club. He simply dare not let Penny down today.

In his four metre by four metre space, laughingly called 'an office' by the Embassy chief of staff, Eric Saunders picked up his red phone. He had two phones in his office. The black one was connected to the Bahrain British Embassy switchboard and the red one was an 'unmonitored' direct line. At least, he was assured it was.

There was no greeting, just a simple statement

'He has just left ... and he met with the General'.

The line was then disconnected. If Saunders had felt so inclined, he could have opened his window in a few moments time, looked up and seen the red and white Cherokee making its way South over Bahrain on the way back to Abu Nar.

The message was simply another piece of this unexpectedly difficult puzzle to put in to place. What the hell was Declan Doyle doing in Basra, meeting with one of the highest figures in the Iraqi Air Force ... at the end of a bloody runway? Since his recent trip to UK and his conversation with Christopher, he had pushed just about as many buttons as he dare without giving a sniff to the Americans of his interest in what he had now understood to be the 'Geneveh Project'. He had learnt many things but none of them from that tosspot Paddy Doherty. He had even flown down to Abu Nar to meet with him face to face, but the Irishman was as tight as a drum.

Eric was convinced he knew much more than he was giving away. He even offered some money, some real money, but Paddy looked as if he was running scared. It

Chapter Twelve – A Trip to Iraq

showed in his face, it showed in his shaky appearance whenever the damn subject was mentioned. It showed mostly in his adamant refusal to take any money. That was the killer for Eric. He knew that Paddy Doherty was a complete damned mercenary where money was concerned and for him to refuse any, especially from the Service, raised many more questions than Eric had repeatedly asked.

However, he knew a lot more now than he did a few weeks ago. On his desk sat the Top Secret file 108.86 sub labelled 'Declan Doyle'. He added a note recording concisely the information he had just received. The file contained many notes, on many subjects, from many contacts, all of whom could add a small byte of information that would eventually compose a clear and comprehensive picture relating to the activities of Mr Doyle.

The next step was to find out what he was doing talking with General Hamad Sadique. He had to be a bit careful here as the Yanks were all over Iraq and if they knew the Brits had any interest in what was going on in their own back yard, they would be putting out so much false clutter around the subject of this well known Iraqi Anglophile that it would take weeks to sort the wheat from the chaff. However, the biggest single advantage to Her Majesties Secret Service was that literally all the officers in the Iraqi military were British trained and what was even better was that many had attended

English public schools. The 'old school tie' network was alive and well in Iraq and all the participants, regardless of political leanings, had an inherent dislike and a certain deep seated distrust of the Americans. That was the fact of the matter; the Yanks knew it and the Iraqis knew it. Eric knew the right people to contact and picked up the black phone dialling in a couple of numbers. 'Get hold of our Embassy in Baghdad and get me an invite there for some reason or other. I need a couple of days … er … and a car'.

~~~~~~~~

Chapter Thirteen
A Friend in Need ...

It was, as usual, packed at Abu Nar airport as Declan fought his way across and through the long lines of irritable individuals queuing at the check-in desks for flights to simply everywhere. He was heading for the British Airways First Class counter, a point from which he would be attended to, whisked away and pampered for the next several hours. The flight to Hong Kong on the red, white and blue liveried Boeing 747 would take around seven and a half hours, with favourable winds. He carried nothing with him but a carry-on bag which he handed to the smartly turned out and quite attractive stewardess, who showed him to his soft dark blue leather seat in the First Class cabin.

He wasn't looking forward to this particular trip, but a problem existed that needed to be settled. He checked his watch. As the big Boeing travelled east, the flight was expected to touch down at Kai Tak Airport sometime around nine thirty in the evening, local time. Declan had a small suite booked on the twentieth floor of the HK Hilton. It was his favourite hotel in the colony and although BA was definitely *not* his favourite airline, Esther had done well to get him a short notice

Chapter Thirteen – A Friend in Need ...

ticket. Lunch came and went; dinner came and went; two films watched all the way through; a rare event for Declan Doyle, and before he knew it the plane was touching down at Kai Tak. Every commercial pilot in the world 'loved' Kai Tak Airport, for it was there, on the approach, most of them had learnt to pray.

A minute or two past ten o'clock, the door closed on a sweetly smelling taxi and the Chinese driver turned a close cropped head to enquire where his European passenger wanted to go. The route to the Hong Kong Hilton would take them through Kowloon, over the Western Harbour Crossing and down on to Queens Road.

The taxi driver dutifully handed the uniformed hotel doorman his passenger's single bag and bowed slightly in a typical oriental sign of respect as he pocketed his fare and the more than reasonable tip.

Declan was greeted at reception by Sarah, the senior night service manager. During the many visits the Englishman had made to HK over the past ten years, they had come to know one another on more than first name terms. She beamed as soon as she saw him.

'Welcome Declan ... I hope you've had a good flight ... and I noticed your booking was a bit short notice this time. I had to work extra hard to get you a sensible room'.

She moved quickly but gracefully from behind the

glistening, polished marble counter top and gave out a restrained, but at the same time, intimate kiss on both cheeks. 'Thanks for fixing it Sarah. Esther told me you had worked your excellent juggling trick for me'

'It was no problem. We are always pleased to see you - you know that' she said in a relaxed reply as she moved back behind the counter to fetch a room key attached to an oversize brass tablet.

Some years back, both had embarked on what could be called some sort of affair; an affair they both knew was going nowhere. Sarah was a beautiful, in fact quite stunning looking half English, half Chinese girl with a massively appealing personality and a heart to match. They were both single and over twenty one, but for various reasons the initial, quite intense involvement, seemed to turn naturally, over a period of time, in to a much calmer and probably more rewarding friendship. No doubt they would have lunch tomorrow.

Declan took his key, blew Sarah a departing kiss and headed for the lift to the twentieth floor. His suite consisted of three rooms; a bedroom, a bathroom and a quite substantial sitting room. It would do, he thought to himself and he quickly unpacked his small bag, hung up three crisp white mixed cotton shirts and threw some underwear in to a drawer. The lightweight dark blue suit he was wearing would have to last. If he had time he would pop down to Nathan Road. This was

Chapter Thirteen – A Friend in Need ...

Hong Kong. Whatever you wanted, you could get and you could get it twenty four hours a day, including some of the very best tailoring in the world.

Declan had a call to make. He picked up the telephone on a long lead and settled himself down on a well upholstered pale green sofa. He grabbed a pen and a sheet of hotel paper from the well stocked desk unit and dialled a London number. He quickly checked his watch. It would be middle afternoon there. The phone was answered by a quietly spoken male with an estuary accent.

'How can I help you?' There would be no identification, no preamble, and there didn't need to be.

'It's Declan'

'Yes Declan, what can I do for you?'

'I am in Hong Kong and I need some assistance. Do you have the phone number of a contact here?'

'Just a moment please' there was silence lasting about twenty seconds.

'Yes we have a reliable contact for you Declan. Please take down this number'.

The number was read out and read back.

'Payment for any services will be in the normal manner and we will cover our contact from this end'.

'Thank you' said Declan 'Can this contact put together a collection of resources if required?' he questioned.

'He most certainly can and you can ring him anytime'

'Thank you for your help and I hope we can get together for a while when I'm next in London'

'My friend and I will look forward to it'. The line was disconnected. Declan raised himself from the confines of the surprisingly comfortable sofa, grabbed his key and took a quick look round the room, mentally plotting where everything was placed before he left. It was an old habit when staying in Hotels; one that took him back to another life and something he had never been able to break. When he came back, he would know instantly if anything had been disturbed. The door clunked reassuringly behind him as he headed along the corridor in the direction of the elevators. A large whiskey and soda in the downstairs bar would finish off a long, unproductive day.

Breakfast began at six thirty and Declan was the first there. After consuming a perfectly cooked and well presented 'full English', washed down with two cups of black tea and a couple of rounds of toast, he was ready to face the day. On his way back upstairs he checked at the front desk to find a message from Sarah advising him that she would be in the lobby at the Peninsular Hotel at twelve thirty and had reserved a table for two at Gaddis restaurant for one o'clock. At the bottom of the note, in scrawled capitals, was the warning 'and don't be late!' He smiled to himself. She knew him well.

Up in his room, he rang the number he'd scrawled on

Chapter Thirteen – A Friend in Need ...

the hotel notepaper the night before. It was answered quickly. The gentleman on the other end listened without interruption to what Declan had to say as he verbally presented his credentials and advised the stranger of his association with his London contacts.

'... and you need some help here in Hong Kong Mr Doyle - is that correct?'

'Yes, that is correct' replied Declan. '... and I will need a surveillance team for maybe a day'

'You have the details of the individual involved?' the stranger asked.

'Yes I do' replied Declan.

They agreed to meet that morning at the entrance to Ocean Park around eleven o'clock. It was a Saturday morning and the popular Animal Park and Marine Oceanarium would be busy.

Declan replaced the handset of the telephone and sat in quiet contemplation for a moment. He searched in his inside jacket pocket for his wallet and fished around for a small sheet of paper with several telephone numbers written on it. The one he was looking for was at the bottom. He placed the paper loosely over the microphone of the handset and rang the Clearwater Bay number. It was a very old trick but it normally worked. An Ni answered and listened with waning patience to the annoyingly muffled and distorted enquiry.

'I'm so sorry, but I cannot quite understand you ...

can you speak up please … this is a very bad line'

Declan spoke a little louder.

'My name is Peter Britten - and I'm so sorry to disturb you on a Saturday, but my company has marine insurance with Mr Swale's company - and I understand that this may be his home number'.

'Yes' stated An Ni somewhat frostily. 'I am his wife … and he does not *normally* take business calls at home … at the weekend'

'Please accept my very sincere apologies Mrs Swales, but it is imperative that I speak with your husband today. I have a real emergency I am trying to deal with'

An Ni paused for a moment.

'Hang on and I'll see what I can do'

She walked through to the lounge where Tony Swales was enjoying his second cup of tea of the day and reading the morning newspaper. An Ni explained about the mysterious caller. She was unable to hide her agitation. The name rang no bell with Tony, but that was not unusual as his staff dealt with hundreds of clients and Tony himself would not necessarily deal with them all on a personal basis. He sighed outwardly as he put down the tea and the paper, levered himself up from his position on the sofa and walked in the direction of his office.

'I'll take it in here' he shouted back to An Ni and then picked up the handset on his cluttered desk.

'Hello … Tony Swales'

Chapter Thirteen – A Friend in Need ...

'It's Declan' came a voice.

'Jesus Christ ... Declan ...'

The brittle, grinding tone interrupted.

'Listen you asshole ... you need to speak to me about putting that fucking insurance back in place ... and quickly' he paused. 'Look what bloody stupid lengths I have to go to ... to get you to simply *speak* to me'

The word *speak* was shouted so loudly, Swales pulled the vibrating receiver away from his ear in an involuntarily nervous reaction, reeling from this unexpected confrontation. He thought of the body guards outside. Should he call them? What could they do? The man he needed protection from was on a bloody telephone, not his front doorstep!

He stood there mutely, not knowing quite what to do. There followed a delayed and sharp intake of breath. Tony Swales had suddenly lost all colour; heart rate jumping, clammy perspiration breaking out literally all over; the horrific events of Tuesday now rushing back. He nearly dropped the telephone. Good God ... not again.

The question was driven not by curiosity but a simple gut reaction.

'Where are you?'

'I'm in the Gulf, where the hell do you think I would be. I have everything going tits up here ... and it's all down to *you* ... you useless bastard'. Tony actually breathed a short and audible sigh of relief. At least the maddened Englishman with an Irish name and temper to match would not be turning up in his living room anytime soon. The next words came with the confidence of new found courage.

'Look Declan, I have to tell you, you are playing with some big boys now ... much bigger than you think.'

His voice was trembling with a combination of anger and fear.

'My family has been *threatened*, my life has been *threatened* - and I can assure you that I am no damned hero. *You* of course, may think you are, but take these, the final words you will ever hear from me, as friendly words of advice. Whatever you are involved with ... get *out* of it *now* ... and never, ever make any attempt to contact me again....' he paused, still shaking with emotion '....and if you do, I will have your fucking guts for garters!'

He spat out the final few words, slamming the handset down and slumping back in his desk chair, hands a shiver, a coldness now creeping over his whole body. In the background, he could hear the comforting and precious high pitched sounds of an excited young Jonothan Swales, accompanied by An Ni's unmistakable laughter. It was coming from the kitchen, where some game or other was probably in full swing. Tears began to form. He knew Declan's reputation. He

Chapter Thirteen – A Friend in Need ...

had to protect his family. He needed to get them away. As he wept quietly to himself, he picked up the telephone and started to make arrangements.

~~~~~~~~
~~~

Chapter Fourteen
A Murder Most Foul

Declan replaced the handset, sitting motionless and thoughtful for several minutes. He was not a vindictive man, or so he considered himself to be, but something had to be done about Mr Swales.

The Volvo hire car had been pre-ordered and the paperwork only needed a couple of signatures. The car was waiting at the front of the Hotel and a quick check of the magnificent Art Deco foyer clock, on the wall behind reception, told him that he would be in plenty of time for his meeting at Ocean Park.

As expected and especially as it was a Saturday morning, it was busy. He knew that whoever was meeting him would find him. They were probably watching him at this very moment. He was right. At exactly eleven o'clock, a small stocky looking European with close-cropped hair and a sun tan walked up to him.

'Mr Doyle?' was the question in an unmistakable Glaswegian accent. This was not the person he had spoken to on the phone earlier making him instantly wary and somewhat uneasy. Declan looked around cautiously before replying. It was an awkward moment as the two men stood facing each other. There was no obvious spotter on the horizon and he searched the

Chapter Fourteen – A Murder Most Foul

crowds quickly for anyone with a hearing aid connected to a wire disappearing down a shirt collar. There thankfully appeared to be no one preparing to create obvious danger standing nearby. He had a pre-purchased ticket in his pocket and an escape route planned.

'Yes' he replied, succeeding to suppress any give-away signs of nervousness. The Scot turned sharply and walked away.

He felt the warmth of human breath before he heard the words.

'Good morning Mr Doyle' the voice reached him from behind and into his right ear. He recognised it as belonging to the person he had spoken to that morning. He relaxed a little as the person moved casually to Declan's front. The voice belonged to a quite tall, clean shaven man who offered an outstretched hand.

Declan spoke.

'Pleased to meet you Mr – er - what should I call you?'

'Mr Smith would be fine' his contact replied

'Well Mr Smith, here is as much detail as I can give you relating to a person who I need to speak to'

Declan pulled a sheet of hotel paper from his jacket pocket and handed it to his new acquaintance. Mr Smith studied the scribbled information for a minute and said 'How do you wish to speak with him, in private or in public?' 'In public - I need to know what his planned movements are for the next forty eight hours; where he is scheduled to go and if possible who he is arranging to meet. Do you think this is achievable?'

'We can only try Mr Doyle' the retracted smile came quickly again.

'I will ring you in your room at nine o'clock this evening'

'My room number is ... '

Mr Smith interrupted.

'I know what your room number is Mr Doyle - just be there at that time. OK?

'OK' Declan replied. That was the end of the conversation as the stranger with the name of Mr Smith turned and was immediately swallowed up in the growing crowds of Ocean Park's excited punters. There was time for a quick visit to Nathan Road before what would hopefully be an excellent lunch with Sarah.

In room twenty twelve of the Hong Kong Hilton, Declan checked his watch. It was just before nine o'clock. He pushed the plate away from him. The well prepared omelette and toast had been served in his room and was all he could handle after a tremendous lunch with Sarah.

The phone rang. The voice was instantly recognisable. There was no greeting.

'Do you have something to write with?'

Chapter Fourteen – A Murder Most Foul

'Yes' replied Declan.

'We are watching his house and he is currently at home. Do you want us to let you know if he moves tonight?'

'No'

'Right then … tomorrow we know that he and his wife are having lunch with family at the Happy Valley club house of the Jockey Club. Do you know who that *family* is?'

'Well, I know that An Ni is somehow distantly related to the family of Robert Wang' Declan replied thoughtfully.

'You are correct Mr Doyle, but unfortunately, not so *distant*. It is difficult to fathom old Chinese family links in the round, but the Robert Wang connection is a close one. He is a voting member at the club and it appears that the target is being sponsored by him to also become a voting member'

This was news to Declan. The Hong Kong Jockey Club was just about the most exclusive club on the planet. It was limited to twenty thousand members worldwide and the powerful closed-shop of voting members was limited to two hundred. Robert Wang was into most things legal in Hong Kong, such as Real Estate and Shipping, in a big way. He was also rumoured to be behind a substantial number of business ventures that were not quite so legal. The confirmed billionaire was by anyone's measure, a self made man. Now Declan had learnt that there was some sort of strong family connection between him and An Ni. This was news indeed. He would have to be careful. The last thing needed right now was half the Hong Kong Chinese Mafia on his case. Mr Smith continued.

'They are meeting at twelve o'clock and eating in the first floor restaurant' he paused. 'Did you know that he has made arrangements for his wife and child to leave HK for an undetermined amount of time?

'No, I did not'

'They are both on the mid morning flight to Beijing on Monday'

'Carry on'

'We understand that after lunch, the whole party of around fifteen people will drive down to Lei Yue Min Harbour and board Wang's boat. They are then planning to cruise round to Clearwater Bay and drop of the target and his wife. We don't expect it to be much before eleven that evening.

'… and the boy? Declan questioned.

'He is being looked after by the nanny, who is sleeping in and two body guards, also living and sleeping in. You should also know that he has two further body guards who have travelled with him everywhere for the past day or two' There was a short silence.

'Is there something we need to know Mr Doyle? … the body guard business for example?' 'I don't think so'

Chapter Fourteen – A Murder Most Foul

Declan replied firmly. 'Thank you Mr Doyle'

The line was disconnected without a further word. Declan placed the telephone back on the coffee table and sat back in to the yielding cushions of the restful sofa. He was absorbed for some time before picking up the phone again and dialling zero.

'Can I speak to the senior night service manager please?

'Is there a problem Mr Doyle?' came a concerned reply.

'No ... if you could put me through please?'

'Hello, Sarah speaking, how can I help?'

'Sarah, its Declan ... and I need a favour'

'Well then Mr Doyle ... I shall need a favour in return ... I'll be up in three minutes' she giggled childishly

'You most certainly will not and you know it' Declan declared.

'I need to gain access to the Jockey Club restaurant facilities at Happy Valley racecourse tomorrow lunchtime'.

'Is that all - will I be coming too?' she purred.

'No, you big tease - I need to get in to the club and speak to someone'

'No problem darling - if you're sure you don't want to take me. I know the manager very well. I get people into the club all the time. There will be a guest pass waiting for you at the main entrance from ten o'clock; just one thing. Please don't cause any trouble. I don't know what the hell you are actually doing here with just a bag and no real reason ... or more to the point, no reason you are willing to tell me'.

'Sarah, please believe me. All I need to do is talk to someone face to face. That's the whole reason I'm here ... and whilst on the subject, can you please see if you can get me booked on the mid morning flight back to Abu Nar on Monday' She blew a kiss down the telephone as she said

'Leave it to me. Good night, sleep tight ... my mystery man'

Sunday morning came with a rush. Declan had experienced a restless night and was woken by an urgent tapping sound at the door. He quickly looked round to get his bearings and shouted 'OK' to the door knocker. His watch told him it was eight thirty.

'Bloody hell' he shouted to no one as he stumbled out of bed in the direction of the shower. It must have been all the wine from the previous afternoon, in combination with the several large whiskies consumed in the downstairs bar from ten till late. His head was fuzzy as he plunged himself into the heart stopping, stinging coldness of the shower on full power. After half a minute, he gradually turned the heat up until he could bear it no more. A minute or two later he was drying himself off, fully awake and ready to go. He had to pay a visit to Nathan Road at ten thirty to pick up his

Chapter Fourteen – A Murder Most Foul

new suit and two cotton shirts. Declan Doyle felt comfortable, relaxed and confident in his new, perfectly fitting charcoal grey suite and pale blue shirt as he pulled up in the Volvo outside the Happy Valley Jockey Club main entrance. The eager, uniformed doorman jumped in to the stationary vehicle to park it and gave out a numbered ticket.

He walked assuredly up to the perfectly presented, gently smiling Chinese doorkeeper, blocking any further progress. 'My Name is Doyle, Declan Doyle … and I understand that you are expecting me'

The doorkeeper checked his list.

'We certainly are sir. You are the guest today of the Manager Mr Yao Ming.'

He bowed slightly as Declan walked past to enter the magnificent interior of the most exclusive family club in the world. The time was eleven thirty and the whole place appeared to be getting busy. He needed a strategy; be seen or not be seen, that was the question! He made his way to the far end of the bar, as far away as possible from the entrance but with a barely interrupted sight line through to the entrance door. He ordered a long chilled lager beer and waited.

Although he didn't know Robert Wang personally, he had seen enough images of him over the years to be able to recognise him as he made his entrance. Heads turned; people whispered as he and his accompanying entourage were busily attended to by waiters and house staff offering guidance to a soft seating, mini lounge area with easy accommodation for fifteen to twenty people.

Declan sipped patiently at his gradually warming beer.

A light tap on the shoulder indicated the presence of Mr Yao Ming who politely introduced himself and assured Declan that as his guest, if he needed anything, to please let him know. Assurances were given to pass on the Manager's respects to Sarah and then he was alone again.

A second, chilled Tiger beer was ordered. Just as Declan looked up from checking his watch, Mr and Mrs Swales entered. They were shown over to the Wang party and with hands shaken, cheeks kissed; they sat down. The Swales were accompanied by two athletic looking, smartly dressed Chinese men who sat away from the gathering at a discreet distance. No one needed to be forgiven for thinking that these two accompanying gentlemen were part of a protective team. Approaching Tony Swales at the family table today would not now be an option. He would have to be careful. He didn't actually know what he was going to do that day to get a face to face with Swales, but whatever the plan turned out to be, it had now been made more complicated with two eagle eyed body guards mixed in to the proceedings.

Ten minutes passed by. Declan was in luck. Tony Swales was making his way, on his own, to the bar,

Chapter Fourteen – A Murder Most Foul

presumably to order and collect drinks for himself and An Ni. He turned his back slightly on the stool so as not to be instantly recognised. Tony Swales was about to collect a large Gin and Tonic from the counter top as Declan moved up close behind him.

'Good afternoon Tony'

Swales froze and all colour drained from the man in an instant as he was engulfed in a tidal wave of fear. He turned quickly, leaving the tall ice filled crystal glass on the bar counter. They were very close to one another now, literally exchanging breath.

'Before you shout for your bright eyed minders over there, I'm not here to harm you, I just need to understand what the hell has gone on here. Now why don't we both stroll calmly along the bar and down to the other end, out of sight of An Ni and her family gathering?'

Swales, after a second of slight hesitation, succumbed to the request obediently and without a word in reply; a disturbingly dull look in his eyes.

'Ok, tell me the story'

It all came tumbling out, tears welling up with anger the controlling emotion, underpinned by a mixture of fear and bewilderment as to why Declan Doyle, thought of as a friend for some years now, should allow his family to be put in this horrific situation.

'Now listen to me' said Declan as the distressed insurance broker reached inside a trouser pocket for a white cotton handkerchief to attend to dampened eyes.

'I had nothing to do with the situation you found yourself in last Tuesday and to simply withdraw from our arrangement and then refuse to speak to me is not acceptable. I have had to get on a fucking aeroplane and travel god knows how many miles just to have this three minute conversation. Do you know how damned mad that makes me? Do you know who you are actually pissing about with?' The tone was controlled but menacing. Swales knew the mood music of the situation was not about to improve. Declan's fists were clenched. It was an indication of frustration rather than anger. By clenching them, it stopped him from grabbing the pathetic figure in front of him and giving him a bloody good shake. 'Tony, I can give you protection. I can …' Tony Swales interrupted speaking firmly and with growing strength.

'I have protection … my own protection … but not from *them*, whoever *them* are, but from you … you bastard. Your insurance is now dead as you will be if you come anywhere near my family … and I …'

It was Declan's turn to interrupt.

'… and is that why you are sending them to Beijing tomorrow?'

The blustering agitated figure looked shocked.

'How the hell did you know about …?'

'I know everything there is to know about you, you little shit' Declan hissed. The fists began to unclench.

Chapter Fourteen – A Murder Most Foul

He was losing control. 'Hi Tony…we've given you up for dead'

The words caught them both unawares. They were spoken by Robert Wang who was only a few metres away, making track along the bar counter towards them. His face was smiling – his eyes were not - and instantly the two adversaries fitted themselves out with a suitable cheerful expression in response. 'Oh Hi Robert' Tony Swales replied hesitantly. '… er … this is an old friend I have just bumped in to here at the bar … and we were chewing over old times for a minute or two' Wang was right up to them now, he could see the signs of distress in Tony's contrived expression.

'Are you OK Tony?' he questioned with some concern.

'Yes - yes of course – Robert - can I introduce you to … er … Charles Braithwate, a gentleman from the Arabian Gulf who visits us regularly here in Hong Kong'

His tone was forcefully and deceivingly bright. The two men shook hands and exchanged a few polite words, the searching smoked slate eyes of the Chinese billionaire ready to pursue any hint of a lie.

'An Ni is waiting for you Tony and we are going up for lunch any minute now' Wang stated coolly, his gaze not wavering from its fixation on the unrevealing face of the English visitor. 'I'll be right with you Robert … please just go ahead and I guarantee I will definitely join you in a moment' The host of the family Sunday lunch turned his back and moved away to the other end of the bar to collect the waiting drinks and return to the gathering. He looked back only once. Swales turned to face Declan once again, his expression now firm. He had gathered himself together and gained yet a little more courage during the disruption of Robert Wang.

'Do you see the kind of people I mix with? Do you have any idea what Robert Wang can do to you? He is not a man to mess with ... one damned word from me and he'll have your balls cut off ... Capiche? Declan moved his face an inch closer.

'So let me completely understand you Tony. Are you telling me definitely and finally, that you will not re-instate my insurance on Geneveh?'

'Absolutely correct my friend. The premium is back in your account. Whatever happens to *you* now is in *your* hands, not mine. My conscience is *clear*. Do you understand?'

The once moist brow was now dry, the angry red eyes now settled, the colourless cheeks now revitalised, the finger daring to point as the necessary resolve came rushing over him. 'This is an action you may live to regret Tony'.

The statement was made by Declan with no real bitterness, but more an air of resignation. The fury had departed to be replaced with exasperation. He had done all he could do.

Chapter Fourteen – A Murder Most Foul

'My advice to you now Doyle, is to exit this place as quickly as you can … or I will have you thrown out!'

It would be the very last time the two men spoke to one another or saw one another again.

Declan arrived back at the Hotel just after one thirty. There was a message waiting for him from Sarah to confirm a seat for him on the eight thirty morning BA flight to Abu Nar via Bangkok. It would do. The message also invited him for some drinks later that afternoon at the Mandarin Hotel, if he was back in time. Sarah knew it was a favourite drinking hole of Declan's. He smiled as he read the neatly hand written message signed with a lipstick impression of a full pair of lips. He had one more thing to do before heading out again and that was to make a final phone call to Mr Smith.

That Monday morning in the offices of the Far East Maritime Insurance Group, things were proving to be a little bit hectic. It was as if every bloody phone was ringing at once and everyone on every bloody phone wanted to speak with her bloody boss … right now. Elizabeth Cox was the Executive Personal Assistant to the head of FEMI and Tony Swales was at the airport for some reason or other on this very busy day. She didn't know why, it wasn't in his diary and she had been advised of the situation by a voicemail waiting for her when she arrived at the office just before nine o'clock.

Messages were dutifully taken, numbers efficiently stored. She had not actually seen her boss face to face since the previous Tuesday. He had been absent from the office and he was not answering business phone calls. Her office and home phone had been bombarded with rude communications from a company in the Arabian Gulf concerning some business or other relating to a cancelled marine policy. To restore a reasonable level of sanity, Elizabeth eventually took the initiative to block all the offending incoming numbers so that normal office work could continue.

Most of the previous week had been a nightmare and if it continued today, she had made up her mind she was leaving. There were plenty of good, well paid jobs for European PA's in Hong Kong.

Suddenly, there was a lull in activity as Elizabeth thankfully turned her attention to the pile of Dictaphone recordings sitting threateningly in her 'In' tray. She was listening to the second one when the shrill sound of a ringing telephone interrupted her again.

'Far East Maritime - office of Mr Swales - can I help you'

A strong Glaswegian accent came back with information from the Jockey Club that some new silver and enamelled member's badges were being produced and as Tony Swales was the head of the financial committee, some samples were being sent to him for comment and possibly approval.

Chapter Fourteen – A Murder Most Foul

'Are you from the club Mr …?' 'No, I am calling from Whampoa Advertising. We do all the below the line advertising and promotional work for the Jockey Club - and my name is Peter McBride by the way. I'm the promotions manager here. Can I send them over to you?'

'Yes. I don't see why not. Mr Swales is out at the moment but I am expecting him back, possibly after lunch'.

'Ideal. I am just packing the samples up now in a small padded bag with our label on the front and marked for the personal attention of Mr Swales. Is that OK?'

'That seems fine' Elizabeth confirmed. 'Will you post them?'

'No … no … I will send them by our courier … if you have no objection. The package will be with you in about an hour. I have put a big 'fragile' sticker on the front … we don't want someone dropping the package and treading on it do we?'

He let out a small chuckle to which Elizabeth responded in kind.

The conversation over, she called down to the building's front security desk and spoke to the day time manager, advising him to expect a package, sign for it and send it upstairs. Tony Swales entered his office building at a few minutes past twelve with his two stone faced, inscrutable shadows in tow. He quickly explained to Elizabeth that for reasons too involved to go into right now, the two smartly dressed men invading her office space were his body guards and were to be accommodated somewhere in the main office area. He also advised his hard pressed PA that his wife and child had left that morning for China and would be on holiday there for a few weeks. He was curt in his explanations, agitated and short tempered and Elizabeth knew him well enough not to enquire further.

With the short passage of time, she would find out what was going on. She advised her boss that his mail was on his desk and on the top was a packet to do with the Jockey Club, which she didn't open because she had been told what was in it earlier that day. Tony Swales was actually hardly listening as he closed his private office door, his mind many miles away on a China Airways flight heading toward Beijing.

The small brown padded envelope was covered more or less completely by a white sticky label containing Swales name and office location in heavy black type. Down one side was fixed a large red 'fragile' sticker. He felt it. There was something lumpy inside. He stretched across his desk for his letter opener and slipped it under the sealed flap on the rear.

The chemical fuse flared immediately with a half second pause as the magnesium flash set of the explosive thermite mixture of iron and aluminium powder. The

Chapter Fourteen – A Murder Most Foul

letter bomb had been designed to do damage but not to kill. However, the bomb maker had resorted to the use of steel staples to hold together the thick cardboard cover protecting the crystalline fuse matter from accidental ignition.

With the force of the explosion, one of the fourteen millimetre staples flew out of the package and headed, unswervingly toward the neck of the victim. It was a million to one chance. With the speed and energy of a bullet, it slashed a deep and jagged line up his neck, cutting straight through the common cervical carotid artery.

Due to his office being so well insulated from all the day to day noise of the general open plan working area outside, no one heard the muffled explosion and the initial agonising scream. Tony Swales died minutes later, on his own, gurgling a final cry for help; head resting in a pool of dark red, thickening blood; part of his face literally missing and right hand burnt nearly black.

~~~~~~~~
~~~~

Chapter Fifteen
The Saboteur

The Intercontinental Hotel in Abu Nar was extra busy on the morning of August 7th. The fifth Gulf Chess Championships were taking place there with the lobby full of people checking in and the path to the elevator block littered with luggage obstacles of varying types. The tall, tanned, athletic figure of military bearing, moving effortlessly amongst the mêlée of arriving guests, already had his room key and decided to take the stairway to the sixth floor. His destination was room 602. The clock above reception confirmed to Colonel Oliver Gresham the time to be nine thirty. He had booked the room for a meeting and with normal military precision he was half an hour early. The Middle East Region CIA Director for Covert Operations sat back in the comfortable couch, part of the elegant furnishings of the executive class suite - and waited.

The expected knock at the door came. It was three minutes past ten. The Colonel opened the door and without any words of greeting ushered Roger 'Chuck' Peterson in to the room.

'Coffee?' was the question to which Chuck replied in a slightly apprehensive tone 'No thanks' and sat down in a chair opposite the couch. He did not really want to

Chapter Fifteen – The Saboteur

share a space with his host this Thursday morning. No hand of welcome had been extended as he entered the room and he felt that somehow, this could turn out to be a 'bad hair' day.

Chuck was officially the Communications Manager for the Hall-Burton Company, a major International American oilfield service business with a regional office in Abu Nar, working out of the McDaniels yard. Both Hall-Burton and McDaniels, another US oilfield construction company, were well known covers for CIA operatives around the world and Chuck was 'the company' man in Abu Nar. He was an expansive, slightly extroverted character with a big smile, an even bigger waist measurement and a huge villa on Chicago Beach where he was well known for entertaining in lavish style.

He was also well known for displaying the sometimes annoying penchant of asking too many questions. Just about everyone in Abu Nar knew that Peterson was CIA, but due to the mind altering psychology practised within the fantasy world he occupied, he was convinced that no one even had a clue outside of the senior management of Hall-Burton.

'The Company' was how the CIA referred to itself internally and many of its operatives were even naive enough to think that this was a secret too. Chuck had been in Abu Nar for about four years and was satisfied he had his finger on the pulse; knew everything that was going on. He had received a phone call late the previous evening ordering him to appear at the meeting with Oliver Gresham. He didn't like it much. The Colonel had a fierce reputation rattling around in the folklore of 'the company' and Chuck had not met him or even talked to him before. As he now sat in the well furnished, climate controlled, luxury hotel suite at the Abu Nar Intercontinental Hotel, his pulse was raised uncomfortably and he felt very, very nervous.

The Colonel had picked up on the discomfort of his visitor. He said nothing for a couple of minutes as he sorted through a few loose documents and maps held together in a pink manila file. Chuck was becoming increasingly agitated and asked cautiously for a drink of water. Oliver Gresham indicated toward the bar with his right hand where a bottle of chilled water and some glasses rested, but said not a word. Finally he looked up.

'So Chuck … you are our man in Abu Nar'

'I most certainly am Colonel and it's a great pleasure to meet you' he replied effusively. Chuck extended his hand toward the Colonel, but it was ignored.

'I want to talk to you about the Geneveh Project' Oliver Gresham continued. 'I want you to tell me everything you know about the project from day one. Don't leave anything out!'

Chapter Fifteen – The Saboteur

The Colonel pulled out some blank sheets of lined legal paper from the pink file and sat with pen poised. Chuck took a deep breath, his mind in top gear as he searched the edges of it for all the detail he could remember about the Geneveh Project. He had received no warning that this was to be the subject of conversation that day and although a little flustered, he talked, more or less continuously for the next hour and a half.

The litre and a half bottle of chilled water had been consumed completely during his verbal briefing and Chuck asked his interrogator if room service could bring up another. The answer was …

'No … you won't be here long enough to finish it'.

The Colonel was writing furiously and had resorted to using hotel headed paper to record his continuing and extensive notes. Finally, Chuck sat back in his chair and told Oliver Gresham that he was finished.

The Colonel was now absorbed in reviewing his scribbles and Chuck thought he may well be in for a bit of a grilling. He was right.

'There are some things we need to know here, such as, what is the total amount of money that AOS is getting paid for this job. Do you know?'

'Well, not exactly' replied Chuck.

'Well, not exactly is not exactly good enough. I want to know who is getting paid what for what, to the cent, on this fucking job and I want to know by Monday'.

Chuck was slightly taken aback to be talked to in this very rude and explicit manner by another member of 'the company'. He was about to respond when the next question came at him like shrapnel.

'What defences are being employed by the Iranians to protect the job?'

'Er - I think ...' Chuck started.

'Don't think Peterson, damned well find out ... again by Monday' the Colonel looked back down at his notes.

'What's the score with insurance on the Manifold?'

'It's covered by Far East Maritime for the full amount and our estimate is around $30 million plus for a replacement with towing charges but without any salvage costs for the original one ... which could be considerable!'

The Colonel was becoming impatient.

'Did you or did you not break in to Doyle's office to get all this information? I don't want to hear figures that are *around* ... I want to know exactly ... that was the whole point of that break-in being approved ... do you understand what I'm saying?' Oliver Gresham was angry, his voice raised, sharp, unforgiving and Chuck was quietly shitting himself. 'To be fair Colonel' he replied indignantly 'I did *not* know what this meeting was to be about this morning, so I do *not* have all the detail with me ... only what is in my head. If you want, I can go back to my office, collect all my papers and be

Chapter Fifteen – The Saboteur

back within the hour'. The offer was ignored ... leaving Chuck with a slight sweat on. Gresham studied his notes. This tosspot of an agent he had in front of him wouldn't last five minutes in the hard reality of his world. He would be out of his depth in a damn puddle. He was overweight, overpaid and unfortunately over here. This man had two good, undisturbed hours in the AOS offices for God's sake and appeared to have gleaned practically nothing except a few photographed drawings and some technical manuals. Didn't he know what he was going in there for? There was no commercial detail in all the verbiage, no handle on what real money was involved, who was actually providing it, how AOS were getting paid and what possible profits that cunning bastard Doyle may, in reality, be stuffing up one of his offshore bank accounts.

'The whole thing was a bloody mess' he told himself.

'Well, there's not much here that you've told me that I do *not* already know. But I can tell you that there is no insurance in place on the subsea manifold ... and that my friend ... is a frigging fact!'

Chuck looked up startled, shaking his head slowly in disbelief.

'That can't be correct. If there was a lack of provable insurance on the most delicate and costly part of the job, the banks wouldn't be able to provide facilities. If it all went tits up, any institution covering the finances could end up being hurt ... for some pretty big bucks!'

'Well I can assure you that as of two days ago, FEMC withdrew insurance cover on AOS'. Chuck was lost for words

'You need to find out what the hell is going on with the bank Chuck and you need to get on to it today'

Chuck felt the fierce tone of delivery indicated this was not a request - but an order.

His mind was trying hard to focus. That sly son of a bitch Doyle used the ABR because he knew that his business was substantial for the size of bank, and due to how it uniquely positioned itself in the market place, none of the American oilfield companies used it. If it had been any of the local Arab Banks or even some of the major Internationals like the HSBC or BBME, he could have had the file pulled and copied in a minute. ABR Findlays was a different kettle of fish. It only operated major business accounts, was fussy about who it let through the door and had a relatively small staff for an institution handing hundreds of millions of dollars each year.

Chuck Peterson was well out of his comfort zone. His transfer from Italy to the desert state of Abu Nar some five years previously had been seen as a sort of 'hardship' posting, but it turned out to be anything less. He had a fantastic house, servants, more money than he could shake a stick at and the advantage of being a

Chapter Fifteen – The Saboteur

rather big fish in a somewhat small but strategically, very important pond. Everyone knew 'Chuck' in Abu Nar and most of the other Gulf States as well. He was everybody's best friend. That's how he worked and as far as he was concerned, he got the right results. At least, that's how his 'desk' back at Langley seemed to see it … but not the visibly irritated military example sitting in front of him today.

'So … can you do it or not?' The sharp words interrupted Chuck's pensive train of thought as he instinctively replied 'Yes Sir … you better believe it!'

'Good' replied the Colonel as he started laying down some more notes on further sheets of hotel headed paper. Oliver Gresham handed the papers to Chuck, looked him squarely in the face and said

'Get me the information I need written here and get back to me by Telex at the MENA desk, Directorate of Operations. This number is not in your directory of offices so I have written it on top of sheet one' Chuck began to study the list.

Oliver Gresham, Middle East Region Director of Covert Operations for the CIA stood up quickly and said

'That's it … this meeting has ended' and without further elaboration, showed his flustered visitor out the door of Room 602.

Chuck breathed the word 'Asshole' out loud as he

stuffed the scribbled sheets in to his back trouser pocket and navigated the corridors on the sixth floor, heading toward the elevators.

~~~~~~~~
~~~~

Chapter Sixteen
An Unexpected Visitor

Final engineering for The Geneveh Project was now in full swing. The Sabeen Road offices of Contec overflowed with AOS Contract staff. Hours were long and tempers short. Andy was doing his normal conjuring trick of being in just about every required place … just in the required time and keeping the lid on any possibly fractured internal and external relationships. Work on site was due to start officially on Thursday August thirteenth. That was tomorrow. The camp was there, the men were there but the infrastructure required to support the pipe welding programme on the shore side of the works was not.

Declan had decided to go and have a look for himself. He turned up at the Oilfield Supply Centre with an overnight bag and a pile of drawings. The two thousand seven hundred ton 'Sea Ranger' was finishing loading. She looked magnificent in her dark blue livery and spotless white superstructure. This was the lead workboat on the contract. This was also one of the finest examples of the 'P' Type offshore support vessel around and Reg Green, an Australian adventurer to the core, was its proud owner. Reg and Declan had worked together many times before and Reg had been

Chapter Sixteen – An Unexpected Visitor

appointed marine manager for all offshore works on the Geneveh Project.

The two men shook hands as they met on the crowded open cargo deck of Sea Ranger. It was full of large welded steel sections, and all in all, this particular cargo made up the sections that were missing to enable the 'wet' side of the pipe support system to be put in place.

'Good-ay Decs' A cheerful, mahogany tanned and fit looking Reg offered as a greeting … along with a rock hard handshake and a refreshing smile.

'Hi Reg' Declan replied equally happy to be in this extraordinary man's company. Reg was one of the few individuals allowed to use the 'Decs' moniker - and he knew it. He had a history of adventuring going back to the Vietnam War where he carried out regular covert activities on behalf of the Americans between the Paracel Islands and the coastline area of Da Nang. Reg Green was a hard man: someone who would shake a problem to death, like a Jack Russell with an old sock, until it was resolved - one way or another.

'Just the man you need on a job like this' Declan reminded himself as they both climbed the internal stairway to Declan's cabin. The first beers were ceremoniously pulled open and both men savoured the ice cold amber liquid quietly in contemplation of the scale of the current adventure. After this quiet, reflective moment, Declan was first to break the silence.

'How long to get there today Reg?'

'If we can get away by ten this morning, we should be anchored up on site by about ten o'clock on Thursday night'. He glanced at his watch. It was a shade past nine thirty.

'Sorry Dec's, but you'll have to make yourself comfortable. The fridge is full of beer and I've got to go and kick ass to get the Ranger out of here before the tide turns'

With another broad and meaningful grin he was gone.

Declan flipped open another can. With a sigh, he realised he would have to get down to going through the drawings he had brought with him, for the umpteenth time. He was known and generally respected for the fact he was as well briefed about the detail of engineering works on all of his projects as any of the individual section managers. If it was on a drawing, Declan would make sure he had his head round it. If it was not on a drawing, it was not on the job. *It* - was as simple as that.

On Thursday evening at twenty two hundred hours local time, Reg ordered the anchors to be dropped and the main engines fell silent. They were on station. Reg had done the journey many times over the past few weeks, bringing men and equipment to site to build the onshore camp and manufacturing facilities. This last load of fabricated steel should complete the job and now he would concentrate on ensuring all the marine

Chapter Sixteen – An Unexpected Visitor

works were properly co-ordinated. At around six o'clock, about fifty miles out from Geneveh, the boat had been buzzed at low level by an Iranian Phantom, bristling with missiles and about five miles out an old, but still menacing, Bell UH-1 'Huey' helicopter gunship came out to 'greet' them. It was good to see that air defences were up and running, but "would they really be enough" was the still unanswered question?

It was dark as the Sea Ranger swung at anchor. Declan felt safe, well as safe as one could reasonably be expected to feel sitting in full sight of the enemy on the front line of a major International conflict. Therefore, he had decided to turn in early. Tomorrow would be a long and possibly tiring day on site and he wanted to be up bright eyed and mentally sharp, fully prepared to take it on.

At six thirty the following morning, one of the service tugs pulled up alongside the Sea Ranger and Declan jumped aboard. He was met on the after deck by Harry Wright. Harry was the Project Manager, the most senior manager on site. From using him before on other projects, Declan knew he could also be a pain in the arse; but he was good at what he had to do - and that was to get this job finished on time and within budget.

'Morning Mr Doyle' Shouted Harry above the beat of the powerful eight cylinder diesel as the tug pulled away. Although Declan and Harry had known one another for many years, Harry always called Declan 'Mr Doyle' … in front of the men … and in private. It was one of his little ways.

'Morning Harry' Declan replied 'Is everyone up for it?'

'They certainly are. All the managers are waiting in the conference room. We shall go there straight away if that's OK with you'

'No problem Harry; can't wait to get going'.

Harry revealed nothing by his bland expression. He was a five foot six tall, four foot six wide, red haired ex-shipyard manager from Glasgow. Harry regarded everything in life as 'serious'. Whether problems were stacked high on Harry's shoulders or he was totally pissed at one of his famous birthday parties, Harry's expression never changed. He showed little or no emotion. He was a machine – and he got things done. He was also an expensive machine to hire by the day, but worth every penny.

As the two men entered the crowded conference room situated in the centre of the 400 man camp, known simply as 'The Compound', a murmur gently rose up amongst the assembled managers, supervisors and foremen. Some had worked with Declan before, but many had not. Declan had a certain reputation in the oil business and so some were curious to get a measure of the man. Before Declan left this room today, every man

Chapter Sixteen – An Unexpected Visitor

in it would have to sign up to stay with the job until it was finished. This would sound a fairly simple and straight forward request to some, but the more experienced managers and supervisors would know that for the next twelve weeks there would be no slacking, no days off, possible air raids on the compound on a regular basis, a punishing schedule to maintain and no complaints.

Each man had his own contract with AOS, one that had been signed before arriving on site. This was the time to actually stay or go. The men who signed up today received 50% of a substantial bonus paid directly in to an offshore bank account. The other 50% would be paid when the project was signed off by the client. It was worth having

Declan looked around the room at this collection of young and old oilfield mercenaries, the continuing buzz tapering away as he began to speak.

He liked what he saw.

'Ok Guys, welcome to project 112/406, better known to you all as the Geneveh Project. By now you will all have realised what you are in for. Today is bonus sign up day. This is your last chance to withdraw. You all know the rules and looking around me, I can see quite a few who have worked with me before' A short lived verbal response confirmed the fact.

Declan continued. 'All of the boffin engineers tell us – that on paper - this *can be done*. However, pulling a pipe of this size off a beach in to over 100 feet of water has *not been done before*'

The final words carried an emphasis that was not lost on the assembly.

'We are already one day behind on installing the pipe cradles and rollers from the welding plant to the water entry point. We now have the cradles and they are being offloaded as we speak. *You ...*' he stated pointedly as he scanned the room to check reactions. '... have to catch up this lost day within the next forty eight hours – and we start as soon as this meeting is over' He paused.

'I now have with me your individual bonus contracts and I want to take them back with me tomorrow signed by every one of you'

Now he had a real reaction. A spontaneous cheer went up from all the men in the room except Harry. He stood behind Declan, silent and expressionless.

'Gentlemen, there is a lot of money at stake here as well as the future of AOS. You hold it all in your hands and when it's finally successful, you will all share financially in that success - so good luck... and try hard not to piss Harry off any more that he is right now'

The whole assembly let out a knowing chuckle. Harry remained impassive. Declan's job with the men was done. Time to go through the long and complex site operations check list with Harry and the relevant section managers as each part of the process was finally fired up and linked together. The whole start-up

Chapter Sixteen – An Unexpected Visitor

operation was timed to take six or seven hours, but Declan knew from experience that this was wishful thinking.

At eleven o'clock that evening, Declan was comfortably settled into the small single man sleeping accommodation provided for him by the camp boss. It had been a long hard day. The temperature had barely dipped below thirty degrees and humidity had remained at a stubborn, energy sapping seventy plus percent. One very positive note was that the temporary airstrip had been completed that very day and so in future, Declan would be able to fly back and forth at will, and men movements could now take place by air directly to the site.

His deep and dreamless sleep was disturbed by an increasingly loud commotion right outside the sleeping cabin window. He awoke with a start and for a second or two, confused by his surroundings. The room was dark but the sounds of revving vehicle engines and lots of shouting in English and Farsi quickly confirmed where he was … but not what was happening. Declan hastily raised himself out of bed and fumbled round the unfamiliar room layout for a pair of shorts and a shirt. The cabin door burst open pushing a shaft of dull yellow light in to the gloom, followed by a shabbily dressed, mean looking, bearded individual, thrusting the end of an AK47 cautiously through the opening and shouting

'Salam, lotfan bebakhshid' Please excuse me.

'Salam' Declan shouted back.

His grasp of Farsi was not good but he knew enough to understand that the words he was hearing were not threatening. The unexpected visitor was indicating with short sideways movements of the gun barrel, that Declan was to follow him. With shirt now half buttoned he was led outside. A collection of mud splattered white four wheel drive pickup's, wearing the standard clenched fist and rifle logo, crudely impressed in black on the cab doors, were surrounding the cabin and inhabited by crews of roughly attired and bearded Iranian militia.

The poorly applied stencil on the cab doors indicated that these were Rev Guard but the standard issue AK 47's were not pointed in his direction and this was interpreted by a cautious Declan as a good sign. Out of the dust haze and murkiness surrounding one of the vehicles emerged a familiar figure. Mohsen Raza, Head of the IRGC and paymaster on the Geneveh Project had decided to pay Declan a visit. Out of nowhere, two canvas folding chairs appeared followed by a collapsible steel table, an ashtray, two standard issue white ceramic Arabic coffee cups and a thermos flask full of the necessary steaming liquid. Declan must have looked somewhat dazed just being woken up from a deep sleep

Chapter Sixteen – An Unexpected Visitor

in such a startling manner. Mohsen Raza spoke first.

'My apologies for having to visit you so late Mr Doyle'

He was dressed in an immaculate grey military uniform with no markings of rank. In Iran, he probably didn't need to give anyone such a clue, or in fact who he was; everyone knew. As usual, his English was perfect and the first cigarette was quickly on the go. The ritual pouring of the coffee had already begun as Mohsen indicated to Declan that he should sit in one of the canvas chairs. The Head of the IRGC continued.

'Have no fear Mr Doyle, I am not here today to discuss the project, even though some reports reaching me indicate that you are a little behind on your programme'

The words had been carefully chosen to be stinging and Raza knew they had achieved the required result. Declan was about to reply - but then thought it would be better to hear his visitor out. Through a practiced and generally engaging smile - not extended to the eyes – Mohsen Raza continued.

'You are leaving us tomorrow I understand and returning to Abu Nar on the Sea Ranger'

Declan nodded his head in agreement.

'Excellent Mr Doyle' Mohsen Raza rubbed his hands together in a slightly theatrical manner.

What was coming next Declan wondered.

'Being loaded right now is a cargo of approximately

one hundred and fifty kilos of Beluga and Sevruga ...' he paused for effect '... and approximately eighty kilos of Ossetra caviar'

He looked pleased with himself and was still rubbing his hands together in his obvious excitement. Comic looking grins had suddenly become infectious as they were taken up eagerly by Raza's surrounding, protective henchmen.

'All of the packaging is legal with the correct stamped export sealing tape around each tin' he announced proudly.

Declan remained coolly silent. There was something going on here that was bound to cause him a degree of hassle and probably cost some money.

Mohsen paused, studying Declan closely for a sign of how well the one sided conversation was going so far.

'In turn for providing you with this fabulous *gift* from the peoples of the Islamic Republic of Iran – when the Sea Ranger sets sail again, I would hope that it will be carrying return gifts from the brotherly state of Abu Nar, such as TV sets, refrigerators and wall air-conditioning units'

The hands had stopped in mid 'rub', all traces of a smile eradicated. Most of the echoing 'grins' had also disappeared. Declan really knew at this point he should say something, but he also held a belief he was being 'done up like a kipper' so engaging in a discussion may sink him even further in to the 'lake' of caviar he had

Chapter Sixteen – An Unexpected Visitor

suddenly become the proud owner of. Raza continued in a firmer less affable tone.

'Just in case someone becomes confused with the mathematics, on the open market the Beluga and Sevruga is currently changing hands at six hundred US dollars a kilo and the Ossetra at over two thousand US dollars a kilo'

So, not only was the man sitting in front of him a torturer, murderer, terrorist financier and religious fanatic, Declan felt he could now comfortably add 'International smuggler' to the list. It looked as if someone was going to be busy sourcing a few hundred thousand dollars worth of TV's - first thing in the morning.

Mohsen Raza must have thought that Declan had taken the news just delivered to him rather well. The two men sat at the table through a couple more cigarettes and several more cups of sweet Arabic coffee, then, as if he had suddenly realised he should be somewhere else, Raza got up from the table, turned and was gone without literally one word of excuse or explanation. The militia guard immediately snatched up the table and chairs, clambered aboard their vehicles and with much shouting, screeching of tyres and labouring of poorly maintained engines, they too were gone.

Declan stood there for a moment in the swirling, settling dust cloud. Had he really just had this ridiculous conversation with the second most powerful but definitely most feared man in Iran? If the deck of the Sea Ranger was covered in fish eggs the following morning he would soon know.

As Declan jumped energetically on to the quayside at the Abu Nar Oilfield Supply Centre, he noticed Andy waiting for him. He checked his watch. It was seven thirty but the OSC was still busy on this humid Sunday evening. Andy's greeting was a firm handshake minus a smile. He got to the point straight away.

'Hi Declan … I've sorted the caviar problem' he advised bluntly.

'Well done Andy' Declan replied encouragingly - what about the electrical goods?'

'I've done a deal with the major dealers here for around a hundred and fifty thousand dollars worth as we agreed and they will be ready to load by lunchtime tomorrow.'

'What about the paperwork? We have to be extremely careful there or else we'll end up being done for smuggling ourselves!'

'Officially the cargo will be going to Nigeria as a final destination to get round the Iranian embargo'

'Excellent news Andy!'

'I fucking well hope this doesn't come back on us Declan'. 'No problem Andy, I think we have all the angles covered'

Chapter Sixteen – An Unexpected Visitor

Declan knew that in Iran, a country suffering western trade embargos for several years now, a hundred and fifty thousand dollars worth of TV's, fridges and air-conditioners on this side of the Gulf would translate in to more than four hundred thousand dollars worth of resale value on the other side of the Gulf

'Make sure you have someone sensible supervising the loading. We don't want any complaints from our 'customer' at the other end!'

Both men laughed out loud at the thought as Andy made his way to have a quick chat with the captain of the Sea Ranger and Declan waved goodbye, heading in the direction of his waiting car. As he opened the driver's door, the internal lights flashed on revealing a stone faced Penny sitting in the front passenger seat – waiting. Words were not necessary. The look was enough.

~~~~~~~~
~~~~

Chapter Seventeen
The Langley Decision

Colonel Oliver Gresham sat outside room six zero six situated on the sixth floor of the Langley CIA building. He was in full dress uniform. He looked immaculate. The silver star, bronze star and two purple hearts stood out amongst the two rows of colourful medal ribbons. His cap was clamped under his left arm and he sat bolt upright. The sign on the door to room six zero six simply said 'William J Carstairs'. This was a temporary office for the head of the CIA. His own seventh floor suite was being fitted out with some new bits of electronic wizardry designed to guarantee all conversations in that office to be even more secure than they were now. A petite, blonde and very attractive young lady exited the office and told the waiting Colonel that he could now go in.

The room was not large and the single, enormous Georgian English mahogany desk seemed to half fill it. Oliver Gresham stood to attention in front of the Director of the CIA. He refrained from saluting as the man seated at the desk did not hold any military rank, unlike his predecessor.

William, who preferred to be called 'Bill' Carstairs, indicated to the Colonel by a wave of the hand to be

Chapter Seventeen – The Langley Decision

seated. Other than the two men, the desk and two chairs, the room was empty.

'Morning Oliver'

'Morning Bill' the Colonel replied. Bill Carstairs finished scribbling on the front of a beige file cover, pushed it to one side of the desk and looked up. 'Good to see you again old buddy'

'Good to see *you* again sir, it's been a while'

The calendar clock on Bill Carstairs desk indicated the time and date. It was 08:30 on Monday, seventeenth of August. Oliver made a mental note of the date and meeting time. When the meeting was finished, he would immediately go to his office on level B3 and write up the relevant notes. The Colonel knew that in the CIA, if you wanted to survive, in the long term, you covered your ass in every direction, *all* the time. Since officially joining the 'Virginia farm boys' from the National Security Council earlier in the previous year, Oliver knew that all conversations would need to be backed up with a record of some sort. This had stood him in good stead in the past and although he didn't know it yet, would play a major part in saving his 'bacon' in the very near future.

'So Oliver, tell me more about this Geneveh thing'

'Well sir, it seems as if it's going ahead'

'I thought you said you could handle it, so to hear that this is not the case is something of a disappointment'

His words were stern, flatly delivered, his gaze

unflinching. Oliver Gresham was feeling the heat.

'To be frank with you Bill, I really thought that by pulling the insurance on the manifold, that asshole Doyle would have to walk away. Our man 'Chuck' in Abu Nar cleaned out the offices of Contec and AOS and came up with next to nothing else worth having a go at. The key to this whole bloody mess is the manifold'.

The head of the CIA remained impassive and deep in thought. After a substantial pause, he spoke again.

'What worries me Oliver is the fact that if this project goes ahead, the Iranians will probably be forced to use the Hawk's they've been keeping under wraps for some time now. They will definitely have to use the upgraded Phantoms against those *damn* new 'Frenchie' machines and even a child airplane spotter will be able to identify them!'

He paused for a second 'It's the Israelis who bother me most Oliver. As soon as they spot them, they'll scream imminent attack, the great Islamic monster, in fear of our lives, the end of a nation … and all that bullshit' The Colonel interrupted.

'Don't we have some influence there Sir?'

'The last PM, Shimon Peres is a friend, but his influence as an elder statesman looks to be waning significantly. With all the turmoil in Israel recently, we think a new government of national unity will not last much longer than the last one. This means that we will

Chapter Seventeen – The Langley Decision

be dealing with the Likud man, Yitzhak Shamir - whether we like it or not. He's no friend of the west; was imprisoned by the Brits in forty two, led the Lehi underground for a long time, too long some say - and is generally considered a right wing hard line bastard. If he starts shouting, the shit will definitely hit the fan'

Both men knew the worrying background subject matter well and were acutely aware that if the brown stuff did hit the rotating fan, it would spread far and wide within the United States and beyond. Bill was 'in charge' during the Iranian hostage crisis, when fifty three Americans had been held for over four hundred and forty days by a group of Islamist students and militants who took over the American Embassy in nineteen seventy nine.

Oliver was in charge of planning the attempted rescue mission named Operation Eagle Claw … and Bill Carstairs was the man who actually approved it. The result was a total mission failure, the destruction of two American aircraft along with the deaths of eight American servicemen and one supposedly Iranian civilian.

The secret and humiliating exchange agreement with the Iranians in 1981 resulted in the sale of arms to Iran for the release of the hostages. The Israelis were used to move the hardware to Iran and the money paid by the Iranians was used by Colonel Oliver Gresham to secretly fund illegal arms supplies to some left wing rebel organisation in South America. They were both up to their necks in it and since the leak in a Lebanese magazine in early nineteen eight six, had needed to keep heads low and lips tight. A confused President Reagan had taken the public hit for the arms-deals, but denied any links with the hostage crisis. However, both men, looking across from one another today, knew that was untrue and by anyone's guess, there was much more to come. If the full and detailed story got out in to the public domain, the whole near fantasy scenario of lies, deceit and corruption at the highest levels of the US Security Services would shake the Intelligence offices of the free world to the very core. Conversation ceased as each man studied the situation carefully in his mind. There could simply *not* be any more cock-ups in the Middle East. They needed an answer to the Geneveh problem.

The director of the CIA was a bruised animal. He had a conscience and a pension to nurture. The man sitting before him had no conscience. That was why Bill Carstairs had pushed for his transfer from the NSC many months earlier. He wanted to keep him close. The whole hostage situation had been an embarrassment to the American government and its people and Oliver Gresham's secret use of Iranian money to fund the Contras had only come to light as a theory long after the event. The whole can of worms was still bubbling,

Chapter Seventeen – The Langley Decision

and could possibly blow open at any time. One or perhaps both of the men sitting in that room on that fateful day may soon be standing up in a court of law to defend their not so secret actions. Bill Carstairs broke the silence.

'Let's look at what we've got Oliver'

The Middle East Region Director of Covert Operations shook himself out of a mood of contemplation and paid attention.

'We're dealing with that damned fanatic Mohsen Raza ... and he is very unpredictable Bill. However, he is a good military man and he will not want Hawk missiles on full view each side of the Geneveh straits. They have managed to camouflage their nuclear activities very well up to now; they know what they are doing. Don't forget we still have a man inside the Rev Guard at a high level. We could use him to push to ensure any new installations are suitably hidden from overhead surveillance. But I have to tell you, this is not for sure. Raza is running this show himself and tackling him on any subject whatsoever that may question some of his strategies, can be a delicate matter, even for those very close to him'.

'Do we know yet what the Englishman Doyle was doing in Basra a week ago?' Carstairs questioned.

'All of our contacts in Iraq are tight lipped and either know and won't tell us or simply have not got a clue - which indicates to me that he was meeting someone very high up, either politically or militarily. He's a cunning bastard and I'm pushing to find out what's going on. It might mean another break in to his offices and maybe his house but I don't think we'll find anything'.

'Ah yes, our beloved friends and allies; the Iraqis. They hate our bloody guts really, but we've taken a gamble on Saddam and so must tread carefully. Stick with it and report to me as soon as you find out anything'

'Yes Sir' the Colonel replied.

'So, we need a plan to literally blow this whole damn shenanigans out of the water … let's look at the options; Coffee?'

'Yes Sir' the Colonel replied once again and then they got down to it.

Four hours later, a plan was in place. Was it a good plan? The Colonel thought so. It was decisive, it was military, it was pretty final and with a fair wind, no one would know what the hell had happened. The head of the CIA was less enthusiastic, as he always was when there was a military 'go-get-em' element involved. He preferred much more subtle techniques to be employed in his kind of problem solving, especially considering the vast resources he had at his disposal. However, time was tight.

'Thank you Oliver - I think we have everything

Chapter Seventeen – The Langley Decision

covered and from now on I want regular reports directly to me on burst radio - and good luck'

'Thank you sir' the Colonel repeated for the last time as he moved smartly out of the CIA Director's office and closed the door silently behind him.

Bill Carstairs picked up the telephone and asked to speak with Admiral James Warkin, Head of the US Navy. After a few seconds wait he was put through directly to the Admirals office.

'Hi Bill, long time no hear. What can I do for you?'

'Hi James, yes it has been a while but I have a little problem that I think you can help me with' he paused '....and I would like to visit with you as soon as possible'.

~~~~~~

An interruption to a morning management meeting was unusual. But as Declan sat in the Sabeen Office meeting room, listening to an engineering update recently arrived from Singapore, the phone rang. The discussion stopped and fifteen short sleeved individuals in the room all looked toward the President of AOS Inc. Declan picked up the phone impatiently. It was Esther. He listened for a few seconds and then said

'Ok. I'll be straight there' He put the phone down gently, a puzzled expression on his face.

'Sorry gentlemen, you will have to carry on without

me for a while'. He moved his chair back from the long Ash veneered conference table and left the room.

Lieutenant Samir Awad of the Abu Nar criminal police was sitting in Declan's office and got up to offer a hand as Declan entered.

'Good morning Declan' It was a cheerful greeting.

'So sorry to disturb you on this bright Wednesday morning and I do understand you are very busy but ...'

'No problem Samir – It's always a pleasure to see you, you know that - in fact I was due to come and see *you* soon about your bar bill at the Country Club'

Both men laughed out loud. The bill would rest behind the bar for a few weeks yet.

'So what can I do for you?'

'Well, it's rather a delicate matter Declan, but I have had a call this morning from an Inspector Herbert Lau in Hong Kong'. The Lieutenant searched for a reaction, but couldn't spot one, so continued.

'He informs me you were there on Sunday August ninth. Is that correct'

'That is correct - and I left on Monday the tenth - on the eight thirty flight. It was British Airways'

He replied calmly – but what was coming next?

'We understand that you had some discussions with a ...' he pulled a small black notebook from his uniform tunic pocket. '... with a ... Mister Anthony Swales' he looked up, dark eyes bright, alert and questioning. 'Is

Chapter Seventeen – The Langley Decision

that correct?' 'It is Samir. We bumped in to one another in the Jockey Club'

'You had business dealings with this ... er ... Mr Swales?'

'Yes, we did have some insurance arrangements under discussion'

The hard smile from the policeman was deceiving.

'Did you know that Mr Swales was now dead Declan?' The question was a genuine shocker - and it showed.

'Good God man ... no I did not ... this is a bit of a jolt my friend. I knew his family ... I don't really know what to say' The searching look continued. Lieutenant Samir Awad was no fool. He was a highly trained investigator and had spent over a year on secondment with the London Metropolitan Police.

He wasn't sure. The next one would probably reveal more.

'Well, I can tell you Declan that the way he died - was not very pretty' he paused. The face on the man in front of him was taut, the expression noticeably strained.

'He had half his face blown off ... with a letter bomb'

It hit Declan like a brick. He flushed involuntarily and broke out in to a sweat. Lieutenant Awad was still not sure.

'It happened on the Monday morning ... when you would have been somewhere over ... let me see now ...

Burma … I believe?' 'I simply don't know what to say Samir … I am absolutely … totally shocked!'

'Hmm – well, I have to inform you that the Royal Hong Kong Police may want a written statement from you … at some stage. Will you be prepared to give one?'

'Well Samir, if it would help you … or them … in any way … of course I will be happy to, but I don't know what else I can really tell you'.

The policeman studied what appeared to be a genuinely distressed and surprised Mr Doyle and he would convey that thought to his colleagues in the RHKP as soon as he got back to the office.

'Thank you for your time Declan - and now I will let you get back to managing your busy empire' This evoked another smile that passed equally between the two men as hands were shaken and the Lieutenant left the office.

Declan fell back in to his chair.

'Jesus Christ' he mouthed out loud 'What a fuck up'

He grabbed the telephone and rang a London number.

~~~~~~~~
~~~~

Chapter Eighteen
A Fatal Error

It was another miserable day in the middle of a hot, bare and unforgiving landscape located many miles south of nowhere, unless of course the small settlement town of Dalaki could be called somewhere; a desolate place inhabited by several hundred peasants living literally in the dark ages. There was not a beer for miles and the food was shit. Even Dalaki village was several miles away from the old airstrip that had been made good in a hurry to accommodate Commander Javad Jananari's squadron, consisting of four fighting fit Phantom F4E's.

As a result, his command now consisted of a runway too short to make a mistake on, a collection of rotting pre-fabricated huts serving as offices and accommodation, four temporary canvas and steel tube covered aircraft bays, a generator that had been left behind by some sort of oil expedition twenty years ago and a cook that had been trained in what was listed in his service papers as a 'military prison'. The only light in Commander Javad's life at this moment in time was the fact that his aircraft were still flying. This was something of an achievement in Iran in nineteen eighty seven, as from his point of view, the country was

Chapter Eighteen – A Fatal Error

financially bankrupt. This was an opinion that could not be voiced but was whispered regularly among the intelligentsia in Tehran.

There was no money for anything. Half of the Iranian Air Force complement of aircraft were unflyable and being used for spares to keep the rest in various states of airworthiness. It was all a complete bloody mess, but at least in Tehran, a well connected individual could lay his hands on some small pleasures such as a beer or two, watch American movies, take out some girls and have uninterrupted electricity for most of the day.

Javad was not a good Moslem. He saw corruption all around him, running in parallel with the pious hypocrisy of the clerics and as a result kept his head low and took with both hands anything good that was offered to him. The 'good' in this case was the promise of making Colonel if he did 'desert' duty with his squadron for some three or four months. He grabbed the opportunity, although on this Monday morning, he wished he maybe had thought twice.

With just a creaking ceiling fan to tackle the oppressive heat in the leaking timber and corrugated iron building serving as an operations room, Commander Javad Jananari sat up in his dilapidated mobile office chair, ran his hands through his hair and shouted 'Come!' in response to a loud knock on the office door. Two pressure-suited and 'bone-dome' equipped air crews entered, followed by chief sergeant Masoud Paywar, leader of the aircraft maintenance team and Lieutenant Mohammad Memarain, the Squadron Intelligence Officer. The six men shuffled around the room until each had found a 'perch' of some kind as the Commander moved listlessly over to the wall map. This showed the extended local area including a large MTZ Military Fly Zone, taking up a substantial part of the map area. It was outlined in red. Everyone in the room seemed relaxed although not one of them really wanted to be there. All were thinking back to a few weeks previously when they were comfortably installed in good quality barracks, with significantly better food than they were eating now and right on the doorstep of Tehran. The base at Doshan Tapeh was regarded as home to the men and also the home of Air Force Headquarters.

The Air Force had never really recovered from the effects of the nineteen seventy nine revolution and the failed coup that followed it which had begun at Shahrokhi Air Base. This had brought about another deep and sweeping purge of the Air Force, from which it had never really recovered.

Today was another day and everyone in the room knew they simply had to get on with it. The squadron worked closely with a similar military facility on Kharg Island. This unit was commanded by Colonel Masih Vandati and he was the overall commander of the

Chapter Eighteen – A Fatal Error

protective cover operation named 'Sharban'. Colonel Vandati was one of the new guard. He was not a pilot. He was an administrator; someone who had seen a meteoric rise through the ranks from lowly corporal in nineteen eighty to full Colonel today. His mentor was one Mohsen Raza, head of the IRGC and therefore could do nothing wrong. He was hated by all the pilots and few remaining career officers of the old guard, but with the protection of Mohsen Raza, he was omnipotent and he made sure everyone he came into contact with knew it.

The telephone on Javad's desk rang and he leant back to answer it. He listened for about two and a half minutes and then put the phone down. He looked up at his assembled staff and said despondently

'Vandati' All eyes in the room moved skyward in a single response and Javad Jananari moved back to the wall map.

'Right gentlemen, today's patrol will leave at eleven thirty local'. He tapped the wall map to a position in the middle of the red marked MTZ.

'Today we are flying top cover to Colonel Vandati's *bottom* cover' The word 'bottom' was emphasized slightly sending a small ripple of laughter throughout the room as the crews visualised Colonel Vandati's bottom. The two navigators began to make notes.

'This means that you will fly at fifty thousand feet in cruise mode with a mission time of two hours.

Fourteen squadron will have two aircraft flying *bottom cover'* again a little snigger '... at twenty thousand feet. As usual, the same rules apply. Nothing - and I repeat - *nothing* is to fly in this zone ...' Javad tapped the map again indicating the red outlined area '... without the permission of Central Command ATC. Any aircraft without a transponder signal will be regarded as the enemy and is to be pursued. You are aware now that the Iraqis have the upgraded Exocet capable Mirage and although we haven't seen one yet, today could be your lucky day'

This raised another smile.

'You may smile gentlemen, but the Mirage is a different sack of potatoes to those clapped out Mig 23 Floggers. They are lighter than you, they climb quicker than you, their service ceiling is greater than yours and what is more relevant is the Iraqi crews have been well trained. These are not shit pilots. If they are coming in with Exocets, they will be low so leave them to fourteen squadron. You need to watch top cover and see if you can nail a couple of Mig's. You know the patrol pattern and today Lieutenant Mohammad Khatami will be the leader and Lieutenant Daywar will be wing man'

Commander Jananari looked around at the crew for questions. There were none. He focused his attention on chief sergeant Masoud Paywar.

'Are all aircraft one hundred percent serviceable?' he

Chapter Eighteen – A Fatal Error

asked. 'Yes sir' replied the chief engineer. 'Good' said Javad with a slight sigh of relief. Fourteen squadron already had one aircraft down with maintenance and his own aircraft had been lucky to survive in these harsh desert conditions without a problem…. so far.

'Intelligence?' he looked over toward Lieutenant Memrain.

'Yes sir' the slow talking Lieutenant mumbled in reply. He checked his notes.

'Meteorology is OK and all pilots have had a weather briefing. We know of four patrols at the moment outside of the MTZ, probably Mig 23's by the radar signatures and all at around forty thousand feet running about one hundred and fifty miles south of Basra. They do not have the range to get down here now, but we are monitoring all air activity and will advise of any further air movements to the pilots as usual'

'Call signs Lieutenant?'

'Today we are Blue Leader and Blue One. Bottom cover is Green Leader and Green One

'Thank you Memrain. Right gentlemen, I think that's about it. Good hunting'.

With that, the two crews left the office followed closely by the chief mechanic and intelligence officer, leaving all quiet except for the continuous rattling of the ancient ceiling fan. The ten foot climb up the aluminium access ladder in to the cramped cockpit of the F4 Phantom was made awkward by the wearing of a full Anti Gravity Suit and parachute, but once slotted in to the pilot's seat Lieutenant Khatami felt comfortable and completely at home. His crewman, Masih Farajwan, slipped in to the equally restrictive navigator's seat at the rear and eager ground crew started strapping the two, supersonic air crew, firmly in to place.

'Another day at the office' Khatami muttered in to his intercom to no one in particular and then it was down to the business of shouting out checks to his partner prior to switching on the main power modules and firing up the twin fuel hungry J79 turbojets. Each would bang out twelve thousand pounds of thrust capable of powering twenty seven tons of aircraft to over one thousand six hundred miles an hour.

At eleven thirty local time, Blue Leader was fifty feet off the deck with undercarriage tucked away and accelerating rapidly. Once the runway was seen to be fading in to the distance behind them, Lieutenant Khatami pushed the throttle forward to the stops with his left hand; the afterburner kicked in. He pulled the stick back hard between his legs with his right hand and the nose of the Phantom pointed skyward. Climbing at a rate of over twenty thousand feet a minute, and with his wing man right behind him, within seconds, the Blue patrol providing air cover over the Geneveh Project was on station, nearly ten miles above the earth, leaned off in to cruise mode and settled down to its designated patrol pattern. A quick radio check to

Chapter Eighteen – A Fatal Error

control on Kharg Island along with Green Leader thirty thousand feet below, and the day's work of seeking out the enemy had begun.

Nearly one hour into the patrol, Khatami's navigator gave a warning that a trace on the look down radar had no responder; was moving quickly at about forty five thousand feet and coming at them from the North. Hopefully the radar countermeasures pods that Blue and Green patrols were carrying would block out their electronic shadow from the incoming hostile target, now moving in fast from nearly fifty miles and closing to their position. The trace was showing on Khatami's radar repeater, situated right in front of him. Masih switched all missiles to armed.

'Call it in Masih' Mohammed Khatami shouted in to the intercom as his eyes nervously scanned his instruments and radar. Every reading had to be right. He may have to throw more than twenty five tons of red hot aluminium around the skies like a balloon in a force ten gale any time now. He needed to know that the killing machine he was jockeying would not let him down. He spoke again through gritted teeth.

'Green leader do you have him?'

'Affirmative Blue Leader I have him closing on you fast, I think …'

At that moment the high pitched warning sounded in Khatami's cockpit to confirm his aircraft had been 'lit up' by the approaching enemy missile radar. His crewman instantly switched to missile lock. They were ready for him. It looked like a Mig 23 and was coming up from underneath them at speed.

'Green Leader, he's above you … come up from below, paint the target and stay behind whilst I suck him in'

'OK Blue Leader … hold on, *I'm lit up* like an Eid Mosque here …'

'So am I …. Oh shit … he's let one off …. No … it's now two'

'You must be behind him … so let off a couple of nine's which will hopefully chase him up the ass and whilst he's worrying about that … we'll have him'

'Will do Mohammed'

The active lock-on warning was now becoming louder as the Adder heat seeking missile, on track, raced toward them at Mach 2.0. The annoyingly bleating red warning siren, indicating a missile attack at less than three miles, now echoed around the cockpit. Khatami's crew man calmly read out

'Three miles and closing'

'Time to get the hell out of here!'

'Hang on!' He shouted over the intercom, as he pushed the throttle forward in to afterburner, searching for one thousand miles an hour, quickly. Five seconds later he smashed the throttle back hard and pulled up on the stick. The 'G' force slammed the pilot and crew

Chapter Eighteen – A Fatal Error

man of Blue Leader back in to their seats as anti gravity suites inflated, stall warning sirens sounded and leading edge control surfaces deployed automatically. The aircraft had literally come to a near dead stop. Lieutenant Khatami pulled the heavy Phantom in to a roll; shouted to his crewman …

'Lock on the Sparrow's'

The four green illuminated buttons on the weapons console indicated that all four AIM-9 Sparrow radar controlled missiles were ready. He pressed two buttons and one missile was released from each fuselage pod. The fight was now on. Khatami was a skilled pilot and knew how to get the best out of his Phantom. He looked earthward through the top of his canopy and saw a vapour trail pass some two or three hundred feet below him. His crewman calmly confirmed.

'Two away'

'Check' Khatami shouted back. He was excited now - and it was infectious.

'Green leader … pull back and get down to two five'

'He's let off two more Blue Leader'

'We've got it' Khatami replied as he now rolled out level and pushed the throttle forward again, thankful to hear both engines fire to full thrust. It was now essential to keep the aeroplane level to enable the crewman to track the missiles toward the target. Six seconds later, the hostile painted blip disappeared as

Khatami's calm and collected Navigator confirmed a hit. Looking down and to his left, Lieutenant Khatami saw the explosion. It was a Mig 23 and now the second aircraft of this type he had shot down since the beginning of the war. The old marks of Mig 23 were no match for the Phantoms in a real fight although the pundits would tell you differently. The F4EJ was a brute to manage but tough to shoot down.

'Second release looks like air to ground, probably KH-23's Mohammed' Masih advised. 'With no control now the Mig is down, they'll be running wild' The Navigator was agitated.

'We can't do anything about them now' Lieutenant Khatami replied in a calmer tone '... except pray and hope to fuck they don't hit anything down there ... or else our lives won't be worth a shit'

Mohammed Khatami was smiling once again and had about him a self satisfied look as he told his crew man to ...

'Call it in, log the time and tell them we are back on patrol pattern'

'Will do' came the navigators reply.

'Green Leader - you OK?

'Fine Blue Leader - good shooting!'

~~~~~~

Reg Green stood in air conditioned comfort on the

Chapter Eighteen – A Fatal Error

bridge of the Sea Ranger, a cup of hot steaming tea balanced carefully on the binnacle and his sea binoculars raised as he scanned the activities of the fleet of small vessels under his care on that significant Monday. His eyes were drawn to one of the diving support vessels seemingly experiencing trouble launching a semi rigid. One of the Iranian forty foot 'Banoosh' dull grey patrol boats was lingering a few metres away, it's twin 350 Mercruiser outboard engines spluttering awkwardly in idle mode.

Suddenly, a wild, frantic waving of arms from the sergeant standing in the shade cover of the small fibreglass wheelhouse was observed. The heads of the remaining six crew members scattered around the deck of the Banoosh turned in his direction and then looked up to the northern horizon.

All this was taking place in silence as the soundproofed bridge blocked any understanding of what the commotion was all about. Reg moved his powerful lenses up toward where the gesticulating red faced sergeant was pointing. The sky was not cloudless, but pretty near so and initially he saw nothing unusual, then, growing out of a pale blue dusty background came a small dirty grey contrail with a second corkscrew contrail appearing slightly further behind and to the left. Reg had seen many similar sky trails in his life and knew exactly what they were. Instinctively he reached up for the lanyard controlling the air horns and hung on it. On every boat in the small encirclement, all eyes turned in the direction of the Sea Ranger to see the Captain running out on to the open bridge and pointing northward.

The Iranian Banouch sat on its stern for a second or two before powering forward as the screaming, epileptic sergeant hit the throttles and swung the small boat toward the north. Then all hell was let loose. With every gun firing, the approaching trails were now being camouflaged from direct view by exploding anti aircraft ammunition and tracer shells. Reg, still on the bridge of the Sea Ranger was anxiously attempting to predict an outcome from the trajectory of the two, possibly three incoming missiles.

Unexpectedly, there was a substantial explosion in the air about half a mile away and the fairly stable westerly trail disappeared. Maybe the Iranians had gotten lucky. However, the corkscrew trail was getting larger in diameter as it got nearer and lower. It was heading in the general direction of the Sea Ranger. Reg had it locked on in the lens of his binoculars and his mind was in turmoil in a desperate attempt to compute where the hell it would land. If the diameter of the corkscrew got any bigger, it would hit the water about a hundred yards in front of him. If not, it could possibly fly over the Sea Ranger.

Chapter Eighteen – A Fatal Error

Reg turned quickly on the open bridge. Shit. The two thousand ton workboat 'Morning Tide' was stationed about three hundred yards behind. Then, too late, there was a 'swoosh' accompanied by a high pitched whine as the Russian made, two hundred and ninety kilo KH-23 Grom missile, streaked overhead and slammed right in to the deck of the Morning Tide. There was complete silence for about one and a half seconds and then the one hundred kilo high explosive warhead erupted and a ball of fire, as big as the vessel itself, rushed skyward dragging with it a mushroom cloud of death and destruction. Reg stood there, glasses dropped, gazing uncomprehendingly at the scene of slaughter in front of him. There were twenty crew on the boat; how many could survive a detonation of such concentrated force? Suddenly there was another explosion as the aft fuel saddles went, ripping the stern section completely off.

The Morning Tide immediately started to sink by the stern with bow raised to nearly ninety degrees - and then, she stopped. Rescue boats were already racing to the scene. The boat finally settled with her prow nearly vertical and her bridge just about on the water line. His own two semi rigid fast boats were already being lowered as he finally came alive again. Reg raced the five decks down to the cargo area just as the last of his two boats was pulling away. Too late! He lowered himself on to a nearby bollard and took his head in his hands. The cacophony of noise surrounding him faded quickly in his mind leaving him voluntarily deaf to the reality.

What the hell happened?

~~~~~~~~~
~~~~

Chapter Nineteen
An Uncomfortable Matter

A black Mercedes pulled up at the gates of the Evin prison, located in north western Tehran. The darkened windows hid the occupants, but as the front driver's side glass dropped with motorised smoothness, just enough to show the guarding, expressionless militia corporal the black edged pass of the head of the IRGC, things started to happen. The guard jumped to attention and simultaneously shouted out to another uniformed individual to open up. The gate, set between two plain and un-plastered double story block buildings, provided access to the interior of Tehran's infamous landmark, built by the last Shah to house 'political' prisoners. Some fifteen years on, it was still serving the same purpose although the number of inmates had been swelled considerably since the start of the war.

The government plated vehicle stopped outside of the entrance to the reception wing and two plain clothed body guards jumped out, looking around cautiously. Satisfied, they provided the remaining passenger the necessary wordless clearance to leave the comfort of the rear seat.

As Mohsen Raza strode through the reception block and in to the main body of the prison, flanked by his

Chapter Nineteen – An Uncomfortable Matter

body guards, his crisp uniformed figure drew the attention of all in his path. He moved unwaveringly, like a man who looked as if he was on a mission. He was. He knew where he was going and who he was here to see. He wore a determined expression as he threw open a freshly painted, grey steel door branching off a long but narrow corridor leading to the back of the prison property.

The room was windowless, with walls completely covered in large format industrial white ceramic tiles from floor to ceiling. One simple, low value light bulb, hanging from the centre of a grey and dirty plaster ceiling, struggled to light the room and the steel, metre square table and straight backed chair, were bolted to the cold, damp concrete floor. Sat in the chair was a dishevelled looking, unwashed and unshaven figure who smelt badly of urine. There was little or no ventilation in the room and more unpalatable smells were rising up from what was a drain of sorts located directly beneath the table and leading out to an open sewer. The two body guards screwed up their faces as they followed their charge into the stinking and claustrophobic space.

The man in the chair, head bent, did not look up as Mohsen Raza entered. He was wearing a khaki military shirt and trousers, no belt, no shoes, no jacket, no insignia. This person, right now, was a no-body; a someone without identity. One of the body guards moved quickly behind the unfortunate prison inmate and pulled his head up by the over long, unkempt and unwashed hair.

'You wanted to see me' Raza stated in a calm, controlled tone.

There was no audible response from the prisoner.

'Colonel Vandati - listen to me' he shouted 'I have come a long way to see you - what do you want?'

The dried and cracked lips began to move but no sound could be heard. The guard tugged at the hair again as a sign of encouragement. Then the words came spilling out. The eyes, now fully opened, were fiery and full of resistance.

'God have mercy on me … please Mohsen … please get me out of here. Please get me back to my family … please … please ….'

The strained voice tailed off.

Mohsen Raza ordered one of the guards to fetch some water. Colonel Vandati grabbed at it feverishly and threw it down his neck in one long gulp as his mentor looked on. Raza had not seen his protégé since he had ordered his de-briefing and detention after the events of Monday, August thirty first. Colonel Vandati was responsible for the safe air cover of the Geneveh Project. It was a job he begged for; to be on the front line of a real war and not the paper one he had been fighting for several years at Air Force Headquarters. Against his better judgment, Raza had given in, but not

Chapter Nineteen – An Uncomfortable Matter

without advising the Colonel of the consequences of failure. He had screwed up, big time and allowed the enemy to penetrate the air cover guaranteed *personally* by the Head of the Revolutionary Guard. For Vandati, it was a bad career move.

'What have you got to say to me my friend' Mohsen repeated.

The desperate reply came spitting out.

'It was not my fault … it was not my fault …!'

The words were disjointed and difficult to make out. He was talking as if to himself.

'It was them … it was that bastard Jananari's men … missiles were running wild … simply out of control. I warned him … I warned him … his men are lazy … they are indolent … they are rude to me … to my bloody face …!'

'Listen Vandati' Raza interrupted

'*You* were the responsible officer. Your job was to ensure that *no one* and *no thing* got through to the working area of the Geneveh project. It is as simple as that. The damage caused to vessels and the loss of life on that day is down to *you*'

The Rev Guard leader pushed his face near to the pitiable, pleading human being in front of him but then recoiled immediately at the smell of sickly sweet, stinking breath. Suddenly the desperate Colonel jumped up and screamed hysterically.

'You … you bastard … I …' His arms moved, but

the body guard standing just behind and to the right of Mohsen Raza moved quicker. The heel of a hand came from nowhere and smashed down on the bridge of the nose of the completely desperate and defeated Air Force Colonel. Everyone in the room heard the sharp crack of splintering bone followed by a shriek of agonising pain; the momentum of the unexpected blow carrying the flailing body of the prisoner over the back of the restrained chair leaving him laying on the blood stained concrete floor in a crumpled, whimpering heap.

'Get up … Get up … Get up you asshole … Get up …!' Raza shouted frenziedly as the body guards grabbed the shuddering body of the man and pushed him roughly upright in the sturdy steel chair. His face was a complete mess with bright red blood pouring down from a smashed nose, covering a set of lips issuing a vibrating, gurgling noise and a stubble chin that trembled with excruciating pain.

'You gutless piece of shit … how dare you speak to me like that?'

Raza was now bent close to his victim's right ear and whispered.

'It is because of *you* that the project you were *sworn* to protect is now possibly two weeks behind schedule. Do you realise just how much such a delay will cost our country? A country that could very well lose this bloody confrontation we are engaged in up to our necks'

He stood up, speaking louder 'In fact … have you a

Chapter Nineteen – An Uncomfortable Matter

fucking clue about anything?' The humiliation was complete. The once proud and often loud Colonel Masih Vandati, had until only five very long weeks ago lived a lifestyle substantially above his rank and status in the military. He enjoyed a fully furnished and sizeable Government Villa located in the fashionable and wealthy north district of Tehran, where he entertained young, up and coming high flyers in government regularly with his beautiful, well connected wife Asal.

Her name in Farsi meant 'honey', which was a fair description in any language and it was she in fact who everyone turned up to see. She was always well presented, had a UK University education and a distant cousin as number two at the NIOC, along with a father who was a minor official in the Ministry of Economic Affairs.

How such an astute, attractive and educationally well rounded woman as Asal should ever have become involved with Vandati, only God himself knew. Mohsen Raza's wife Khorsheed, who had a particular affection for Asal, had persuaded him, some years ago, to take the dull, boring and sometimes pretentious young lieutenant, who had come up through the ranks, under his wing and become a sort of mentor. As a result, the now beaten, snivelling and sorry looking individual seated at the bloodstained steel table in interrogation room nine at the Evin Prison, needed all the friends he could get and for him, as Asal had now realised, they were in very short supply. 'Sit up ... sit up and look at me when I'm talking to you' Raza shouted. A guard pulled the prisoner's head back by the hair again. His bruised and bleeding mess of a face came up, hostile eyes fully exposed, staring through and beyond the stony expression of Mohsen Raza, ex-mentor and now possibly executioner.

'You will stay here until the Geneveh project is finished' Raza said sharply. 'In the meantime, I will give considerable thought as to what will happen to you. Asal and the children will be safe and are being looked after. So, at the moment, think yourself lucky to be alive ... and do not expect a visit from me again'

Colonel Vandati remained wordless and in tears as the head of the IRGC left the interrogation room with his two body guards who closed the door firmly behind them. There were no thoughts in his mind, no feeling in a now numbed and nerveless body. He had given up. They could do as they wished with him. He simply didn't care anymore. One more day or one year in Evin held no further fear and at that point of realisation he felt the warming flow of urine running freely and somehow comfortingly down his legs as the smell and the wetness at least confirmed he was still alive.

~~~~~~

Friday, October sixteenth was no normal day in Tehran.

Chapter Nineteen – An Uncomfortable Matter

The weather was unusually cold with violent winds picking up dust and dry earth, flinging it in all directions. Four major demonstrations were under way around the fourth district. Even Mohsen Raza had been obliged to release some of his ninety thousand strong Basij militia for peacekeeping duties. They did not like that and neither did he. The convoy of four white Nissan Patrol vehicles, all carrying the feared Rev Guard logo, travelled with difficulty down Mostafa Khomeyni Road. It was a wide avenue packed nose to tail with early evening traffic, slowed even more by the expected number of collisions along its length, due to the effects of the dramatically reduced visibility.

Raza was in the second vehicle of the small procession as it crawled past the Sepahsalar Mosque and then the Majalis building until finally he was at his destination. He checked his Gold Rolex. Only forty minutes late, but late for what? Mohsen Raza, absolute head and unquestioned leader of nearly a quarter of a million highly trained military, had been summoned to meet with the Supreme Leader, Ayatollah Khomeini.

He had not been requested by a phone call or personal message, as was usually the case when the Supreme Leader required his presence; he had been curtly *summoned,* in writing and this had left him a little confused and most certainly wary. He would know better what was likely to happen as soon as he saw who would be sitting with the Ayatollah. However, having an untrusting nature and by way of initial insurance regarding the outcome of this obviously necessary meeting, he had brought ten of his personal body guards with him. They had half covered faces, AK 47 assault rifles, side arms and three stun grenades each, clipped to an ammunition belt.

All occupants of the four dusted and muddied trucks scrambled out as they pulled up outside the Refan School building. This was the Ayatollah's headquarters and had been since the revolution some eight years previously.

With the body guard contingent began making a path through a crowd of people, all clamouring for an appointment to meet with the clerics and other religious members of the Council of Guardians, hoping to resolve some issue or other of perceived injustice.

Mohsen Raza quickly exited his vehicle and entered the building. Two armed policemen jumped to attention as the head of the IRGC passed by and within seconds he was at the doors of the Majalis of the Supreme Leader. Another policeman opened the folding door just enough to see who was outside and upon seeing Raza, quickly opened it fully and sprang to attention. Mohsen Raza indicated to his guards that they should wait outside. He prepared to make his entrance.

'This will be interesting' he thought to himself as he entered the room, simply furnished with a very large, ornately carved, gold leaf encrusted table and matching

Chapter Nineteen – An Uncomfortable Matter

twenty chairs that had once graced the main dining room of the Shah's favourite residence, the Niavaran Palace.

Apart from the policeman who had let him in, still standing bolt upright, waiting for the head of the Rev Guard to pass completely by, there were five other people in the room and all seated at the elegant and possibly priceless dining table.

At the head and farthest away from him sat the Ayatollah. He was smiling a welcome as all heads turned to face the visitor. On the supreme leader's left sat two clerics, both members of the Council of Guardians, an elite governing body of only twelve people; six clerics and six from the judiciary. On his right sat the Minister of Petroleum, Ghasem Jahanbani and the Deputy Head of the Iranian Oil Company, NIOC, Nosrat Tamouri. He was satisfyingly relieved to see that the Council of Guardians representatives were from the religious cleric contingent and not the judiciary. If it had been the other way around, it might have indicated some decisions were planned to be made today that could have some life shortening consequences for someone in the room. The Ayatollah stood up. Everyone else followed him.

'Welcome my brother – welcome - please take a seat in the name of Mohammed - peace be upon him!'

There followed a murmur of PBUH from the rest of the assembly as Raza took up an indicated seat next to the two clerics. He was now able to look directly in to the faces of the Petroleum Minister and number two at the NIOC. They both fidgeted nervously. The Ayatollah was beaming, as were the two clerics. The obligatory tea and coffee appeared as Raza explained and apologised, for his rudeness at being late. This was brushed aside by the Ayatollah as he began to enquire about the recent activities of one of his most senior military commanders.

The conversation between the two men carried on for nearly fifteen minutes in a generally relaxed atmosphere. As he spoke, Raza was carefully studying the expressions of the two silent, uncomfortable looking men in front of him. This scrutiny would not have been a pleasant experience for either of them and the Ayatollah had noted it. Raza sipped at his tea during a natural point of pause in the conversation, not taking his eyes from Nosrat Tamouri. The man directly in front of him was building up a sweat and it wasn't the temperature of the steaming hot tea that was causing it.

'So bother leader' he said to a very relaxed Ayatollah 'Is there any special reason why you have requested my presence here today?'

That was it. The trigger had been pulled and Tamouri's eyes became wide and fearful, the perspiration now visibly falling down the side of his face. It was noticeable and he knew it. He put down his glass of tea as the hand holding it became

Chapter Nineteen – An Uncomfortable Matter

conspicuously shaky. Raza looked questioningly toward the Ayatollah, who, in response, raised an arm in the direction of Minister Jahanbani. The Minister was fidgety, but his voice was calm and controlled as he began to speak.

'Well brother Raza' he offered 'We have some pretty serious situations building up around us right now and we ...' he paused and indicated a flushed Nosrat Tamouri next to him. '... we feel we should make you aware of them'

Mohsen Raza replied thoughtfully

'Well, perhaps as you have taken it upon yourself to inform me of these *serious situations* in the presence of the Supreme Leader and members of the Council of Guardians, you had better get started ... I have limited time available'

This was ominous and the Minister knew it. He replied apologetically.

'Then my brother, for the sake of expediency, I will hand everything over to Mr Tamouri ... who has all the facts, figures and detail in his head'

The Minister smiled. As far as he was concerned, he was off the hook. The bullet fired from the still smoking gun was rattling round the room and had no particular target as of yet, but this was to change very shortly. The number two at the NIOC cleared his throat. It took a few seconds. Everyone around the table waited expectantly. When he spoke, the voice was noticeably croaky. 'I wanted to bring you up to date brother Mohsen with the rather chronic situation regarding oil production. Last week, our average refined product output was less than three hundred thousand barrels a day. Due to the requirements of our armed forces, we are now at a stage where we will have to ration fuel for all civilian activities. I have to …'

Raza interrupted

'Can I ask where Doctor Rahoul is?'

This stopped Tamouri dead in his tracks. Dr Rahoul was the President of the NIOC. He was a well respected figure and one that Mohsen Raza knew well. The two oil men looked at one another. Who would reply to this delicate question? As the Minister remained tight lipped, Tamouri responded nervously.

'Er … he … in fact … he is not well. We fear he may have had a stroke of some kind and has been ordered to his bed'. 'I had not heard of this' said Raza.

He leaned forward across the table to emphasise his carefully enunciated words.

'Yes my brother, this happened two days ago and we do not expect him back to work for several weeks' Tamouri replied shakily. Raza turned his gaze towards the Ayatollah, looking for some sign of confirmation. He remained expressionless.

'… and if I may continue … we have an even worse situation with maintaining commercial production. In fact, as of today, only the Rafsanjan and Kerman fields

Chapter Nineteen – An Uncomfortable Matter

are delivering anywhere near a full output. The biggest problem is income. We have stockpiled crude and refined product to sell but simply do not have the required ability to export it'

'This is nothing new that you are telling me. Every week there is a crisis of some description. As I understand the situation, *you* as the Minister of Petroleum' he pointed to Jahanbani '…. and *you* as the …' Raza paused '… as the *acting* head of the NIOC, are paid to ensure that such crises are managed. You do of course have the authority to do this … or perhaps this is why you have called this meeting … because you feel you do not have the authority?'

The conversation was not going the way the Minister and Tamouri had expected.

'No … no. … my dear brother …' the Minister quickly responded '… this is not the case. Surely we do have all the authority we need and of course we are employing our very, very best people in the Ministry to resolve the situation'

He paused and looked to his left.

'My Ministry will come up with what is required … I feel sure of that … and I want you to know that the reason for this meeting is to air some concerns raised by Mr Tamouri that he felt would be much more quickly resolved in a meeting of this nature'

A close observer would have been able to detect a look of substantial relief passing over the grey toned, dark eyed face of a Minister who, from his point of view had completely removed himself from any danger of having to catch the now quickly accelerating bullet.

All eyes turned in the direction of the acting head of the NIOC. Tamouri looked shocked and then confused. Everyone in the now silent room was waiting for him to speak. Sweat poured in warm rivulets down his face but he looked determined.

'Well … my engineers are struggling with a scheme of some merit that you brother Raza have something of a hold over' he paused, quickly looking round the assembly '… called the Geneveh Project'

The room remained silent. He continued.

'We understand that this project has been delayed and was in fact attacked by a *massive* Iraqi force from the air … which could have caused irreparable damage!'

He paused again, waiting for a reaction, waiting for a sign of any description from the fearsome head of the Iranian Revolutionary Guard. There was none. He had no choice now, he had to carry on but knew instinctively that the hole he was digging was surely getting deeper and deeper.

'We understand that our heroic airmen fought them off … without any casualties, which is to be highly commended brother, but what is of concern to us is the unfortunate fact that Iraqi aircraft did actually get through, despite your *personal* overseeing of the defences of the working site … and …' Tamouri

Chapter Nineteen – An Uncomfortable Matter

glanced nervously round the table. Raza now had him locked in his gaze, boring uncomfortable holes in the politically motivated tapestry he was now committed to weaving.

'... and ... we at the NIOC, who have *no input* to the management of the project ... need to know when this loading facility will be coming on line'

The response was an uncomfortable silence. He felt he had to continue further. This was a mistake and he appeared to be the only person in the room who didn't know it.

'As all of us sitting round this table today are fully aware of our brother Raza's well expressed competence in managing complex projects that the illustrious Revolutionary Guard have undertaken over the past years ... to the glory of the revolution ... of course ... and therefore an update on where we actually are on this project ... so *essential* to the survival of our country in this terrible time of war .. er ... would be very much appreciated.'

It was out now. The speeding bullet was turning in one single direction. The room was still and quiet again. Then Raza spoke.

'You may have to remind me brother Tamouri, what particular aerial incident are you referring to?'

The NIOC man coughed and then looked up.

'The one on August thirty first - I believe'

'... and who gave you this highly restricted

information?' 'Well … I do actually have some contacts within the Air Force and it just happened to slip out in some conversation or other … and I think …'

He was cut off by Raza's next question.

'… and when this information just … *slipped out* … would it by any chance have been at one of those excellent lawn parties given by your most beautiful and intelligent, University educated cousin - Asal?'

'Well … yes … as you come to mention it …' he tailed off.

'… and would this very competent and persuasive cousin of yours be married to one Colonel Vandati, the senior officer in charge of air defences for the Geneveh Project?'

The path of the speeding bullet was now confirmed. Tamouri had to answer.

'Yes my brother … that is exactly the situation'

'You are aware of course that Colonel Vandati is currently being debriefed regarding the incident to which you refer. Although exaggerated, as one would expect from Vandati, there was some damage and I am afraid some loss of life on the project due to one loose missile penetrating Colonel Vandati's air cover. He is now working closely with some of my intelligence staff to ensure that such an event does not take place again'

'So … am I correct in understanding you now have de-briefing facilities at Evin Prison?'

It was a shocking statement, fed purely by emotion

Chapter Nineteen – An Uncomfortable Matter

and resulting in total silence throughout the room.

That was it. The target had been confirmed and the bullet now unstoppable. The Ayatollah and the two clerics looked on at this verbal tussle without interference or comment.

'I most certainly do my dear friend and if you wish, I will most happily make arrangements for you to visit them ... at any time'.

Mohsen Raza got up quickly from his chair, everyone else in the room stood as well except for the Ayatollah, a wry smile now clearly visible on his face.

'I think that this meeting is unnecessary and therefore terminated ... with of course the permission of the Supreme Leader'

He looked in the Ayatollah's direction and received a small nod of approval as he then turned finally toward Tamouri.

'If you wish to know anything further about the Geneveh Project, I suggest you look eagerly for your invitation to completion and first loading celebrations - to be held shortly in Bushehr. However, as you have taken so much time and trouble to arrange this important gathering, I can tell you that the project is programmed to be finished on Thursday November fifth ... and it *will* be finished on that date'

With a slight bow to the Supreme Leader and the two members of the Council of Guardians, Mohsen Raza turned and left the room. The bullet smashed home. Mr

Nosrat Tamouri, currently acting head of the Iranian National Oil Company was a marked man.

~~~~~~

Two days later, it was only just light at seven thirty on a cool, cloudy Monday morning. The white Range Rover, carrying the carefully applied insignia of the NIOC, pulled up beneath the covered pergola type structure providing shade to the entrance of the spacious, walled villa located in an up market area in the south district of Tehran.

Nosrat Tamouri left the villa by the front door. The armed and suited driver waited patiently for his charge to get in to the rear of the vehicle. All senior government officials in Iran had a driver bodyguard. They all carried nine millimetre hand guns and in the boot of the transportation vehicle would normally rest a well oiled AK47 and several clips of ammunition. It was rumoured that all of the driver bodyguards in Iran were somehow appointed or controlled by Mohsen Raza. It was probably true. In Tamouri's case it was definitely true.

Tamouri was not in the best of moods and hardly acknowledged the greetings of his regular driver as he slammed the rear door shut. He had not left the house all weekend after returning from the disastrous

Chapter Nineteen – An Uncomfortable Matter

confrontation with Mohsen Raza on Friday afternoon. He was visibly angry when he arrived home that night and headed straight for a carefully concealed wall cabinet where a stock of hard liquor was kept. He managed to gulp down a large whiskey before the inevitable questioning from his wife and resident mother-in-law.

The driver glanced back in to the rear view mirror. His passenger did not look well today. The eyes were sunken, the skin tone a pale grey pallor, the hair slightly dishevelled. He looked as if he had not slept properly for a few days and such observations were not deceiving. The route to the NIOC Vice President's office within the Isfahan Refinery was changed every day and this morning's route would be via the Tondguyan Highway and then further south on the Beneshte Zahr Highway.

All roads making up the thirty to forty minute journey were normally busy, as were just about all main roads in Tehran at that time of day. As the journey progressed, Tamouri found himself deep in thought. He was a worried man and one who had knowingly crossed the most fearful figure in the country. No one ever questioned Raza's actions, motives or abilities in front of the Supreme Leader and got away with it and frighteningly, he knew he would be no exception. Would they be waiting for him his at his office? Would he receive the summoning phone call? Would he simply be bundled unceremoniously in to a car as he stepped out of his house one day? It was the not knowing that caused the most distress.

The traffic was worse than usual as the heavy four wheel drive vehicle crawled through the narrow choking road system of the south district to access the Tondguyan Highway. The roundabout providing a route to the highway was just up ahead. As the Range Rover pulled cautiously on to the roundabout, for some reason the engine faded and the vehicle came to a stop with a slight judder. It was enough of a change of momentum to make Tamouri look up questioningly at the driver now turning to face him. It was to be the last face he would ever see. The first dilapidated, fully loaded, three ton Nissan pick-up truck, hit the left rear passenger door at over thirty miles an hour, initially pushing the reinforced aluminium door in toward the seated passenger some thirty to fifty centimetres. This action had the effect of distorting the protective box frame to pull the roof down on to the head of the occupant.

When the second vehicle, an old cream Mercedes 190, hit the other rear passenger door at a slightly greater speed, the frame buckled completely, the door ripped itself from the restraining hinges and now, having gained some kinetic energy of its own, smashed in to the breathless body of Nosrat Tamouri.

Chapter Nineteen – An Uncomfortable Matter

It was over in seconds. The front section of the Range Rover was more or less intact and although he had to kick the door open after unbuckling his full safety harness, the grey suited driver exited unharmed and apparently unflustered. He carefully inspected the body of his passenger for a pulse. He was unmistakably dead, literally cut in two by the imploding aluminium bodywork.

The chauffer's expression remained implacable as he held a short conversation with the two drivers of the offending vehicles. When the conversation ended, the two men walked casually away in different directions. The sound of two tone sirens could be heard in the distance.

~~~~~~

That Monday, October nineteenth, 1987, would become engraved on Mohsen Raza's memory for many years to come. It was three thirty in the afternoon as he sat slumped in his office chair. The second most powerful man in Iran worked mostly out of a barely furnished, nondescript room in an even more nondescript office that was in fact an apartment in a residential block in the northern district of Tehran. The single desk top was home to two telephones, a Farsi typewriter and a small battery driven calculator. A twenty two inch TV sat on an ended timber ammunition box in one corner. It was on, with the sound turned down. Having been called to his office earlier that day, the black telephone on the left of the smooth topped desk had not stopped ringing. He now had it off the hook.

The first piece of intelligence received related to the unfortunate accident that had occurred earlier that day, in which Mr Nosrat Tamouri had been involved. By the time the emergency services had arrived, he was pronounced dead. His driver had explained what had happened to the local police force and that the two drivers of the vehicles involved in the collision with Tamouri's Range Rover, had simply run away. He provided them with what he thought was an accurate description and the police were investigating. Raza had already informed all of the media not to run a story on the demise of Mr Tamouri and this blackout would stay in place until he personally released it. No one questioned it. Mohsen Raza would make arrangements for the man's family.

The Tamouri situation however, was not the one that had called him out to his office and left him in a very pensive mood. The light had begun to fade in what was already a poorly lit room. He sat there in the approaching darkness disturbed only by the flashing, near hypnotic light emanating from the practically new colour TV. At one thirty that day, he had received information from one of his command and control

Chapter Nineteen – An Uncomfortable Matter

centres located on two shut down production platforms in the western Gulf at Rashadat Oilfield. It was disturbing at the time.

The Americans had announced to the occupants of the platform they had literally twenty minutes to leave the structures and that after such time, the US Government could not guarantee their safety. A reluctant Raza gave the order to evacuate and at two o'clock precisely the Americans attacked. Four warships pounded the two structures until they were well ablaze. These fires would eventually die out but the humiliation would live on for a very long time.

This was a whole new set of circumstances in the conflict with Iraq. Did this mean the Americans were now officially backing Iraq and were prepared to actually do battle on their behalf? It was a very worrying situation. However, what was flashing up on his TV screen was now even more worrying. The world financial markets had gone in to a nose dive with the American Dow Jones index losing over twenty three percent of its value during the past few hours. The rest of the worlds exchanges were following suit with commodities moving in all directions.

Raza was glued to the flash messages scrolling across the screen. The red telephone to the right of his desk had rung once about an hour ago and he had confirmed to the Supreme Leader he would be with him after evening payers that day. What he was expected to say he did not know but having taken a year for crude oil to rise from a trading value of around fourteen dollars a barrel to the current nineteen dollars a barrel, movement of a dollar or two either way could spell great fortune or total disaster for the stricken Iranian economy.

The Geneveh Project was now even more important than ever to his plans and perhaps the very survival of his country. With news circulating about the American military action, described on TV as Operation Nimble Archer, the Russians had made it clear they regarded the events in the Rashadat oilfield to be an act of aggression and would be holding council on the matter. The Far East financial markets were tumbling at the prospect of World War Three breaking out in the Middle East and no one knew what was supposed to happen next. The experienced and resolute Mohsen Raza had learnt many things in his relatively short life. One thing he knew for sure was that 'the art of politics is not to *react* to events but to *shape them*' … and *'shape them'*… this very day … he would.

~~~~~~~~
~~~~

Chapter Twenty
A Mysterious Enemy

The middle of October had come soon enough. Declan had been moving on a regular basis over the past few weeks from a state of total frustration to sheer panic and was physically feeling the strain. Keeping the Geneveh Project on track had been a massive undertaking. Four men had died on the job, one work boat had been lost and the PLEM had left Singapore two days late. The Iranians were doing a generally good job in protecting the area except for a really bad day about two weeks in to site work. The final conclusion of what actually happened on that particular day was that an Iraqi Mig 23 had been taken on by the Iranian Phantoms and destroyed immediately after releasing a couple of Russian made, air-to-ground missiles.

The incident had brought a sense of foreboding over the men on site and Harry Wright was earning every penny of his substantial salary keeping all the wheels on the cart and works up to schedule. However, after that particular event, although there had been one or two attempts to break through to the land site and work camp, these attacks had all been repelled remarkably well. The site crews had seen several ground-to-air missiles released over the passing couple of months and

Chapter Twenty – A Mysterious Enemy

lots of aircraft activity, but nothing too disturbing. In fact, except for the very poor and generally unexpected performance of Intek Marine, the whole job was going remarkably well. The contract handover date was Thursday November fifth and this now looked very realistic.

Declan now had confirmation that the massive twenty two thousand horsepower, ocean going tug, Maybech Rotterdam was off the horseshoe inlet and port of Chabahar in Baluchistan. It would shortly be entering the Gulf of Oman accompanied by her sister vessel, the Maybech London. In tow was the all important PLEM manifold structure and SBM. This meant that the vessels should be on station in around eight days time, only a day behind schedule.

It was past six in the evening and already dark outside. Most of the late staff were now packing up to go home and the night crew just arriving to cover the twelve hour evening communications shift. The telephone rang. It was Penny.

'Before you say anything … I'm on my way right now'

There was a strained silence at the other end

'I really mean it … I am just locking my office door and should be with you in about fifteen minutes … oh … and by the way, I have confirmed with everyone for the boat trip next Friday … we are definitely going to have the *whole* day out! Are you pleased?'

The reply was short and to the point. 'Dinner will be on

the table in twenty minutes ... and twenty minutes later, it will either be in you ... or be in the dog'

The line was disconnected abruptly. Penny didn't have a dog. Declan was smiling to the point of near laughter as he locked the office door and strode out of the building with a determined step, nodding goodnights to everyone. Penny was obviously in a good mood.

~~~~~~

It had been a quiet day so far in the Boundary Street offices of Robert Wang. The sign over the shop simply stated 'Wang Import Export' in English and Cantonese. However, hiding behind the plain, triple fronted façade of 'the shop' was a Tardis like structure consisting of several floors of modern offices, a large packing and processing operation and a distribution warehouse. This busy Hong Kong business based on the boundaries of Kowloon, as the name of the location implied, was in fact the centre of a massive shipping and distribution operation feeding kilo upon kilo of dried food goods to every single Chinese restaurant in the UK.

This was only a small part of Robert Wang's empire, but it was also his very first company, his very first business premises and directly behind the entrance door to the triple fronted shop had been his very first office. Therefore, some thirty five years later, if you wanted to

Chapter Twenty – A Mysterious Enemy

do business with Robert Wang, this is where you would have to come. He owned skyscraper office blocks, a small private airline, various manufacturing facilities within China, a substantially busy commercial shipping line and a few world class golf courses scattered throughout the western world and the Far East.

He was a successful horse breeder and because of that singular consuming passion, rubbed shoulders with Royalty wherever they happened to alight on the most famous race courses in the world. The face of Robert Wang, to an interested audience, was one of benevolence, philanthropy, a ready smile and general politeness. To the Royals, he was *'that very nice little Chinaman'* who knew his place. To just about everyone else, he was someone to be admired, respected and to those who knew him well - much feared. Crossing swords with the self made multi-millionaire often left visible scars at best and terminal, wounds at worst.

He sat at the head table with the mafia securely ensconced in China and was provided, by them, with his 'gift' business of controlling all dried foodstuffs of Chinese origin in to the UK as a very young and promising trader. They had educated him, trained him, nurtured him and protected him for the past forty plus years and their investment in time and money had paid off handsomely.

Robert Wang had had a bad few days. He sat in his reasonably sized office at the back of the building on

Boundary Street, mulling over the horrific events surrounding the death of Tony Swales. Since the man had been killed by a letter bomb on that unbelievable Monday several days ago, his substantial contacts had been working overtime in an attempt to find out what had happened, why it had happened and who had caused it to happen. He had gotten nowhere - and he was very annoyed. Tony Swales was the husband of An Ni and An Ni was the first cousin of his wife, Chao-xing. This was family and a cold blooded murder in his family could not go unpunished. Chao-xing had been the one to fly to Beijing, break the news and bring An Ni and Jonothan back to Hong Kong.

She was completely distraught, her heart plucked clean from her body, leaving it an emotionless husk. She had only left the house for the funeral, the rest of her time spent in her bed, a total disinterest in everything around her except Jonothan, her son. Robert and Chao-xing had the best doctors in HK and the very best in China, placed at her bedside in attempt to keep her from simply fading away. It wasn't working. Chao-xing was constantly in tears and Robert Wang, with all his money, all his power, all his influence, could seemingly do nothing. Getting the evil bastard who planted the bomb would not bring Swales back or provide the magic recipe for An Ni's recovery, but it would do a lot for Robert Wang. Robert felt that something had happened to An Ni a week before the

Chapter Twenty – A Mysterious Enemy

murder of her husband. He had raised the question, very gently, many times and on one occasion quite forcibly since Tony's death, but she remained tight lipped. There was a thread of some description through it all that had the name of Declan Doyle attached to it. He had asked Inspector Herbert Lau of the Royal Hong Kong Police, to have Doyle interviewed in Abu Nar by a local policeman. He had reported back that Doyle had shown a level of genuine surprise when he was advised of Swales death and especially the manner in which he had died. Was he a damn good actor - or was he genuinely surprised?

There was a light knock at his office door and Robert Wang shouted as a sign to enter. Longwei stood before his boss, well groomed, beautifully suited, hands crossed in front of him, awaiting recognition. Wang put down the light grey manila file on Declan Doyle he had been studying. The conversation began in English.

'Take a seat Longwei' he stated simply 'I need you to do something for me. I want you to take the company plane and go to a place called Abu Nar'

Longwei sat upright in his high backed chair, facing forward, mentally 'to attention' as his boss spoke further. 'There is a man there that we have an interest in called Declan Doyle'

'Is he Irish?' Longwei questioned.

'No. He is as English as you or I'. At that, the two men smiled as they savoured the irony of the thought.

Both had been educated in UK, both at Charterhouse and then on to Cambridge. They knew the British sense of humour very well. Were they not being 'ruled' by them right now? Longwei had been by Robert's side since they were boys. He was Robert's first lieutenant, totally loyal and where necessary, totally ruthless.

'Is this something to do with Tony? He questioned further.

'It is. In fact, I have to tell you I have *no* evidence that leads me to believe that Doyle was involved at any level. However, there are lots of coincidences. Tony cancelled a marine total loss policy on one of Doyle's companies very recently and for days his office staff were bombarded with threatening phone calls and telexes from Doyle's offices demanding that Swales rescind his decision. I've talked to the company underwriters and they tell me the decision was made by Tony because he felt he was too exposed – and I suppose at one third of many millions of dollars - he was absolutely right'.

Longwei picked up the file from the desk and opened it. Robert Wang continued.

'The day before the cover was withdrawn, something happened at the Swales house and as a result, Tony hired body guards for him and the family. An Ni will not discuss it. What is completely curious is that Tony met with Doyle the day before he died. It was at the Jockey Club. I actually met him myself, although Tony chose to introduce him to me by another name for

Chapter Twenty – A Mysterious Enemy

some reason or other. I know the meeting was not planned, or that's what Tony told me. I know it was Doyle he was meeting and I also know that Doyle is not a member of the club, so somehow this was not a casual meeting as Tony said it was – but contrived by Doyle. When Tony arrived back at his office from seeing An Ni and Jonothan off at the airport on the Monday, Doyle was already on a plane back to Abu Nar.' He paused, waiting for some reaction from Longwei who was studying the contents of the file. He looked up.

'So, what am I looking for in Abu Nar?'

'We have some good contacts there at the Summer Palace Restaurant. Chonglin, the manager, will assist you with anything you need. I have already spoken to him. I want some top level surveillance on Declan Doyle day and night. I want to know who he talks to, when he talks to them and about what. If there is even a hint that he was in any way involved in Tony Swales sickening, gruesome murder, then I want to know straight away. If necessary we will deal with him on the spot, but …' he paused to emphasize his words '… we must be absolutely sure!'

~~~~~~

As the silver grey Mercedes pulled in to the car park at the Um Suqeem sailing club on a beautiful crisp clear

Friday morning, the sky was clear blue, the sea outside the little rock walled harbour flat calm and Declan was really looking forward to a day out on his pride and joy, the forty two foot, ketch rig motor-sailer, 'Esmerelda II'. She was swinging gently on her mooring. The gleaming, glass finish lustre of the jet black hull and unusual stern cabin design had given way to the nickname 'The Black Pig' by all the members of the club. However, she was no 'pig' in the water. With full main, mizzen and both jibs tight, her razor profiled bow would happily carve a way through the warm waters of the Arabian Gulf at between seven and eight knots.

Two of Declan's mechanics were making their way back from the boat to the slipway in the inflatable tender and waved as Declan and Penny came in to view. Today was to be a full day of uninterrupted relaxation. No doubt more than a few alcoholic drinks would be consumed and with the return of the tender, the last of the food and drink was on board along with Saskan, Declan's house steward and Rajan the cook. Declan had invited a few friends for the day but as he checked his watch, now reading just past seven o'clock, he knew they would be late.

Within minutes, the hard bottomed inflatable tender had deposited both Penny and Declan on to the deck of Esmerelda II to make preparations to leave the harbour. There was no real plan for the day except to cruise about ten miles offshore and get back in to the

Chapter Twenty – A Mysterious Enemy

harbour for about six in the evening. The tender and one of the mechanics waited at the slipway for the first of the guests to turn up.

Penny shouted up from below.

'What time are we leaving Declan?'

'As soon as everyone is on board, we will be off. Tom will want to get some fishing in before the surface water get's too warm … and no doubt the decks will be awash with Hamour by lunchtime'

Declan knew well that no one really ever had to 'fish' for Hamour. Tom had convinced himself he was a good if not great 'fisherman' and as he was likely to haul a few catches on board that day, fish was definitely on the menu at some stage during the trip.

'Is Harriet coming?' Harriet was Tom's wife and 'Tom' was Tom Wilkinson, CEO of Coastal Marine. Coastal had been in Abu Nar since the late sixties, initially dredging the creek area, then building harbours and now building islands in the sea. Tom was well liked by all who knew him and he and Harriet were Declan and Penny's best friends on a completely social basis.

'Yes' Declan replied '… and Peter Broussan and Jill … and Derek Lawless and Angela'

Peter Broussan was the Middle East General Manager of the accounting giant Price Waterson and Derek Lawless was the General Manager of the Abu Nar Intercontinental Hotel. Everyone got on well with one another. It was Friday. The weather was looking good with all on board planning to have a great time; and that was how it started.

A shout from the slipway announced the arrival of Tom and Harriet and as he looked up toward the quay side, Declan noticed that Peter and Jill were bringing up the rear. Derek and Angela's car was just pulling in to the car park. He waved as they all jumped aboard the tender before disappearing below to the engine room to get ready to go to sea. The space where the substantial one hundred and twenty horsepower marine engine was fitted could be described as cramped and at a push a small man could crawl all the way round the installation if needed. The on-board electrical generator was located in another compartment under the centre cockpit and hummed away quietly, supplying main electrical power to the boat whilst in harbour. Declan was checking the oil, water and hydraulic levels and he could hear the clamber and excited chatter as his guests came on board.

He could also hear the distinct clink of glasses as Saskan poured generous drinks for his guests. The engine room was spotless, as was the rest of the boat. The two Indian mechanics who maintained it were meticulous in their work. All copper and brass-work always left highly polished, all cables clipped as per original builder's specification and the engine bilge dry and gleaming clean. If it hadn't been for the extremely

Chapter Twenty – A Mysterious Enemy

high standard to which the boat and all of its fixtures and fittings were maintained, Declan may not have noticed it. In fact, someone had gone to a great deal of trouble to conceal it, but it was definitely there.

The very, very thin, nearly invisible grey cable was glued in some way to the rear of a section of galvanised conduit taking the engine instrument repeater cables up from the control panel to the cockpit. Unless someone was on an actual inspection, or didn't know the boat as well as Declan did, it would have been missed.

Firstly, this piece of carefully concealed flex was not part of the original wiring specifications of the boat, so what was it?

Secondly, who put it there and why?

He grabbed the waterproof torch from its storage clips screwed to the bulkhead, switched it on and traced the line of the mysterious wire. It followed the route of the conduit downward and disappeared in the bilge. Upward, it followed the conduit and vanished behind the bulkhead. Declan pondered for a second or two. This could be a link to a trigger of some description or a feed to a surveillance device such as a camera, microphone or radio transmitter.

'Better not start the engine' he thought as he turned off all isolator switches. The generator was running and had been for nearly an hour so hopefully, whatever it was, it was *not* linked directly to the generator. Declan made a last check as he climbed up the small access ladder out of the engine room and in to the rear lounge. Penny and his guests were all sitting out on the rear deck just above his head.

He moved out of the lounge cabin and in to the centre cockpit to amused shouts of 'Why are we waiting?' from Tom and giggles from Harriet. Declan just waved a loose hand.

'Not long now, just got a couple more checks to do' he shouted as he dropped down in to the front cabin. He turned to a polished hardwood head panel just above the door hiding all the electrics and cabling for the external cockpit instrument pack. It was held in place with industrial Velcro fixings and after getting his fingers just underneath a lifting recess, he pulled the panel off. There it was. The fine grey cable that had left it's fixing on the conduit had now disappeared back in to the front cabin under the headlining. Declan carefully felt under the padded material, located the thin cable, followed it and nearly in the centre of the cabin roof, the cable terminated in a small thimble size lump. Just by looking at the headlining, no one would have known of its presence. It must have been installed by a professional. The miniscule object had been let back into the padding of the material and yet there was no sign that the headlining itself had been disturbed. Declan knew what it was immediately ... a radio microphone. By feeling carefully around the thimble size lump, Declan was able to detect another cable

Chapter Twenty – A Mysterious Enemy

leaving the object … about five centimetres long. This would be the aerial and no doubt it would have perhaps more than one partner on board.

The shouting continued up on deck. Declan's brain fell into compute mode for several seconds and then the decision was made. He poked his head back in to the open cockpit and shouted

'Sorry about this, but got to go ashore for a minute or two and pay a visit to the club chandlery. I need a new cable crimp before we set off. Nothing important really … just me being ….'

'Just you being mister perfectionist … as usual' came the response from Jill as Declan dropped in to the tender, kicked the little fifteen horsepower Evinrude in to life and sped the short distance to the slipway. Once out of the tender, he walked quickly in to the clubhouse, swinging left to the secretary's office and asking to use the phone. Declan was the biggest single sponsor of events at the club and had nearly assumed the status of 'local hero' amongst the sailing fraternity. Nothing Declan wanted, within reason, would be refused here. Bill Deverage, the club secretary waved toward the telephone and politely left the room.

Declan stabbed Andy Peters home number in to the button dial instrument and waited. The phone cut off twice after ten or so rings but Declan persisted. Eventually the connection was made. It was silent for a few seconds until a weary, sleepy sounding voice said in a low and slightly annoyed tone 'Hello' 'Andy, I want you to do something for me and I need it done right away!'

'Declan ... is that you? ... it's Friday morning for fucks sake ... I was trying to have a bit of a lay in ...' Declan cut him off

'No time for all that Andy, get hold of our electronics man and tell him to get his little bug sweeper box of tricks out and scan all the offices ... top to bottom ... especially your office and mine. When he's finished that, I want my villa and your villa done as well. When he's finished that, I want your cars done and then he can do my two at home and the Mercedes when I get in to the office tomorrow. If he finds anything, anything at all, tell him not to remove it, electronically block it or play about with it in any way. Just take a note of the location and then make sure you see me first thing tomorrow morning'

'Do you think we have a *problem* Declan?'

'The answer to that is I don't really know. I don't think it's a *real* problem, but someone is definitely looking for something as the boat is bugged and probably my car too - and it's a 'pro job' Andy. Keep this to yourself and tell that electronics man the same'

'Will do Declan. I'll get on it straight away'

With that, Declan put the phone down, left the office, paid a quick visit to the Chandlery and made his way back to Esmerelda II. His guests were becoming

Chapter Twenty – A Mysterious Enemy

impatient. Declan pressed the starter button on the six cylinder Perkins power house and the magnificent marine diesel kicked in to life. He waited, as he always did, until the engine temperature indicated normal before signalling Tom to untie the bow mooring. A course was set for Sir Bu Nu'ar island off Dubai and the auto pilot locked on. There would be no sail up today as this limited safe deck space. Today was a *fun* day not a *serious sailing* day. The steady, rhythmic beat of the diesel engine faded in to the background as breakfast appeared. The smell of bacon and eggs was particularly inviting and even too much to resist for the constantly dieting Harriet. During the course of the day, Declan established the presence of another listening device in the main rear cabin.

With the ice machine generating ice for some hours, by ten o'clock, the fish store was packed with it, ready to receive its first live cargo from the fishermen on board. Declan spent the day just lazing around the boat and swimming for an hour or so whilst moored for lunch just off the gleaming white sands and deserted beaches of their destination island. Penny was spectacular and in her element entertaining their friends. She also *looked* pretty spectacular in a very revealing two piece pastel blue bikini, which had turned in to a one piece as soon as Esmerelda left the Abu Nar shoreline over the horizon. Declan tried hard not to be distracted by the discoveries of earlier that day. This was Penny's time. She deserved a good day out. She was having a great time. She was happy … and it showed. Peter had nudged up to Declan at one point and quietly let him know that 'Penny looks fantastic … you lucky old bugger!'

The day had gone well. Esmerelda II was back on her mooring and Declan and his guests had noisily invaded the sailing club bar to tackle a few last drinks. Calls had been made for drivers and cars to come back down to the club ready to take everyone home and Saskan waited in the Mercedes to drive a slightly inebriated Declan and Penny. As coffees appeared and the final brandy poured, Declan was able to sneak off to the secretary's office and phone Andy.

'What's the result Andy?' was the straightforward question.

'Not good news Declan' There was a short pause.

'Your office, my office, the Telex room, your villa, my villa, both my cars, your Range Rover and DeLorean … er … and one can only assume the Mercedes … all bugged. We know where they are and we know what type they are. Some very sophisticated stuff our man says. Top of the range FM transmitters, built in, using a lithium power source. Our man reckons they definitely have a range of a mile and maybe even more, which means that whoever is behind all this must have a set of listening stations located within range to pick up the

Chapter Twenty – A Mysterious Enemy

signals. This is a bit bloody scary'. Declan thought hard for a second. Declan didn't have a phobia about security, in fact, he was often the culprit when sensitive information was found laying about the office. However, on a particular trip to the UK, he was having lunch, as he did regularly, at the Pall Mall restaurant of the Institute of Directors. He had become involved in a conversation with a government senior civil servant who told him some interesting tales about the current and growing levels of International Industrial Espionage. This prompted Declan to go out and buy the necessary equipment to scan his own offices and now he was damn glad he did.

'OK Andy. Keep a lid on it all and from now on watch what is being said. Leave the bugs where they are. Don't discuss any business at home or in your car and don't use your car phone to discuss anything to do with the Geneveh Project'.

'You think it's *just* the Geneveh job they're after?'

'I don't know Andy, but it's a fair bet. As long as we know the bugs are there, we are in control of what they think they know. If we remove them, they will come up with something else and this time we may not find out what it is … or even worse … find it too late'.

'OK Boss … see you tomorrow'

With that, Declan put down the phone. He had been pondering the subject of the covert surveillance operation against him all day. There was no clear path to the identity of the instigator although there appeared to be a few candidates. Whoever it was, they had access to top quality kit and top quality installers.

This was no cheap operation. The candidates so far were number one, that asshole Paddy Doherty and his cloak and dagger friends in the British SIS.

But why?

That particular contender already knew just about everything there was to know about the Geneveh Project and was in fact the broker in the whole deal.

Number two, that even bigger asshole Mohsen Raza, but once again why? Mohsen could be checking up on the whole deal, but really, his complete but simple interests spoke for themselves. Either the job was finished or not. If it was, then Mohsen was a hero and if not, Declan was a dead man.

The third entrant in the 'asshole of the year' competition could well be the Hall & Burton crowd. They had possibly two niggles to satisfy. One was the fact they did not get any work on Geneveh, as they thought they possibly had a right to. The other was the well known close involvement of that business with the CIA and their operatives buried within Hall Burton's extensive world operations, at all levels. Declan, like many others, knew of the activities of Chuck Peterson. He had an open invitation to Chuck's regular and extravagant Saturday night Bar-B-Q's. It was rare for him to appear at such events, but he had decided that

Chapter Twenty – A Mysterious Enemy

tomorrow night would possibly be an exception.

It was time to rejoin the party. Everyone was ready to go. A fair bit of drink had been consumed throughout the day and all the girls were showing the significant signs. Tom was well on his way but Peter and Derek seemed quite sensible. So, with much hugging, kissing of cheeks and over long handshakes, the party finally broke up and Declan and Penny fell into the back of the Mercedes quite exhausted.

'My place or yours' Declan asked as Penny snuggled in to his side.

'Yours' she replied sleepily.

~~~~~~~~
~~~

Chapter Twenty One
Silent Surveillance

Commander Alan Victor Dillaneo, US Navy and Captain of the Los Angeles Class hunter killer submarine, the USS Augustine, ordered his crew to diving stations. The 362 foot long, 7000 ton state of the art attack-sub, with vents open and little or no fuss, slid silently beneath the warm waters off Masirah Island in the Indian Ocean. The log was entered as Saturday October 24th, 0600 hours, on patrol, heading 030, depth 220 feet. Dillaneo wore a broad and engaging smile. It was good to be back at sea again. The Augustine had spent several days restocking supplies at the American military facilities located to the north of the island. Masirah was not a 'rest and recreation' base but it was one of the most strategically positioned military facilities the Americans had in the Middle East. It sat just south of the entrance to the Hormuz Straits providing the only access to the closed off sea known to Commander Alan Dillaneo as the Persian Gulf.

At its narrowest point, the straits were only fifty four kilometres wide and bounded on one side by the unpredictable Islamic Republic of Iran. On the other side lay the Arab state of Oman, the ruler of which had been put in place by the British in nineteen seventy and

Chapter Twenty One – Silent Surveillance

was still being propped up by the British both militarily and politically.

The British SAS were roaming the mainly desert south of the country in small motorised groups, practised at blending in to the landscape and even more practised at raiding and destroying Yemeni rebel tribesmen infiltrators and their resources in the border country.

It was time for a conversation. Commander Dillaneo called his Executive Officer Dwain Shulman into his cramped cabin and ordered the door to be closed. A fresh pot of steaming coffee and two cups were waiting.

'Sit down Dwain and grab yourself some coffee'

'Thank you Sir'

Dwain sat across from the Captain at a fold down table.

'What are we doing right now Dwain?' Dillaneo asked casually.

'We are embarking on patrol for approximately three weeks fully submerged in the Persian Gulf sir' stated Dwain confidently.

'… and what is the purpose of our patrol Dwain?'

'To report on the activities of the Iranians and Iraqis, who are at war in every sense of the word and protect American shipping moving in and out of the Gulf'

'Correct Lieutenant Commander Shulman … and that is what will go into the log'

'I don't quite understand sir' the executive officer

queried. 'You have just stated what will be entered in to the ship's log but in fact we have a particular mission to undertake ... and I am about to reveal to you orders for this mission ... as they were given directly to me ...' Commander Dillaneo paused, studying Shulman's face for any sign of enlightenment as he finished the sentence '... verbally by Admiral Warkin, Head of the US Navy'

There was a short, non expressive silence as the XO took it all in.

'You mean we have no *written* orders sir'

'You are correct Mr Schulman!' the Captain announced.

The XO's face remained implacable. He was trained to take orders. He was used to taking orders. Written or not, whatever the Captain was talking about, these were just another set of orders.

'Whatever you say sir, anything you need from me or this crew you will have sir, let me assure you of that'

'That is the kind of assurance I need Mr Schulman, but you had better hear the details of the mission we are to be engaged upon and the likely consequences of success ... or failure ... first!'

The Lieutenant Commander sat drinking his coffee without further engagement.

'It will not be news to you that in this so called 'Gulf War' there are two sides involved and in effect the United States Government policy in this matter is to be

Chapter Twenty One – Silent Surveillance

politically neutral' Shulman nodded his head. The captain of the Augustine continued.

'However, you and I both know that we favour the Iraqi position and without being seen to becoming involved in any military assistance, we are helping the Iraqis with intelligence, training and *some* arms supplies. This mission takes us outside of this public policy and as a result will never be acknowledged as to have happened … *whatever* the result …'

Shulman interrupted.

'Can I ask a question sir'

'Sure you can'

'Will the crew be in any *extraordinary* danger on this mission?'

The question was a fair one. The word 'extraordinary' had been expressed in emphasis.

'Unless something untoward happens, the crew are in no more danger than being on patrol in a closed off sea with a fairly major war between two fanatical nations going on above them'

'Thank you sir'

Shulman was satisfied with that. He and Dillaneo had been together a long time - and he trusted him.

'Right, let's get to it!'

The Captain of the Augustine pulled a couple of charts from a locker above the table as the XO moved round to a position where he could see the charts clearly. Dillaneo pointed a finger to a position on the first chart. 'There are two large tugs towing an oilfield manifold structure currently positioned about here, in the Arabian sea, some two hundred and seventy nautical miles to the North East and travelling toward the Gulf of Oman. They will then enter the Straits of Hormuz with a final destination being a position in the straits between Kharg Island and the coastal town of Geneveh - about here' Commander Dillaneo pulled the lower chart to the top and stabbed it with a finger in the area of Geneveh.

'This is part of a major oilfield installation, now commonly known as the Geneveh Project'.

Shulman was attentive - taking it all in.

'The mechanics of our mission are simple and straightforward. We are to shadow the movement of these vessels that, at their current speed, will be on station at their destination on or before Saturday, October thirty first. The object of the exercise, by the contractors on the project, is to sink the manifold on the sea bed, connect a submarine pipeline they have been building from a shore station to the manifold and then connect a floating oil loading buoy to the manifold. The result will be an instant near doubling of Iran's current declining oil export capability, with little or no chance of the Iraqis destroying the facility using conventional means' Dillaneo waited for a reaction.

'I am with you so far sir' Shulman confirmed.

'There is a very delicate operation that has to be

Chapter Twenty One – Silent Surveillance

performed in getting the manifold from the decks of the barges, to which it is secured and on to the sea floor in exactly the right position. The manifold, or PLEM as they call it, will need to be in limbo, on the surface, for at least three hours'.

'What kind of protection are the Iranians providing sir?'

'Ground to air, they have our Hawk missiles … and you know they are pretty damn good'

The XO winced visibly. He was well aware of the circumstances under which Iran had obtained substantial numbers of Hawk's.

'… and in the water?'

'Just a few Banoosh type thirty and forty foot fibreglass boats with heavy calibre weapons. I am confident we have nothing to fear from Iranian marine protection'.

'That sounds about right to me sir. So are we to take out the manifold?'

'We most certainly are Dwain'

'Right sir. I think we can handle that' came the confident reply.

'Ok. This is what I have in mind'

The two naval officers began the process of deciding plots, calculating time lines, carrying out risk assessments and discussing the viability of all available weaponry options.

Over an hour and a half had passed when finally the

operational plan was in place. As far as they were concerned, any military undertaking that stung the Iranians was a good operation and just about everybody in the American military would admit to the same. As far as Dwain Shulman was generally concerned, this was payback time for the US hostage debacle and Dwain knew the right people to give the Iranians a damn good smack, were the United States Navy. He couldn't wait.

'This is a very unusual situation Dwain and you are well aware that if any of this gets out, with no written orders or a ships log to protect us, our careers will be sawdust in a matter of days'.

'I am aware of that sir, but to tell the truth, any chance to stick one up those bastards is a trip that I would volunteer for any day of the week and I think I speak for just about every man jack on board this boat'.

A faint smile coloured his words as he spoke softly but firmly in reply to his Captain. After a short but thoughtful pause, he spoke again.

'So what do we tell the men - and probably more importantly, how do we tell them?'

'Call the officers together and brief them as I have briefed you. You must ask them all to confirm that they will follow the orders they are given and that no record of this mission is to be kept in writing, in notes, in the boats log and in any audio or video diary recordings that I know some of the men keep. Get that confirmation from the officers and then come back to

Chapter Twenty One – Silent Surveillance

me. We will then brief the rest of the crew in two watches - together'.

'Aye, Aye sir' The XO finished his coffee in one.

'Do you have any questions Dwain? ... because if you do, now is the time for them'.

'No Sir. I think I speak for every goddamn man on this boat when I say any chance to get back at those bastards will be OK by all of us. We won't let you or America down sir. Whatever needs to be done, be confident, we will do it!'

'That sure is pleasing to hear XO. Get to it right away and then report back to me here'

'Yes Sir!' and with a sharp salute, he was gone. Commander Dillaneo sat in deep thought for a minute or two.

'I hope to heaven we are doing the right thing' he muttered to himself as he put away the charts and poured his eighth cup of coffee of the day.

By eight thirty, the crew had been briefed by the Captain and his XO. To a man, there were no questions about the mission or signs of concern about the false log entry; in fact just the opposite. As Shulman had predicted, every member of the crew wanted a full share of involvement in any operation that would provide a level of revenge for the disastrous result of Operation Eagles Claw.

All personal voice and video recorders had been

freely handed in until the mission was over and with a new buzz of purpose going around the boat, the XO set course to intercept the Maybech Rotterdam and her sister vessel, Maybech London. The mission was on.

~~~~~~

Declan Doyle finished his last whiskey and soda of the day as he placed the heavy, hand cut Swarovski crystal whiskey glass carefully back on the uncluttered coffee table in front of him. The lights in the lounge were low. It was late and he had just put down the telephone. The news was that the tugs and their precious 'tow' were now about to enter the Gulf of Oman.

Not long now.

The whole process of getting oil actually flowing through the line may be delayed a few days, but remarkably, everything had gone to plan so far. Once the tugs approached the Straits of Hormuz, the Iranians would be providing full time protection. Then, when on station, the anchor handling vessels would take the PLEM in hand and the big tugs could be placed 'off charter'. At $300,000.00 a day, Declan wanted this to happen as soon as possible.

He also desperately wanted to be 'on site' when the manifold was positioned and lowered some one hundred or so feet to the sea bed, but the logistics of the project would deny him that particular pleasure.

Chapter Twenty One – Silent Surveillance

Due to so many final payments to so many contractors and sub-contractors being triggered by the event, Declan's presence was required in Abu Nar to sign off and authorise the movement of substantial sums of money.

He had thought the whole thing through and finally decided to send Andy to be his representative. He knew next to nothing about the technicalities of oilfield engineering, but he sure knew bullshit when he heard it and that was the essential element to be avoided on that particular and most important day.

From a technical point of view, Declan knew that with Reg Green on site, the management of the marine works was in safe hands. Andy would provide Reg and the overall Project Manager, Harry Wright, with a simple and local point of authority to refer to if required. Amongst sensible, experienced men, that was all that was needed. Declan fell in to bed. Did he have the right to feel pleased with himself? He thought he did - but if he only knew!

~~~~~~~~
~~~~

Chapter Twenty Two
The Troublesome Turncoat

The last day of October was a Friday. Hamad Sadique was not at the mosque attending to his prayers; he was in fact staring up at the clock on his office wall which told him it was seven fifteen am. The General's Basra office was empty of staff. Friday was a religious day and no work was undertaken in Iraq on a religious day. His desk was strewn with high quality aerial images of the area around Geneveh and Kharg Island and the work being carried out on the so called Geneveh Project. There were also several reports written in English on plain paper provided to him by a particular source within the Basra office of the American oilfield engineering company, Hall-Burton.

These were wide ranging intelligence reports provided to the General by the good grace of his American 'friends' and one of the hand written reports had given cause for concern. This concern was unfortunately not directed toward the safety and security of his country but for the unacceptable size of the dollar balance in his Swiss bank account. He was really quite angry ... in fact deep inside he was fuming. He banged the top of his desk with a closed fist as he shouted out in frustration 'How dare he ... that little shit ...'

Chapter Twenty Two – The Troublesome Turncoat

The General picked up the report on the top of the pile headed 'Hall–Burton Economic Intelligence Division. Strictly Confidential' and re-read it - yet again.

Hamad finally threw the disappointing document back down on the table. He had done the figures time and time again. The worst costs he could come up with for Mr Declan Doyle on this project were ninety eight to one hundred million. The very best costs were eighty five to eighty seven million. This meant that Doyle was in fact making anywhere between twenty and thirty five million dollars on the deal and that was assuming an included insurance cost. The big question was whether he was even paying that!

He banged the table again, with an already bruised hand in his frustration at being such a fool as to accept the measly amount of one hundred and twenty five thousand dollars for guaranteeing the success of a project that could net the cheating Englishman a possible thirty or forty million.

He took a small set of keys from the pocket of his light grey thobe and unlocked the bottom left hand draw of his desk. There were several papers inside along with a specially manufactured miniature tape recorder setup with wire microphone extensions. This was a gift from his American friends and had become an essential accessory to meetings with any 'brother' members of the ruling Baathist party; any military strategy meeting with his senior officers and most of all, any meeting with the acknowledged wild and untamed animal named Saddam Hussein.

He recorded everything and sent the original tapes immediately to his house in Surrey, England with copies kept securely in a safe buried in the garden of his Basra villa.

Hamad Sadique shuffled through more documents in another draw until he came across one single sheet of notepaper with dates on the right hand side and figures on the left, all written in Arabic. The figures on the left had been added up and the total was one five five zero. He knew it was not enough. One million, five hundred and fifty thousand dollars in his Swiss UBS bank account was definitely not enough to retire on. Not enough to get him and his family away from this god forsaken place, this unholy war and the madman Saddam Hussein.

When the war started way back in the September of 1980, a jubilant Tariq Aziz told his leader and all the assembled military that with the help of Allah, the war would be over in a matter of six or seven months. Well, six years on, Aziz was not so jubilant and Allah had not appeared to have been of any assistance. Well over three hundred thousand Iranian lives had been lost to date and that figure was still climbing. He placed the hand written list on the desk and stared at it, deep in thought. The house in UK was nearly finished. A major

Chapter Twenty Two – The Troublesome Turncoat

extension had just been completed and in fact his wife was there right now sorting out all the furnishings. It was a large eight bedroom property set in over three acres of private grounds in the heart of the Surrey stockbroker belt. It was all paid for and now he was staring at what he had left.

So, the question needed to be addressed; what did he really need? If he was to escape the clutches of the revered leader of the great Iraqi peoples, he would need to cost in some full time security for a couple of years at least. Saddam would not be happy that one of his senior generals had decided to desert him in his hour of need. No, he would definitely not be pleased.

He would also need a regular income from investments to live to the high standards that his wife and family had become used to. The figure of five million flashed in to his mind as he pondered on the situation. Simply grabbing a few hundred thousand here and there from military equipment suppliers and contractors would take years to get to such a figure. That was it then. Mr Doyle would have to come up with four million. So, how was he going to do it?

Option one was to simply go straight to Declan and ask for another four million. The hundred and twenty thousand was already in the bank. He may get some of it, he may get all of it but having now researched the man in great detail, he was aware that Declan Doyle had a reputation of having especially good connections in the 'money recovery' business and these resources could well be turned against Hamad at some future date. This was a risk.

Option two was to get a copy of the audio tape of the meeting with Doyle in Basra to Mohsen Raza, head of the Iranian Revolutionary Guard. He would tell Raza that the Englishman had reneged on the deal and he now felt free to act as he wished.

Option three was to tell the Americans what was going on and hope to grab what he could from them in turn for ensuring that the manifold structure was decimated. He didn't like that idea much, in fact he hated the Americans even more that the Iranians and knew they were not to be trusted.

The Iraqi general continued thinking through the situation and finally came to a conclusion. He would blow the whole manifold business to shit and Doyle would no longer be flavour of the month with Mohsen Raza - which was not a good place to be. He didn't know how much Mr Doyle was really worth in hard cash, but he had an instinct that deep in the private coffers of this very miserly businessman was an amount much larger than four million dollars, just waiting for a rainy day. Well, as far as he was concerned, the dark clouds were building for a downpour.

There was another important piece of paper, secreted

Chapter Twenty Two – The Troublesome Turncoat

somewhere amongst the documents and images filling the substantial desk top of Hamad Sadique. It was a set of minutes relating to a meeting of the war committee held the previous day. It was the last meeting to be held with General George Hormis Sada sitting in his seat as number two in the Air Force to Air Marshal Hamid Sha'aban. Yesterday the well liked George Sada had retired. George was Hamad's mentor.

With his boss and benefactor now gone there was good news and bad news. No decision had yet been made as to his replacement. Hamad, as General George Sada's number two was being considered for the promotion. However, in Iraq, ability and experience would be voted second place to the particular thoughts, feelings and general mood of Saddam Hussein on the very day the subject would be up for discussion. If he got the job, there would be little or no real extra money involved in terms of state salary. However, there would be much more opportunity to grab some of the proceeds of substantial 'slush funds' budgeted by all the western arms and equipment suppliers, beating down the doors of generals managing a nation at war. That was the good news.

The bad news would be that he would have to attend the daily war committee meeting chaired by Saddam Hussein himself. This was a dangerous position to be in especially if you tended to take an alternative view on any subject to that of the 'great leader'.

It was a difficult time and so any decision he made relating to Declan Doyle could be critical, not only in shaping his future with the senior military of Iraq, but putting himself in a position where he might not have a future at all. More than fifty senior military officers were now languishing in Abu Ghraib, most having committed the grave sin of disagreeing with the relatively unbalanced Saddam - and Hamad was very reluctant to become the next one to join them.

He had made a final decision. If the promotion came through within the next week or so, he would gratefully accept it and suck up to his President in any way required. He would keep his family in the UK so they were distanced from everything happening in Iraq. He would send his best man in one single aircraft to do what was necessary on the Geneveh Project. If he pulled it off, he would deny any involvement from Iraq but that asshole Doyle would know what had happened. He would be in the dark brown and by now rather smelly stuff, up to his eyeballs and with everything in place except the manifold, he would have no choice but to pay for another one, that is of course assuming he wanted to stay alive. That was a decision that Mohsen Raza would probably have to make, or maybe one that Declan Doyle would be so desperately praying to make after spending an hour or so with some

Chapter Twenty Two – The Troublesome Turncoat

of Raza's eager interrogators in the dark and damp depths of Tehran's infamous Evin Prison.

The route was now clear. He would get his money, in one way or another. If Declan Doyle stayed alive after losing the key element of the Geneveh Project to the force and accuracy of an Exocet missile, Hamad Sadique would have his four million within months, if not weeks. If Hamad Sadique stayed alive, under the period of early inquisition that would accompany his elevation to the inner sanctum of Saddam Hussein, then he may be able to grab at least half of his four million within a year. No one would stand in his way.

Quietly congratulating himself, Hamad got up from his desk and moved over to the fridge secreted behind some pine panelling decorating the south wall of his office. It was full of alcohol.

Hamad selected a nicely chilled bottle of Chenin Blanc, pulled a crystal wine glass from the lowest drawer in his desk and sat back to savour the possible sweet success of his planned victory.

~~~~~~

Wednesday November fourth was the circled date staring uncompromisingly out of the desk calendar at Declan Doyle. It was six thirty in the morning and the Sabeen Road offices of Associated Oilfield in Abu Nar were heaving with bodies. Desk tops were strewn with a variety of drawings and the several long wave radio links to the Geneveh Project were all busy. Everyone was tired and it showed. Declan was particularly annoyed as he had tried the previous day to get hold of Hamad Sadique in Iraq. In Basra he was told that Hamad was on his way to the Al Taqqadum Air Base near Baghdad and when he finally managed to contact the air base he was told the general was still in Basra. This negative result had consumed nearly all of one totally frustrating day. There was nothing specific that he wanted to question Hamad about, it was just that he felt naturally nervous now that the manifold was on station. He had just wanted to hear the voice of the man who was now the key player in the final outcome of work that had consumed many millions of dollars and thousands of man hours to bring to this delicate stage. Declan picked up the phone. The ship to shore line was poor.

'Hi Andy ... everything OK there?'

'Everything is just about in place here' came the tin toned, distant and echoing reply. Atmospherics were creating a tediously longer than usual delay. Andy Peters aboard the Sea Ranger continued.

'Reg is off on one of the anchor handling boats right now; we are having a little bit of trouble getting number four to bite, but the other three are fine and in position. We are planning to start at about ten o'clock when we get a slack tide in the straits and the best possible light.

Chapter Twenty Two – The Troublesome Turncoat

The weather forecast is good as you know and we are going for it, first time out. If we mess up in any way, we will have enough time to bring the PLEM back to the surface and make adjustments to the anchors'.

'We've got to get it down today my friend' Andy knew that when Declan used the phrase 'my friend', anything that went before it was less of a request and more of an instruction.

'Listen Declan, you sent me out here to do this bloody job - and I will do it. Rain, shit or shine - I will get this pile of scrap metal on the sea bed, in the right position ... *today!* But if there is a safety issue or a positioning issue, *it will come back up again* ... and we will stay here 'till the damned job is done. That's the score *my friend* and I'm afraid that if you don't like ...' Declan cut him off.

'OK Andy, no need to say any more. I'm just a bit nervous right now, perhaps a little bit more than I should be'

Andy of course had no knowledge of the arrangement with the Iraqis and Declan was now wondering if that wasn't a mistake.

'No problem boss. You sit there and sort the money out and Reg and I will stay here and sort out the job. OK?'

'OK Andy. Try to ring the office every hour for an update and definitely ring me personally if you have a problem'

With that, Declan put down the radio phone handset and poured his third cup of coffee of the morning. It was going to be a long, long day.

~~~~~~~~
~~~~

Chapter Twenty Three
The Attack

Captain Omar Tahir began to walk with a quickening pace toward his Mirage F1E military jet cocooned within its remote, hardened concrete shelter at the Al Taqqadum air base, home of the Iraqi Air Defence Command. He noted it was just past eight o'clock. The polished, pale blue camouflage fuselage was surrounded by half a dozen ground crew all busy completing final ground checks and signing the various flight forms to confirm that the aeroplane was fit to fly.

There was a muted hum throughout the shelter from ground air conditioners keeping the cockpit and vital electronics cool, mixed with the low growl of the mobile electrical support generator, keeping all of the twenty million dollar aircraft's complex electrical systems alive. The second of two Exocet anti-ship missiles were being jacked up to the right side inboard wing pylon. Captain Omar had spent three months in France training on the new F1E. He knew he was the best pilot the Air Force had on this type and he was particularly convinced that the current aircraft mark could out-perform and out-shoot the Iranian Phantoms; he was looking forward to the opportunity. With the Mirage weighing only sixteen tons and with a

Chapter Twenty Three – The Attack

fantastic climb rate, this decorated, well trained Iraqi Pilot knew he was on a 'thrill' run today.

As part of his checks, he paid particular attention to the sea skimming, fire and forget Exocet missiles. These French manufactured missiles were the very best there was against a marine target. Right now, the gleaming white Exocet looked the most beautiful thing in the world to Captain Omar.

The missile looked expensive. It was.

At nearly a million dollars each, there was not much money in the Defence Ministry coffers for practice firings. Today would be no practice; this would be the real thing. Captain Omar climbed aboard his aircraft, and within minutes, was strapped in and ready to go.

There was a restricted traffic order out for this particular day issued by General Hamad Sadique. This meant that there would only be defence patrols approved within Iraqi air space. This was not an uncommon directive and would provide Captain Omar with an unrestricted run to his target that day. General Sadique had briefed him the previous week and the attack plan had been agreed then.

The target was a large floating steel structure with hardly any superstructure, sited in the straits between Kharg Island and Geneveh City. Everyone in the military knew about the Geneveh project in Iraq and some were concerned that nothing was specifically being done to stop it. But as usual, Captain Omar suspected that his celebrated leader Saddam Hussein, the great thinker and military strategist, would have something up his sleeve and so it was that Omar had been bestowed the honour of carrying out the leader's faultless plan. This plan had been transmitted to him directly by General Sadique.

Omar knew he should have been at least a major by now. He had carried out over two thousand missions since the war began. He was a career officer. He wanted to 'get on' in life but he suffered a couple of drawbacks in that he was the wrong kind of Muslim and had not been accepted in to the ruling Ba'athist party, the party of the resurrection. It was definitely no 'resurrection' for the Tahir family. However, maybe carrying out this important mission would bring him to the attention of Saddam Hussein and the religious brotherhood who could get him promoted.

Today he had the opportunity to become a hero in the eyes of his great leader Saddam Hussein. Today he would not be found wanting. Captain Omar had been told that the mission was so secret that only Saddam Hussein himself, the General and Omar would know about it. Omar was sworn to secrecy but told by his General that if successful, he would still have to tell no one, not even his wife. Omar knew how to keep a secret and willingly agreed in the comforting knowledge that his General had intimated his rewards would be substantial.

Chapter Twenty Three – The Attack

The flight plan registered with Air Traffic and the Air Force Intelligence Unit would show a normal patrol pattern over Basra to the south, but the operational plan was to actually *head* south from Taqqadum at fifty thousand feet. The track would take him over Kuwait and follow the Saudi Arabian coast line to Jubail. He would then turn north to his target and drop down low over water at around a hundred and fifty feet using terrain hugging radar all the way to the target area. No one would be expecting an attack from the south and at such a low level. The Mirage would be up to the missile release point before anyone even knew he was there.

At about forty miles out, Captain Omar would release both Exocets. Each missile would switch on its own radar when it neared the target, flying at about one to two metres above sea level and moving at over three hundred metres a second. In this mode they were unstoppable.

Once the missiles were released Omar would pull the Mirage hard back up to fifty thousand feet, turn north-west at Mach two and head for home before the Phantoms could get to him.

It was a good plan for the most part. He had studied the myriad satellite images of the site provided by the Americans and had all the required co-ordinates. He had an ECM Electronic Counter Measures pod fitted to the centreline pylon of the Mirage and this very expensive electronics package should cover his movements enough for no one to be sure where the attack had come from and more importantly, who had carried it out. As he pushed the throttles gently forward to move the aircraft on to the apron, the General's last words on the day of the mission briefing echoed in his mind.

'Whatever you do, make every attempt to steer clear of the Phantoms. I simply don't need to tell you, they are built like a tank and handle like a spitfire on marijuana. If you keep low on the approach and release at near maximum range of the Exocet, they should not be able to catch up with you. If they do, release a clutter trail from the ECM, get up as high as you can and get the hell out of there'

'Yes Sir' was the obedient reply, although Captain Omar Tahir had no thoughts of running away from a fight with an Iranian Phantom. His French instructors had told him that the upgraded Mirage could out-perform the F4 – with ease, and if it came to it - Omar would be very happy to prove it. As the fully loaded Mirage turned on to the end of the runway, Omar pushed the throttles fully forward. When his wheels left the one dimensional comfort of the black tarmac, with afterburners flaming several metres behind him, he joined the three dimensional freedom of full flight and noted the time as exactly 08:30 hours local. He wrote it on his knee pad.

General Hamad Sadique sat in his Basra office alone.

Chapter Twenty Three – The Attack

He had just put down the phone after receiving the patrol reports from Taqqadum. The flight number of the Mirage piloted by Captain Omar Tahir was there amongst only eleven internal flights authorised for that morning. He could hear the clatter of the written reports now coming over the telex machine in the outer office.

Hamad was calm.

Five other aircraft had been authorised to carry Exocets that day, all as part of exercise 'Mawtini' which was recorded in the English versions of Iraqi air orders as 'Homeland'. The General had received approval for the exercise from the General Staff Council two days previously. This was a routine matter as Hamad planned and received approval for missions and exercise events more or less on a daily basis.

If for any reason his determined protégée failed in his mission, the General would put it down to a frustrated, totally loyal officer who wanted to give the enemy a bloody nose. It would not be the first time an Iraqi pilot had launched himself gloriously in to the other world, inhabited seemingly only by virgins, after being wound up by an overzealous Imam at Friday prayers. The inspiring climax would essentially dare the young and impressionable to take on the evil enemy in a glorious Jihad and become a Mujahid. The promise of a magnificent end in Paradise was sometimes too tempting even for the most educated of men and since

1982 the Iraqi Air Force had lost two Mig 32's and one Mig 21, along with the lives of costly pilots, to this unfortunate type of business.

At 09:33 Hrs, the Executive Officer of the USS Augustine called Commander Dillaneo to a massive tracking screen where over three hundred air traffic movements were being logged and plotted simultaneously.

'What's our exact position XO?' the Commander queried.

'We are in sector C459 at this location' the XO pointed to a set of continuously changing coordinates highlighted on the top left of the screen. As Dillaneo was being briefed by the XO he picked up that there appeared to be very little military traffic emanating from Iraq. He questioned it.

'Well Sir' the XO replied 'we have had word that a fairly large military exercise is about to take place in the north on the Turkish border and its usual for military air activity to be considerably reduced a day or two beforehand. This allows for material and equipment movements to the exercise area to take place'

'So you think that this is the situation right now?'

'I do sir, but the reason I have brought you up here is to have a look at this'

He pointed to a plot on the screen which had been locked to a track heading south of Basra to Jubail and

Chapter Twenty Three – The Attack

was turning north. The track had to be decoded as it was surrounded by suspicious electronic clutter. But clutter or no clutter, it was definitely there.

'It's heading straight for us sir'

'What is it? Dillaneo asked, now concerned.

'There is no electronic 'ident' from the aircraft and it's now running at low level very quickly'

'How far are we from our target?'

'Twenty minutes at this speed sir'

'How far away is this possible enemy target?

'Ten minutes at current speed and track sir'

'Options?'

'Could be someone having a go at us - but unlikely. Could be someone having a go at our target - more likely. However, whatever it is and whatever it is armed with, I calculate it's a threat to us and the secure outcome of our operation sir'.

'I agree number one. Arm two SM2 anti-aircraft missiles and lock to this track. Do it now'

'Yes sir. Nine minutes'

'Periscope depth please' shouted the Commander as both he and the XO entered the control and command deck.

Two minutes later.

'Periscope up'

Commander Dillaneo scanned the surface for three hundred and sixty degrees. Nothing in sight.

'Good' he muttered to everyone and no one.

He glanced at his watch. Time was running short. The distant possibility of being hit by a couple of air launched lightweight anti-submarine torpedoes was not the problem. Being exposed ... just minutes before carrying out an attack on his carefully plotted target, now literally sitting just over the horizon ...*was*. Whether the unidentified aircraft was Iraqi or Iranian didn't really bother him. What he was sure about was that it was definitely military, flying at such speed and so low ... and more importantly with no electronic identity. This, combined with lots of electronic 'clutter' around the trace, indicated the presence of an ECM pod. Any aircraft operating an ECM pod, in these particular waters, on this particular day was up to no good. As far as Commander Dillaneo, Captain of the USS Augustine was concerned, this could only be translated as an aggressive posture. He couldn't take the risk and anyway, as far as the rest of the world would ever know, he simply wasn't there. His log book said so, he said so and his crew said so. He simply wasn't there. If he gave the order to fire, the two missiles would be launched and at half a million dollars apiece, they didn't often disappoint. He paused for a second then made his decision.

'Fire when lock confirmed'

Captain Omar Tahir knew of an impending attack only fifteen seconds before contact. His ECM was on and

Chapter Twenty Three – The Attack

flying at literally wave top height, he felt confident he was well beneath any Iranian, Saudi or Bahraini radar. To say he wasn't a little on edge, would be a lie. However, he took some comfort in the fact that the Iranians didn't have the benefit of any useful satellite data.

What his attack interrogation and alarm system didn't tell him was that just over seven hundred kilos of missile, powered by a state of the art solid fuel rocket was travelling straight at him from the south at over eighteen hundred miles an hour. When the cockpit horn actually sounded, the surprise and following confusion took up valuable, fateful seconds.

Where was there to go?

He couldn't fly any lower. He needed air space if he was to attempt a roll out manoeuvre. He hit the heat counter measures and one missile chased a flaming cartridge in to the water, but the further mini seconds consumed in making this decision were seconds he didn't have as the other missile slammed straight in to him. He knew nothing of the following explosion and eye searing fireball. Captain Omar Tahir was already dead.

~~~~~~~~
~~~~

Chapter Twenty Four
Mission Accomplished?

By his wrist watch, Andy Peters noted the time to be a few minutes past ten o'clock. He stood on the bridge of the 'Sea Ranger' riding at anchor but with engines running. He had field glasses in hand in an anxious attempt to map out the substantial dimensions of the complex scene being played out before him.

The dive boats were in place.

The tugs were in dynamic positioning mode.

The anchor lines were connected to the SPEM and the inflatable sea bed crossing pillows were in position. Once the manifold structure was in place, the crossing pillows would be inflated with liquid concrete to obtain a level across the whole installation. Only when the PLEM was level on the sea bed and anchors tied off would the final jointing pipes between the twenty four inch land line and the twelve inch flexible lines leading to the SPM, be attached. Right now the massive steel structure, ninety metres in length and twenty six metres wide, was being gently manoeuvred, inch by inch, in to a position approximately three hundred metres away from the Sea Ranger.

The completed manifold was an impressive piece of steelwork. It contained massive oil storage and

Chapter Twenty Four – Mission Accomplished?

balancing tanks, hydraulic positioning winches and a maze of pipes and valves all set on an open steel framework, surrounded at the perimeter with a ring of water tight tubing for buoyancy control, mounted by massive protective steel fenders.

'How the hell they managed to tow that bloody thing half way round the world without breaking it … I do not know!' Andy muttered to himself. He considered that what he was looking at was probably an absolute feat of mechanical engineering, especially given the amount of time taken to design it and then actually manufacture it. He pulled his shoulders back a little as a small feeling of pride swept over him, knowing he was part of the near miracle spread out ahead of him on these particularly calm Gulf waters. He had to give it to Declan, he could be an absolute asshole at times but by god he was right on this one.

Andy was a little nervous but very excited at the same time. There were still many questions related mainly to the inevitably short design period and the major one was - *would it work?*

The big question could only be answered when all the feed lines were connected and the SPM anchored in place.

The scoured and expressionless face of Reg Green came in to view as he opened the starboard bridge door and closed it quickly again to keep the air conditioning honest. The weather beaten face on the ubiquitous

Australian broke out in to what passed for a smile as he spoke above the suppressed noise of the portable radio hanging from his belt.

'I have confirmation from all the other boat Captains that everything is ready to go Andy'.

Reg was looking to him for confirmation.

'Has anyone checked with the Iranians for any sign of the Iraqis?'

'There's nothing on the Radar and when I give the word, the Phantoms will be in the air to provide some cover directly over the site'

'Are you happy that everything is *really* ready to go Reg. Has every *single* thing been checked?'

The inscrutable looking Australian sensed Andy's nervousness.

'Everything is as good as it's going to get but if we don't start ballasting the manifold shortly, we will be out of slack tide. You need to give me the go Andy!'

'OK' Said Andy as he pulled himself up to full height and crossed his fingers behind his back 'Let's go!'

Reg also crossed his fingers, which signalled another rare smile, as he echoed the command over the radio

The final and most delicate phase of the Geneveh Project had begun and there was now a distinct possibility that within twenty four hours, Associated Oilfield Services Inc would become the toast of the International oil business - or simply become toast.

319

Chapter Twenty Four – Mission Accomplished?

Andy picked up the ship to shore phone and relayed the news to Abu Nar.

~~~~~~

Declan Doyle carefully replaced the receiver after his short conversation with Andy. He looked up at the wall clock. It was ten minutes past ten. Sat on his desk were over thirty financial transfer authorisation documents for the bank. Once these completed documents were presented to the bank, an electronic transfer of monies due to all of the contractors and sub-contractors on site would be made within the hour. The single pile sitting in front of him was worth twenty eight and a half million US Dollars. The trigger for the AOS accountant to get in his car and make the short journey to the ABR Bank would be a clear message from Andy that the PLEM was safely on the sea floor. Declan dutifully signed each transfer authorisation, patted them into a neat pile and sat back in his chair. Everything was now out of his hands. He reluctantly admitted to himself that he actually had no control over anything that was now happening to the biggest gamble he had ever taken in his life. This really was the big one. But what should he do right now? There were two reasonable choices.

One was to stay in the office and wait for the next hour or so, pissing off everyone within shouting distance in the process.

The other one was to go and have a drink with his friend Geoffrey. He pondered for a moment, pushed himself up eagerly from his now suddenly uncomfortable office chair and left the building.

~~~~~~

On the USS Augustine there was a tense silence of anticipation. Messages passing back and forth between the surface work boats and diving vessels on the Geneveh Project were being monitored by a bank of headphone equipped communications technicians. A full and detailed picture of what was happening on the surface, over three miles away, was emerging. The Augustine had been sitting on the bottom in a hundred and fifty feet of water, in full stealth mode, for over an hour. Finally, Commander Dillaneo gave the command.

'Periscope depth number one'

'Periscope depth -aye sir' came the hushed reply.

A minute or so later.

'Periscope depth sir'

'Up periscope'

The barely audible release of compressed air accompanied the effortless vertical movement of the stainless steel tube, inches away from the commander's face. Dillaneo bent down and grabbed the focus and sighting handles as the periscope came up to the lock position. He scanned the horizon a full three hundred

Chapter Twenty Four – Mission Accomplished?

and sixty degrees before turning back north, adjusting the focus until his target loomed large and clear in the sight. At three miles distance, the Sea Ranger was blocking a full view of the manifold as it swung left and right across his sighting screen. He waited until he was able to put a bearing on the centre of the structure and then breathed the word

'Mark'

'Mark two eight nine degrees sir' Dillaneo stabbed the range button.

'Target?'

'Target - six thousand eight hundred and fifty yards sir'

'Down periscope'

'Down periscope aye sir'

'Set number one to fifteen feet' he paused carrying out a quick mental calculation' 'Set number two for twenty five feet'

'Fifteen and twenty five aye sir' It was a quiet, confident confirmation.

'Fire tubes one and four'

'Tubes one and four sir'

The muffled crump of the compressed air shockwave could be heard and then felt as a slight vibration through the control room floor grating as the torpedoes were fired, three seconds apart.

'Two torpedoes running sir'.

The weapons officer spoke in a practised, matter of

fact tone. Everyone on board the Augustine listened over the open intercom; bodies taut with tension at actually being in action. This is what they had trained for; the years of preparation to ensure that a moment such as this should be executed perfectly. On *this* mission there would be no second chance. One of the torpedoes had to make its mark. Once they turned away, there would be no going back.

'Exit time?' shouted the Captain

'Ten eighteen and sixteen seconds sir' replied the calm and collected weapons officer.

The pressure was on.

'All stations dive. Set boat depth … one hundred feet'

'Dive – Dive – Dive … one hundred sir' came the XO's confirmation. Then there was silence.

The stress of the moment was easily read; a distinct smell of sweat now pervading the warm breathing air pumping relentlessly through the control room ducting.

The XO was visibly excited. The hand built destructors cost over two and a half million dollars each and his Captain had just spent five million dollars, courtesy of Uncle Sam.

'Maintain heading, slow ahead'

Dillaneo's crisp words of command cut through the stilled atmosphere. He needed to get in to some deep water and fast.

'Maintain heading and slow ahead sir' replied Lieutenant Commander Dwain Shulman; a small hint of

Chapter Twenty Four – Mission Accomplished?

pride filtering through the words that did not go unnoticed by the boat's anxious Captain. He looked toward the XO standing stock still some feet away on the other side of the control room and smiled.

The first explosion picked up by the hydrophones was exceptionally loud and just over three seconds later was followed by a more muted thumping sound. Commander Dillaneo did not need confirmation from the weapons officer that they had hit something ... but what?

'Periscope depth number one!'

'Periscope depth sir'

The familiar whoosh was followed by the Captain ducking down to grab the handles once again. He scanned the horizon. It was chaos. He did a second quick three sixty, confirmed that there were no visible air movements and clipped up the handles.

'Down periscope, one hundred and fifty feet, full ahead heading green two six three. Right, let's get the fuck out of here!'

'All aye sir - one hundred and fifty feet, full ahead, heading two six three - and let's get the fuck out of here!'

There was a burst of laughter from the boat's crew at this small aside from the XO, the tension of the past few minutes immediately broken.

The Captain's face broke out in to a full-size, infectious grin; the tension evaporated and now back to the normal job of navigating his billion dollar weapon of war safely out of the area. He needed deep water quickly. In submarine terms, one hundred and fifty feet was simply not enough. He also needed to ensure that the boat was confirmed being logged as near to Bahrain as possible, as quickly as possible, providing some evidence of his reported patrol pattern.

As the periscope was being lowered the Ofek 6 Israeli surveillance satellite, in stationary orbit, three kilometres above the Persian Gulf, was busy sending information back to the USS Augustine. Captain Dillaneo and the XO moved down one level to the intelligence centre, a large room where over nine officers and men worked translating a constant stream of intelligence gathered from a multitude of sources.

The first high resolution image pushed its way through the large format thermal printer a millimetre at a time. After nearly a minute, the still hot printed sheet, in vivid colour, dropped in to the receiving tray. A technician carefully removed it from the tray and placed it on the under lit examination table. A second image was on its way.

Dillaneo and Shulman did not need a magnifying glass or an image interpreter to tell immediately that the job had been done, but there was some collateral damage. A lot of smoke covered the target area but it was obvious the manifold had been hit and more or less

Chapter Twenty Four – Mission Accomplished?

destroyed, with what appeared to be only two balancing tanks still left floating on the surface some two or three hundred metres apart.

The large workboat to the south of the target had been hit and the stern of the vessel badly damaged. It was now listing and slightly stern down in the water. The technician placed another warm image sheet on the table. The smoke in this image was clearing and the space in the circle of over a dozen boats, where the manifold structure should have been, was empty. Even the two floating tanks that were clearly there a moment ago were now disappearing. The big workboat was well down in the stern and some of the smaller boats were heading toward it. One of the small boats, probably a diving vessel, was stationary and shown to be on fire.

The job was done. It was a grim satisfaction knowing the possibility that many human beings would have been injured or even killed that day because of the actions of these two men. They looked at one another for a brief moment, a searching and maybe questioning look having fully taken in the carnage wreaked by them on fellow mariners within that fateful hour.

Captain Dillaneo left the XO in the intelligence room in thoughtful mood and returned to his cabin to send a top secret 'burst' message to Admiral James Warkin.

It simply read ... 'Mission accomplished'.

Little did Commander Dillaneo, or Admiral Warkin for that matter, know the action taken that day by the USS Augustine was to have some unplanned and possibly far reaching consequences.

~~~~~~~~
~~~~

Chapter Twenty Five
The Disaster Unfolds

Declan found himself sipping on his second beer, sitting at the bar of the Abu Nar Country Club in the company of no one in particular. Geoffrey, the person who's company he did actually need right now - was not in the club. Declan was disappointed and somewhat frustrated. He wanted someone to talk to. What about? Just about anything other than the Geneveh Project.

He was on his second cigarette, stolen from Rajan the head barman; only the second cigarette he had smoked in several years. A phone was ringing somewhere in the distance.

The light tap on the shoulder made him tense a little but the soft admonishing tones relaxed him completely.

'Declan Doyle … I am flabbergasted … where on *earth* did you suddenly learn to smoke?'

The words, although chiding, were delivered gently by Penny who stood directly behind him, hands resting lightly on his shoulders.

Declan turned quickly on the bar stool to face her, putting his arms around her trim waist. She bent down and gave him a lingering kiss on the lips.

'How did you know I was here?' he questioned through a welcoming smile. 'Where else would you be

Chapter Twenty Five – The Disaster Unfolds

at a time like this - if of course you couldn't be right in the thick of it?'

He laughed out loud. She knew him too well.

'Is everything going OK at Geneveh?' she asked, pulling up a bar stool next to him.

'Well - they should be putting the manifold down right now and in a couple of hours we will know'

She placed a comforting hand on his knee.

'Everything will be fine Declan … have no fear. Everyone knows you have done all you possibly could to make sure this project is a success'.

'Let's hope so Penny … let us all really hope so. Do you want a drink … a coffee or a wine or something?'

She interrupted.

'No darling … I just popped in to see you quickly. I have a client in twenty minutes to look over some apartments at the Trade Centre in Dubai … and so in fact, I must rush. Hopefully I'll see you tonight. Give me a ring'

Declan gave out a kiss as Penny turned and moved rhythmically out of the room. He didn't know it at the time, but it was to be the very last time he would ever see her.

He checked his watch, restless and impatient. Rajan came over toward Declan with a hurried walk and whispered in his ear.

'Message from office sir … got to get back quickly'

'Who rang?' Declan enquired in a muted tone.

'Secretary woman sir' replied a nervous looking Rajan.

'I'm on my way' Declan downed the last of his beer and set off for the car park.

As he walked through the heavy and recently re-glazed main office doors, there was an unusual silence. The sixty or so people in the room were all standing, as if frozen in time and as Declan entered, all heads turned in his direction. What the hell was going on?

Paul Williams, one of the engineering managers on the Geneveh Project walked purposely toward him and in a quiet but commanding tone said

'Your office I think Declan?'

'Of course' came the quick response. As Williams closed the door behind him, Declan sat down at his desk and motioned to Paul Williams to sit on the easy chair in front of him.

'Ok Paul. Something dreadful has happened, but how dreadful?'

'The worst you could possibly expect' came the bitter reply.

~~~~~~

The first explosion came from the back of the Sea Ranger. Andy, standing on the bridge with Reg, initially felt a strong push from the back that nearly made him

Chapter Twenty Five – The Disaster Unfolds

lose his balance. They turned to each other with a questioning look. Milliseconds later the noise of the actual explosion rose to an ear deafening crescendo - and then, carried on a violent rush of super heated air, debris appeared to be flying everywhere.

The world was running in slow motion as Andy hit the unforgiving steel deck plating. Red hot torn and twisted metal shrapnel, some the size of a small car, came screaming through the rear plating of the bridge accelerated to a speed of nearly five hundred metres a second by the force of the high energy explosion and Reg was facing it … full on. It carried on through the bridge and the thick laminated glass weather screens unhindered, taking Reg with it.

Then - as suddenly as it had started – it stopped!

To Andy it appeared he had lain glued to the deck for minutes without moving; waiting for God knows what, but it was in fact only a few seconds. Then, as he raised himself, shaking uncontrollably, up to the now shattered window line … the second explosion came. The pressure wave knocked him back to the deck once more and threw him hard against what remained of the rear plating. As a result, he was thrown physically unconscious, half sitting, and half lying, up against the smoking remains of the bridge steelwork for some time. The circle of boats surrounding the manifold structure were all affected in one way or another by shrapnel and pressure waves from the second explosion which hit the PLEM square on. It simply disintegrated as a quarter of a ton of high explosive material erupted on the south side of the structure directly beneath the main valve blocks. The whole fabrication was literally thrown in the air some seventy to eighty feet as it seemed to hang there for a second or so and then broke up into a myriad of metal pieces showering down on the nearby support vessels and anchor handling tugs.

Of the twenty or so divers, waiting at various depths to guide the manifold structure to the sea floor in the lowering operation, four were killed instantly by the amplified water pressure wave and two more were injured severely by metal fragments from the explosion. There was a black smoke cloud over the area where the manifold had once been but not as large or as dense as one would have expected from an explosion of such force. It was moving out of mushroom status and now breaking up as it began to drift eastward.

The Sea Ranger had been hit with some force in the middle of the loading deck and the resulting mayhem had ripped at least thirty feet of hull from the vessel. She was down in the stern to such a point that her bulbous bow had risen completely out of the water. The thumping beat of helicopter rotors could be heard in the distance, invading the unearthly, stunned silence of the moment. At least four Iranian Hueys were hovering over the area and around seven or eight high speed coastal launches were heading toward the carnage.

Chapter Twenty Five – The Disaster Unfolds

Andy came round slowly but found himself remarkably clear headed as he pulled his bruised and battered body up from a position now cradled by the vee formed where the deck and rear plating of the bridge works met. It was obvious that the bow of the Sea Ranger was now pointing upward.

He knew he had to get out of there fast as he moved awkwardly toward the open bridge doorway, biting back pain and checking himself for any possible life threatening injuries on the way. Miraculously, there appeared to be none.

He clambered and skated down the decking to the water line and with the force of gravity aiding him, gently slid in. The Sea Ranger seemed to be stable in the water at about thirty degrees as the individual buoyancy compartments beneath the loading platform held up. He had his personal floatation device on and it automatically inflated as he hit the water. There were lots of smaller, more manoeuvrable boats milling about on the surface now and within a minute or two, Andy was whisked up from the warm, debris ridden Gulf waters and in to a small semi-rigid belonging to one of the dive boats.

'Get me to a fucking radio' Andy demanded as the boat turned at speed and headed toward its mother ship. Now he was out of the water, he suddenly felt very, very cold and sat in the boat shivering despite being covered with a first aid foil blanket and a heavy plastic sheet. Andy's face was a tightened, expressionless mask as he focused in on the mind numbing situation - and he was angry. He was *fucking* angry. As he climbed aboard the 'Gulf Diver II' the skipper, Billy Barlow, a young Brit, rushed down to the stern to help hoist Andy and two other crew members of the Sea Ranger on to the diving deck.

'Reg is dead!' Andy shouted.

'Bloody hell!' Billy replied – stunned.

'How are you and your team Billy?'

'We have a few holes in the superstructure but all the surface crew are OK and the boat is OK'

He paused with a grim expression.

'We can't make contact with two of our divers and the water is so clogged down there, you can't see a hand in front of your face. I can't move any of my divers in the water right now until it clears a bit more. I fear for the worst Andy'.

'Those bastards' Andy shouted out loud 'Did you hear an aircraft or anything? Did you hear anything coming? Have you any fucking clue what happened here?'

'Absolutely nothing Andy! Everything was totally spot on. I was on the sea-com to my low level dive group when I heard a bang come from the rear of the Sea Ranger and as I turned to have a look in your direction, the fucking world exploded in front of me'

Chapter Twenty Five – The Disaster Unfolds

'Some bastard will answer for this. It must have been the Iraqis but where the hell were the damned Iranians? I just don't understand it. Is your radio phone working?'

'Yes, it's in here' Billy Barlow indicated a short set of steps leading up to the bridge.

'Right Billy' said Andy, struggling hard to maintain a controlled and outwardly calmer manner. He took several deep breaths but the inevitable weeping had begun. He forced the words through the tears.

'As Reg is no longer with us, I'm putting you in charge. Get on the VHF radio and get me a picture of everything that's gone on. I want damage reports, casualties, sea worthiness estimates of all vessels on station and as soon as possible I want an ROV down on the sea bed to inspect the end of the subsea pipeline. You tell every boat captain and every crew foreman that you have my personal authority - and if you have any problems with anyone, put them straight on to me'

'You've got it Andy!'

'Good. Now leave me alone for a few minutes with that bloody phone'

~~~~~~

'I've just put the phone down to Andy' Williams spoke quietly without any sign of emotion.

'The manifold has gone, the Sea Ranger is badly damaged. There are casualties, quite a few serious injuries - and some deaths. One work boat is sinking fast with a gaping hole in her engine room, one dive boat is unable to manoeuvre, and a situation report is being put together as we speak'

'God all mighty' Declan squeezed through tight lips. Williams waited for a few seconds for it all to sink in; then he delivered the bombshell.

'Reg is dead!'

'What?' Declan jumped up out of the soft leather chair in total shock

'Paul, for god's sake tell me that's not true' he shouted, nearly screamed. A bewildering sense of disbelief came over him as he slumped back in to his chair totally overwhelmed at this horrific news - and he knew he was to blame.

'I'll leave you right now Declan. I hope you don't mind but I've sort of taken charge in your absence. Do you want me to carry on for a while - until you've had time to get your head round it all? Until ….'

Declan cut him short. 'Yes. Yes - please Paul. Please carry on until I come and speak with you. Is Andy OK?'

'He's fine, but only just. You know Andy. He's very pissed off, but he's alive with only a few scratches and he *is* trying to hold everything together. There will be the Iranians to deal with eventually, but I've told him that no one is to take any shit from them and all necessary discussions will take place directly between you and Raza. I hope that's OK with you?'

Chapter Twenty Five – The Disaster Unfolds

'Exactly the right thing Paul' Declan murmured '… and tell everyone that I do *not* wish to be disturbed for the next half hour or so'

'Leave it me' he replied and then quietly exited the office.

A requested black coffee fortified with a suitable measure of good Spanish Brandy came and went as the thought processes began to unfold.

There was no doubt in Declan's mind that he had been double crossed by that asshole Iraqi General Hamad Sadique. But what for? How the hell did he really gain anything by destroying the Geneveh Project? Did he get cold feet? Did he want more money? Was there some political issue? What in God's name went wrong?

He continued to scratch at the dark corners of his mind in search of an alternative scenario to the one labelled 'betrayal' on one side and 'double cross' on the other.

He couldn't find one.

Any attack must have come from the air and any attack from the air must have come from Iraq, it was as simple as that. Declan decided that sitting in the office contemplating his future, was not the right place to be. He left the building; left the clatter of Telex machines and cacophony of barely intelligible radio traffic, overlaid with the hum of anxious conversations taking place between sixty or so people, attempting to piece together an accurate picture of what, if anything, may be left of the Geneveh Project.

~~~~~~

Christopher StJohn Briars studied the lazy traffic of the River Thames as it passed beneath Westminster Bridge from his vantage point on the tenth floor of Century House. He was in the office early. In fact he had been woken at home from a well deserved sleep by a telephone call from his man in Bahrain, Eric Saunders.

The Geneveh Project was in a mess!

Someone had been up to no good and it was Christopher's job to try and figure it out. Saunders information had been confirmed only minutes later by a call from GCHQ who had intercepted some communications traffic from several surface vessels on the scene. There would be an inquest within the Service, that was for sure and if he was a betting man, he would have put money on it being no later than lunchtime.

Christopher knew he would need to come up with something and it had better be good. He had already told Saunders to put himself on the first plane out of Bahrain and get his backside in to the office … with every single thing he had on Doyle and the Geneveh Project. Being frank with himself, he knew the events at the Geneveh site could be proven to be seen as

Chapter Twenty Five – The Disaster Unfolds

completely unexpected. However, from a distance, it looked as if someone had purposely blown the whole thing to kingdom come – and he didn't know who! What was even more distressing was the thought that it might even have been some of the 'Gungs' working on an agenda of their own. Stranger things had happened within the UK's top Espionage and Covert Activities business. The Secret Intelligence Service was riddled with a history of cock up's, and purposeful non-communications, some, such as the Buster Crabb affair, that actually led to a change of management - at the very top. Could this turn out to be a similar situation?

As he looked down pensively on the ant-like scurrying movements of the blindly focused commuters pouring out of Waterloo Station as he attempted to formulate the events in some sort of order. He pulled out, from a desk draw, a blank sheet of paper and started jotting down some thoughts.

The primary question glaring from the page had to be what was it that had blown the key element of the project to hell and back and caused such bedlam? What in fact *could* it have been? There were few possibilities. One was an attack from under the water ... and for that you needed a submarine. The other was an attack from the air ... and for that that you needed a pretty quick aeroplane with some state of the art technology to get past the Iranian air cover. The third was some sort of explosive sabotage that again would need some pretty sophisticated operatives and equipment to get in there and do the job unnoticed. However, for the 'Gungs' and their SAS friends, this kind of operation would be just up their street.

The politics were the problem. They simply did not make sense. Christopher had it from the very top, from Curwen himself that British interests were best served by letting it all happen, by letting the Geneveh Project succeed. So that left only the Iraqi's with their new Exocets, or some involvement by the Russians or the Americans. The Russians would have no possible reason to piss off Iran at the moment as literally all the oil being produced right now was going to them. That left the Americans ... and such a thought resulted in a big question mark.

He called down to Peter Stevenson who was head of technical liaison and basically managed all the 'Tecno's' at Century House. Peter was fortunately one of the 'Cats'. Although it was still a bit early, he was at his desk and answered immediately.

'Hi Peter ... can you do me a favour please? Can you give me the movements of all US military surface vessels and patrolling submarines in the Arabian Gulf over the past forty eight hours?'

'It will take a bit of time – but - say about four this afternoon?'

'That will be fine Peter. No need to tell anyone else about this though'

Chapter Twenty Five – The Disaster Unfolds

'I understand Christopher'

The head of the C2 desk carefully replaced the telephone handset with a final thought. He spoke it out loud.

'If the errant Mr Doyle is to survive the next twenty four hours, he may need a little assistance!'

~~~~~~~~~
~~~~

Chapter Twenty Six
On The Run

Declan Doyle sat in the lounge of his luxury villa located in splendid isolation, set back from the Fujeriah road two miles beyond Abu Nar International Airport. He had a whiskey and soda in one hand and a framed photograph of him and Penny in the other. He contemplated the image for a moment as thoughts crowded through his mind. His favourite photo of himself and Penny together, had been taken on Esmerelda II about four years previously. Both were captured sun tanned and laughing, wine glasses raised in a form of salute, enjoying the good life in the land of plenty.

However, that was in the past. Today - he was deeply ensconced in the 'brown stuff' and it was time for some honest arithmetic. He moved over to a low polished mahogany sideboard, opened one of the drawers and extracted a lined pad, a pencil and small battery driven calculator. Saskan the Head Steward entered unexpectedly, enquiring about any possible lunch arrangements and Declan waved him away. He would miss him too. Right, now to work. He placed the pad on his knee and started to scribble down some numbers.

Chapter Twenty Six – On The Run

He didn't really know how much he was worth in cash so now was the time to try and work it out. The stock market crash on Black Monday had left his stock investments severely depleted but in such a situation, the best advice available is to leave everything as it is and simply wait for the markets to recover. That of course was fine if you didn't actually need to liquidate any of them. Only then did the losses show. His private investment stocks were now worth less than half of what they were valued at only a few weeks ago. He knew how much his businesses were worth to the penny. This information was fed to him by his team of accountants on the last working day of each month in the form of a full and detailed set of management accounts.

So, personal bank accounts first.

In his UBS account in Zurich, Declan knew he had a balance of eight hundred and fifty thousand dollars on one month deposit, and a further two hundred and twenty thousand pounds sterling in a Jersey Midland Bank account. Finally there was the 'personal emergency fund' of around one hundred thousand UAE Dirhams held in the Standard Chartered Bank in Dubai.

The AOS Jersey account, operated solely on his signature, held the twenty million dollars from the first payment for the Geneveh Project plus about half a million from previous deposits. Due to the fact that

Declan had not paid any insurance premium on the manifold, there was a surplus on the final payment received from the Iranians of around eight million dollars. Adding all the numbers together, Declan calculated he would be close to eleven million dollars short to salvage the site, repair any underwater damage and replace the subsea manifold.

Now to the businesses!

Putting a value on Contec being a Gulf based company would be difficult as on paper, the local Arab partner held a stake of 51%. On the basis of calculating a sale value of say three times net profit, then Contec should be worth around nine million dollars. Cut that in half, take a bit off and a sensible figure would be say four million dollars for a quick sale.

AOS was a different matter. For a quick discounted sale, a figure of five million should be achievable.

With everything selling quickly – and at the right price, he would still be two million dollars short. With Declan's contacts, this amount could possibly be 'begged, borrowed or stolen' from friends, but then he would have no business left and no way of paying it back. This kind of situation was regularly noted in the oil business as being 'between a rock and a hard place'.

As for personal stock investments, they would probably have a surrender value of less than three hundred thousand pounds sterling and he may have to live on that money for some time to come.

Chapter Twenty Six – On The Run

Declan sat in deep contemplation for a moment or two. 'Bollocks to it all' he breathed as he reached for the phone. He had made his decision.

The first call was to a UK number which was answered immediately. He was absolutely convinced that a certain Iraqi Air Force General had not kept his promise, so Declan must now keep his. The conversation was short; the promise extracted from the receiving party reassuring. The second call was to the Standard Chartered Bank in Dubai to arrange for twenty thousand dollars to be debited to his Dirham account and made ready in cash, in small denomination notes within the hour. The next ten minutes were spent packing one large soft bag with clothes, towels and washing kit and checking his flight bag. He lifted his most favourite framed image of himself and Penny from the side table - broke the frame open and removed the photograph. He placed it with care in a side pocket of his flight bag. Taking a sheet of blank paper from the bag he began to write.

He folded the paper and wrote the name 'Penny' on the front, leaving it resting on the empty picture frame. As he did so, he felt the possibly unwelcome beginnings of an emotion he had purposely denied himself for many years now, but it was too late.

Moving out in to the cool marbled interior of the entrance hall, he took down a framed Picasso print to reveal a small combination lock wall safe. He flicked through the four key numbers and opened the steel door. Inside were a few documents, around ten thousand UAE Dirhams in large denomination notes and his hand gun.

He stared at the contents of the safe for some seconds. He was making up his mind. Eventually, he took the Browning Hi-Power 9mm out along with three box-magazines of ammunition, the money and the registration documents for his aeroplane.

Holding the hand gun for a lingering moment, Declan felt the cold black steel, weighing the one kilo weight of extraordinary firepower in a steady hand. It brought back grim memories and had saved his life in another existence; in another distant time. Perhaps it would need to do so again.

Declan closed the wall safe, replaced the picture carefully and moved back in to the lounge. He looked round the room once, placed the gun, the money and documents in his soft bag.

Saskan was hovering. 'What time will you be back sir?' came the expected enquiry

'Late, Saskan … very late. So don't wait up and if Penney calls, tell her I will ring her tomorrow' Saskan noticed the flight bag at Declan's feet.

'Are you flying somewhere today sir?'

'I have to go over to the east coast on some urgent business … and I'm running late Saskan'

The reply sounded unexpectedly irritated.

Chapter Twenty Six – On The Run

'I'm sorry sir' said the Head Steward apologetically, sensing that his boss's mind was on other things and with that Declan was gone.

In the car, heading toward the Standard Chartered Bank in Dubai, Declan's mind was half on the road and half on his problem. He was not safe in the Emirates; that was for sure. He needed to get out of Abu Nar, even get out of the Gulf, completely. Whatever was happening in the straits between Kharg Island and Geneveh, the Rev Guard and his recently acquired friend Mohsen Raza, would probably be reconsidering their relationship right now. Once they had all taken in fully what had happened, Raza would be looking for some retribution. He had substantial resources at his fingertips, especially the deadly 'Khuds' which acted as the covert overseas arm of the Revolutionary Guard. Declan had no doubt that some of the darker forces under Raza's influence were being briefed right now. Declan needed time to regroup, to consider the total situation and he needed all his physical and mental capacities to do so. Revenge is probably a dish best served cold. Laying beaten half to death in the shallow end of his swimming pool would not solve the problem for him or Raza, so better to remove the temptation.

Declan pulled in to the half empty car park of the bank. He walked up the steps to the entrance of the nondescript building and fought his way through a swarm of Asian workers crowding all the teller points eager to send their hard earnt Rupees back home. He caught the eye of one of the European managers sitting at a desk in the open plan offices, behind the teller stations.

After the obligatory coffee and a quick visit from the bank manager to assure Declan of his very best service at all times; ring me day or night - kind of assurances, Declan quickly did a count. It was all there; twenty thousand US Dollars in a mix of used and unused low denomination dollar bills. It was good enough. The over-helpful young man gave Declan a plastic carrier bag emblazoned with the Standard Chartered bright blue logo. Now he had some cash - he had some options.

The original thought of taking a commercial flight out of Dubai or Abu Dhabi to anywhere in Europe and then travel on to Spain as the ideal place to 'chill out', sort out the grey matter and possibly find a solution to his current predicament loomed large. However, the simple act of taking a commercial flight, even in a last minute booking would place him in a form of quarantine for several hours whilst in the air, giving Raza valuable time to arrange for an unsolicited welcome wherever he happened to land. He felt sure that one of the more fanatical elements of the Rev Guard or Khuds, may already be on their way to have a conversation with him, or even worse, one of the hard line terrorist organisations, with whom there would be

Chapter Twenty Six – On The Run

no conversation at all. The United States had also been considered. Declan had good contacts there and America was a big place to get lost in. However, in general, this option was discarded for the same reason as the first.

The last carefully considered option was one that he hoped Raza and his associates may not have thought of. Instead of putting as much distance as possible between him and Iran, he would sneak up and hide behind its back door.

He would fly himself to Hyderabad, just north east of Karachi and then move up to Quetta, tucked in behind the Afghanistan border where he could simply disappear. He had never flown to Hyderabad before, although he knew his way in to Karachi quite well. The airport was on the south side of the town and easy to find on his charts. There he could buy just about anything he wanted, including a new passport, new identity and anonymity. He could get rid of the aeroplane, get himself a four wheel drive of some description and probably move north to Peshawar where – in exchange for some US Dollars - the Mujahideen would ensure he was protected from prying eyes.

Declan did have a couple of contacts at the main Mujahideen base in Badaber, about twenty odd kilometres north of Peshawar. He had met, a few years previously, a member of the Saudi Arabian construction giant, Bin Ladin whilst attending a contractor's conference in Dammam. Declan knew this tall, elegant, quietly spoken man had some fairly high up links to the Mujahideen, fighting the Soviets in Afghanistan. He was hoping that spreading a little money around would allow him to cash in on these 'connections' and although the CIA was pouring millions in to the coffers of the 'struggle', he was hoping that a few dollars more would always be welcome.

It wasn't the perfect answer, but it was definitely the best one he had come with so far.

Declan picked up his car phone and filed a verbal flight plan from Abu Nar to Fujeriah on the East coast. This would not raise any eyebrows as he often flew over to the tiny landing strip at Fujeriah and would regularly arrange to meet business contacts travelling up from the Oman at the nearby hotel. Once over the mountains, he would drop down and head out over the Gulf of Oman. All he needed was a head start.

The trip through the security gate at the General Aviation section of Abu Nar airport was without any particular complication. Declan received his normal polite salute from the armed guard's upon the production of his security pass. He had phoned ahead to have Hotel Yankee pulled out of the climate controlled hanger and parked on the service apron.

The car park for the GA operations centre was at the

Chapter Twenty Six – On The Run

front of the building and he nosed the Mercedes in to his private and paid for parking space, jumping out of the car and retrieving the two now bulging bags from the rear seat. Acknowledging a wave from the receptionist behind the ultra modern chrome and smoked glass booking desk, Declan turned left in the building to the changing rooms. He opened his locker, took out his old RAF flying suit, stripped off his dark grey safari top and trousers and eased himself in to it. He always wore his flying suit if a particular trip was to be a long one. It was comfortable and tailored for someone sitting down. It had loads of pockets and two plastic covered knee pads, useful for making navigation and approach notes when entering controlled airspace.

Through the window, providing an unobstructed view of the main hanger and apron, Declan could see his aeroplane some hundred or so metres away. He walked out to the reception desk with his two bags, signing for a full load of fuel and his flight plan.

'Have a good trip Declan' the very good looking and particularly efficient female receptionist offered, accompanied by a particularly engaging smile.

'I will. Thanks Angela' he replied.

He was well known to all the staff at Aero Gulf Services. He would normally take time to partake in a bit of banter with Angela, but today was not the day for it. Today Declan was focused. He picked up his bags, one in each hand, tapped his Ray Ban Aviator glasses to the bridge of his nose, pushed his way through the terminal doors and out on to the apron.

Declan squinted in bright sunlight, despite the masking protection of his darkened pilot's glasses. He walked without any particular hurry toward his aeroplane noticing one of the ground staff dressed in a white boiler suit leaving the hanger as he did so.

The boiler suited individual began to walk toward him.

With the sun high and directly behind him, the figure was difficult to make out in detail. It did not appear to be his usual mechanic, Abdulla. This man was much larger than him and moved awkwardly. The two men were advancing steadily toward one another and now Declan had begun to feel a little uneasy. He definitely did not know the individual heading purposely in his direction with what now appeared to be quite a clumsy gait. He was large, his boiler suit was fully zipped up, which was unusual in the thirty degree heat pouring off the apron surface. As he got closer, Declan realised that this stranger was unusually bulky round his middle. The hairs on the back of his neck stood up in warning. His brain sprinted through the possibilities, but for some reason he kept on walking forward, as if in some kind of daze.

The man approaching was now close enough for him to make out he definitely was Asian and sweating profusely. He had both hands in the side pockets of the

Chapter Twenty Six – On The Run

particularly clean and seemingly iron pressed boiler suit. Declan stopped, his brain sending out massive danger signals. *He* was sweating now and it began to pour down his face in a warm uninterrupted stream. Adrenalin was flowing at a pace!

Flight or fight?

He dropped the bags and stood stock still as the dripping, scarily expressionless individual approached and finally stopped two metres away.

There was a moment of frozen silence where all other noise appeared blocked out by the amplified sound of heavy, un-rhythmic breathing emanating from the stranger now standing squarely in front of him. He took his left hand slowly from his pocket and carefully lowered the zip on the boiler suit to waist level.

The four wired explosive packs, each the size of a small quarter loaf of bread were wrapped in brown plastic sticky tape. They were held in custom made pockets added to a crudely made, soiled canvas waistcoat. Strangely, above all the thoughts that were speeding uncontrollably through Declan's mind at that particular moment, the most overriding was that if the packs contained C3 plastic explosive, or something similar, they would make a hell of a bang.

The profusely sweating, impassive Asian man standing stock still in front of him spoke in heavily accented English.

'Mr Declan Doyle?' Declan nodded in silent reply,

fearing what might be concealed in the right hand pocket of the boiler suit.

He was about to find out.

His eyes were drawn down as everything within this terrifying scene was now being assimilated in slow motion. Declan had been in a similar place once before, a place where time stands still and yet - races by as frame by frame, he observed the right hand being carefully removed from the boiler suit pocket, pulling with it one red and one black bare ended wire.

He looked quickly down at the bags resting at his feet, panic welling up inside, a blender of emotions. Was there time? It was too late for 'flight'… so there was only 'fight' left. Would the suicide bomber standing stock still before him shout 'Allah O Akbar' before ……?

Declan knew what was supposed to come next. But was the end to arrive so soon?

~~~~~~~~
~~~~

Chapter Twenty Seven
A Near Miss

Time now physically stood still in a world of eerie silence, all sounds of a busy International airport blocked as the finest milliseconds of time were being calculated; time to dip down and grab the Browning Hi-Power, just visible near the open zip top of the soft bag resting at his feet just to his side; time to grab the vacillating hand clutching the two bare cables and simply wrench it off; time to grab a throat and choke it until there was only a lifeless and inactive body left laying on the shimmering hot tarmac surface in front of him. Where was that oh so valuable time.

The sheer panic welling up inside, ice cold tentacles of utter fright closing firmly round the senses, knowing that this was finally the day his world would come crashing down and he would be consigned to oblivion forever.

The priceless micro seconds ticked by.

Declan was counting them.

In some strange way, as thousands of distorted and cluttered images flashed through his mind, knowing that these were to be his last living seconds on God's earth, he was overcome by an unexpected warming, comforting feeling and an irrepressible smile began to

Chapter Twenty Seven – A Near Miss

form on a grey, drained face as the two men faced one another with death playing a deadly waiting game between them. The bomber did not understand the smile; did not understand the stillness of the man in front of him; he was confused. He was in a semi-trance like state.

It was time.

Declan knew it too, as the bomber's head moved in ultra slow motion, diverting the manic frozen gaze from the face of the unbelieving infidel and down toward his right side. Declan's focus moved in perfect synchronization with his adversary as now two pairs of eyes rested upon the red and black bare ended cables protruding from the bomber's wavering hand.

They began to move gradually closer. The expected shout of praise to a higher exaltation did come, but Declan didn't hear it.

The two wires made contact.

There was a small, barely imperceptible spark. Two hearts stopped, eyes tightly closed, hands trembling uncontrollably. Declan's last thought at that final defining second of that death defining moment was of Penny … and then … nothing happened.

Declan waited for what seemed an extraordinarily long time for something. He didn't know what it was he was waiting for but his eyes remained firmly closed.

It was in fact less than a single second. When he

opened them the bomber was staring at him, eyes wide, bulging and manic in a total and bewildering sense of disbelief. It was a frighteningly haunting, quizzically desperate look on the face of a man totally prepared to die, a look that stamped itself in Declan's mind as if delivered with a flaming red hot branding iron.

He screamed out loud, a long releasing sound as he felt rather than heard something pass very close to his left ear.

It was moving at over twelve hundred and fifty feet per second.

Suddenly a red weeping spot appeared just above the right eye of the panic stricken bomber, now standing shaking violently in front of him. The spot was no larger than the diameter of a ten cent coin and as he watched, it began to change shape and grow bigger.

The bomber's head then jerked back so violently and so quickly that Declan, struggling hard to absorb all that was going on, felt the Jihadist's neck must surely have been broken.

The boiler suited body sank to the floor in a single jerking, uncontrolled movement as Declan, rooted to the spot, turned his head to look behind him and then followed through with a one eighty degree twisting movement until he was down on one knee, left hand in his overstuffed soft bag, searching for the cool, comforting butt of the Browning.

He steadied himself and used the back of a trembling

Chapter Twenty Seven – A Near Miss

right hand to wipe his sweat laden eyes, desperately refocusing on the figure standing about twenty meters away, between himself and the GA Terminal.

His hand remained inside the pale blue bag as the still undetermined, heavy looking character slowly dropped raised arms and placed the silenced nine millimeter hand gun back in to the side pocket of an annoyingly familiar light brown safari suit; a suit that looked from such a short distance, as if the wearer had slept in it for more than a day or two. Finally words were spoken.

'So the old fart … is not such an old fart … after all … young Declan!' the voice shouted in a theatrical Irish accent.

Declan was speechless, partly from fear of what might come next and partly from a dawning recognition of the crumpled suited, grey haired individual standing on the baking apron surface in front of him. The voice came from the gradually clearing outline, now in focus and fully lit by a lowering, early afternoon, carrot sun.

'Maybe I *do* have bad breath boy … but not a bad shot eh?

'Well, well, well, Paddy … did you come to save a life or claim a trophy?'

The delivery was decidedly shaky but the question came with confidence; the 'flight or fight' choice still in 'fight' mode as his hand closed firmly over the Browning, with thumb and forefinger searching for the side mounted safety catch. 'If you are searching for a weapon of some kind in that bloody hold-all Declan Doyle, I should be careful if I were you'

His head turned and looked up to his left.

'You may find that there are some not so friendly and particularly prying eyes focused on you right now … from that control tower'. Declan looked up sharply at the angled and concealing slabs of darkened glass, reflecting the ant like activities of the busy commercial apron below.

Who could tell? Paddy may be right. He relaxed his grip on the gun and flicked the safety catch back on.

'What's the deal Paddy?'

The question was simple and so was the answer.

'There is no deal my greedy and often very rude friend! Yes, if my memory serves me well … very rude indeed. You came here to fly away … so go on - fly away - simply fuck off'.

Declan turned to the body of the suicide bomber now laying motionless in an awkward, graceless and distorted pile on the dusted black surface.

'… and what about him? - You killed a man in full view of possibly hundreds of people. Have you a plan for that?'

'The choice is yours. The longer you stand here talking about it, the quicker someone will realize there may be a dead man on the tarmac and start to ring a few alarm bells. Go! … Go now and never come back here Declan … never …! If you do, you know what will

Chapter Twenty Seven – A Near Miss

be waiting for you. That bastard Raza will never give up. He's lost face - the Ayatollah's money - and now Iran has possibly lost the fucking war. You have purchased yourself a very large bucket of shit Mr. Doyle and I only hope you now have the strength to carry it on some necessarily broad shoulders. Go now for Christ's sake. I am more than capable of handling everything here. My *people* are more than capable of handling everything here!'

His voice had now become raised in a level of heightened frustration.

'My *people* want to give you a chance … you damned idiot!'

Would there be a word of thanks? Paddy suspected not as he watched the Englishman with an Irish name pick up the two bulky bags, turn quickly and head with firmly controlled steps towards his aircraft, sitting waiting with the door open only thirty or so meters away.

As Declan approached he looked round him nervously. One side of the sliding hanger door set was open and parked behind the closed section was a brand new, pristine white, Canadair Challenger executive jet. Unusually, there appeared to be no staff in or around the entrance to the half opened Aero Gulf hanger. He knew he didn't have time to worry about it as he clambered up the short steps and within a minute was strapping himself in to the left hand seat of Hotel

Yankee. He leant over to shut and lock the access door and then, in the sweltering heat of the closed cabin, clipped up his restraints and was ready to go.

Harness pulled tight, fuel primer worked and locked, switches on, fuel pump on, magnetos on, a quick look round to make sure no one could walk in to an unexpectedly rotating propeller - and time to hit the start button.

A couple of stilted half turns and then all cylinders fired in a puff of light blue smoke. Brakes off - then a hard right turn to the exit and on to the General Aviation taxiway. Declan made a radio call to the tower to confirm permission to enter the main taxiway and takeoff runway. He reached down for the flap lever. Second notch: twenty five degrees and ready to go. The scratchy sounding, distant, ethereal voice gave a warning.

'Hotel Yankee. Please hold at threshold runway one-two for turbulence procedures from previously departed BA Tri-Star …'

The words trailed off. Declan was not listening. He was still nervous. He needed to get away … now! His mind was racing as he checked the engine instruments He riskily calculated he should, with a bit of luck, be up, away and above any dropping clear air turbulence swirls. With half flap and full revs, the little Cherokee could be up and climbing hard through one thousand

Chapter Twenty Seven – A Near Miss

feet before covering one third of the runway length.

He kicked the rudder bar hard and pushed the throttle lever forward to the stop. The hardy little aircraft leaped forward and clawed at the air with an eager leap as Declan, anxiously watching the air speed indicator pulled the control column back and both man and machine were off the ground. The earphones were filling with chatter as he heard his call sign being repeated again and again. He pulled them off. He did not want to communicate with anyone just now. His heart was pumping, adrenalin freely flowing; he had done it.

Suddenly, there was a flash and a muffled explosive sound behind him. At only five hundred feet and climbing, Declan banked the aero plane into a dangerous turn as a rumbling shock wave hit him, sending rivet popping shudders through the durable aluminum airframe.

He needed to see what was happening on the ground, but as he looked back the whole of the GA Terminal was shrouded in an ominous black and grey cloud surging upwards in an attempt to form a widening flat topped vortex.

'For God's sake … Paddy! …' he shouted out loud; the earphones resting on his lap emitting a cacophony of sounds as everyone on the open frequencies began to talk at once. 'Damn it … Paddy' he said again, quietly to himself. 'What the hell have you done ... you silly old duffer'

A reluctant tear formed, followed by another as he pulled up the two notches of flap, climbed through one thousand feet and set a heading directly east toward the mountains of Fujeriah.

~~~~~~~~
~~~~

Chapter Twenty Eight
The Escape

Paddy Doherty watched motionlessly as his eyes stared through and beyond the scene of Declan Doyle literally *driving* his aeroplane at speed out of the nearby taxiway. The crystal sound of a high pitched voice, screaming something unintelligible, cut across the hurting noise of the Lycoming engine as it revved louder and louder, pushing the careering red striped flying machine out on to the main runway.

He turned. It was the rather attractive uniformed GA receptionist standing behind him and in front of the terminal doors. He raised his head slightly as some form of recognition toward the near hysterical receptionist before turning back to walk the few metres distance in the direction of the still body of the suicide bomber. He made the approach carefully. The right hand was exposed as were the two bare ended wires still clutched within it. They were not touching.

The body was warm and damp. He bent over the boiler suited figure, took a grubby handkerchief from his pocket, pulled the wires apart and carefully wrapped the cotton material, formed in to a bandanna like dressing, round one wire to act as an imperfect, but what the Irishman thought to be, a well improvised

Chapter Twenty Eight – The Escape

insulator. The entry hole above the right eye of the motionless corpse was that of a nine millimetre bullet fired from Paddy's personal weapon, a Beretta M9 US military issue hand gun. He did not want to disturb the body by lifting the head, but instinctively knew that the high velocity bullet would have penetrated the skull, passed through the brain and exited out the other side. The exit wound would be much larger as was evidenced by the growing mere of dark red, sticky blood now forming a large pool on the ground. The suicide bomber would have died instantly. It was an excellent shot and Paddy knew it.

He turned once again as he heard Hotel Yankee screaming down the main runway, gathering speed at such a rate, the little aircraft was off the ground in what seemed like a couple of hundred metres. Paddy smiled inwardly as he visualised Declan fighting so desperately hard to un-stick the little aircraft from the overheated and blackened ground surface. Turning back to the body, he angled his head to obtain a better view of the bomb material strapped to the unfortunate, but now deceased terrorist. From the red, brick orange colour of the explosive showing between the brown wrapping tape, Paddy assumed that the 'plastique' material was Semtex H - and there was a lot of it. He was right.

The constant shouts and screams of the distraught receptionist were becoming more invasive. Then it happened.

The primary force of the explosion lifted the bodies of the bomber and his executioner high in the air, with instant ignition temperatures of over two thousand degrees Celsius - and consuming both eagerly. The high energy, high temperature shock wave followed in a millisecond, moving outward in a three hundred and sixty degree arc at speeds in excess of seven thousand feet every single second. Angela, the hysterical receptionist, literally only metres away from the centre of the blast, was lifted up whole, carried over several metres back toward the GA Terminal and slammed through the half inch thick glass viewing windows of the departure lounge until her charred, twisted and sliced body was lain inert, thrown carelessly up against a high density block wall that itself was cracked from top to bottom with the resulting, nearly unstoppable explosive force. The closed door section of the Aero Gulf maintenance hangar was itself no match in its attempt to hold back the speeding pressure wave. Initially it held … then buckled in the middle.

Finally it gave way.

When it became airborne, four and a half tons of fragmented steel and aluminium smashed a path through the obstructive four million dollar Canadair jet as if it were simply empty, functionless, shining white cardboard. The part of the shockwave encountering little or no resistance screamed at thousands of miles an hour through the hanger, consumed everything in its

Chapter Twenty Eight – The Escape

path, leaving behind only fire, total destruction and the dead, burnt and dying bodies of eleven mechanics and several other unfortunate hanger staff who happened to be on duty on that hapless, ill-fated day. The oxygen hungry fireball was spreading further, out on to the runway and simultaneously in the opposite direction, toward the main commercial apron; toward a bank of parked aeroplanes, either loading or disgorging some several hundred passengers.

~~~~~~

Colonel Oliver Gresham stood unobtrusively behind the senior air traffic controller in the observation tower at Abu Nar Airport. He had his military high magnification field glasses up to his eyes and was carefully studying the scene at the General Aviation Terminal. The stage was set. The main players had not yet arrived. The Colonel was pleased, though tight lipped. He had driven over from Abu Dhabi earlier that afternoon after hearing about what had happened on the Geneveh Project.

Gresham had information from his paid contact at Abu Nar Air Traffic that Declan Doyle had filed a flight plan to the East Coast for that afternoon. He simply couldn't risk it if Doyle was on the run. He had to stop him. He wanted the cocky little Englishman confined to somewhere where he had control. Perhaps only when

Declan Doyle was a dead man would Colonel Oliver Gresham be assured that the Geneveh Project was finally and totally, scuppered.

An incident with the Abu Dhabi Traffic Police relating to speeding on the way to Abu Nar had consumed a valuable half an hour as he quickly realised that waving an American Military ID at the local police force would be of no assistance whatsoever. Americans were tolerated in the Gulf for their knowledge of the oil business, but American Military were generally unwelcome and in circumstances such as these - it showed. Colonel Oliver Gresham was very pissed off – and unfortunately for him – it had showed.

The lightweight field glasses scanned across the main commercial apron to the General Aviation Terminal where Declan's little single engine aeroplane had been pushed out to sit close by the edge of the service apron, in front of a half open hanger.

Good!

The aircraft was still there, which meant that Doyle was still in Abu Nar. He dropped the glasses and turned to move toward the internal elevator that would take him down to the ground floor and the Met Office. There he could exit air-side out on to the main apron and make the uninterrupted walk to the Aero Gulf hanger. Gresham pressed the call button of the elevator and looked up to see where the service may be among

Chapter Twenty Eight – The Escape

the choice of twelve floors. At that moment, a telephone rang on the desk of the senior controller, who answered swiftly and after listening wordlessly for a few seconds said

'Yes - he is still here'

He waved the handset in the air, advising the American Colonel that the call was for him. Gresham turned back impatiently.

'Gresham?' There was only silence from the other end.

'Gresham here ... who the hell is this?'

A cultured, only slightly accented voice replied in perfect English.

'Leave him ... leave Doyle alone ... he is mine!'

The tone was somehow dark and menacing.

This was no request

'I know what you think you are doing - but you will *not* be doing it today Colonel. There are lessons that some of us have yet to learn my friend and where I come from, we have a saying that ... *"lessons not learnt in blood are soon forgotten"*. Hopefully, I make myself clear. Leave now, or I can promise you this hot Middle Eastern sun will set finally on your non-believing world ... and you will no longer cast a shadow in it!'

The line was disconnected abruptly with only a soft purring tone left to accompany a confused and laboured thought process. Gresham put the handset back on the cradle and politely thanked the controller for the use of it. The elevator bell chimed mutely in the background and he sensed rather than heard the doors slide gently open. Gresham had a feeling. It was a very bad feeling. He ignored the elevator doors and after a delay of a second or two, they closed again quietly. The filing cabinet of memories, holding a lifetime of data collected throughout a career of subterfuge, double cross and assassination finally came up trumps. He had heard this quite distinguishable voice before and on one particular occasion, in the aftermath of the disastrous Operation Eagle Claw. It had been a voice he felt was far too close for comfort. The Colonel was a man who was rarely taken by anything other than cold, sober, analytical thought – and right now, the cold and disturbingly emotionless voice at the other end of the telephone was making him think!

He stood stock still, for a minute or more, eyes unfocused, ignoring all around him. Finally he came to a conclusion.

The Colonel turned again in the direction of the GA service apron and raised his olive green, rubberised binoculars. Although the sun was beginning to sink steadily lower on the horizon, he could clearly make out the exit doors of the Terminal, set in a long wall of darkened one way glass. The doors opened and Declan Doyle walked through. He was struggling a little with what looked to be a well packed flight bag and a large blue soft holdall, the size of a standard navy kitbag. It

Chapter Twenty Eight – The Escape

was bulging and the top zip remained open. He did not appear to be in any particular hurry.

The American military officer smiled imperceptibly as he pulled back the zoom and focus to take in Doyle's mechanic walking across the apron from the hangar to meet him. The man moved awkwardly with hands in the pockets of what appeared to be a 'straight out of the packet' white workman's cover-all. He didn't falter in either pace or direction. Gresham calculated they would meet about halfway between the two buildings.

The figures of interest stopped only a metre or so apart. They both stood unnervingly still, without conversation, for what seemed to be a long puzzling moment. Then, suddenly, the mechanic pulled down the front zip of his white overall with his left hand. The Colonel knew instinctively that something bad was about to happen - and he was right.

He zoomed in hard on the body area exposed by the now fully opened zip. The distance limited ant particularly clear view, but he had seen suicide bombers before and there was little doubt in his mind that this was one.

Gresham instinctively moved quickly right up to one of the dark and angled control tower windows and refocused the fine Bausch & Lomb optics. The two human images now filled the coated lenses. Something was happening. The mechanic was pulling his right hand from the side pocket of his coverall. He was holding something. His mouth opened as if shouting at a motionless Declan Doyle.

'What the fuck ...?' Gresham cried and then the man in the white overalls fell backwards to the ground - like a stone.

'I'll be damned ... what the hell is going on here?'

He refocused the glasses, zooming out to provide a wider view and there, ten, maybe fifteen metres directly behind Declan stood a recognisable figure.

Paddy Doherty was in the act of lowering both his arms and fiddling what appeared to be a hand gun into the flap pocket of a crumpled cotton safari suit. The American was struggling to take it all in. He dropped the glasses and rubbed his eyes. What he had just seen was a suicide bomber, for now he was sure that's what he was, being shot dead at near point blank range by a retired ex British Army pensioner, in the middle of the afternoon, on the apron of an International Airport; in full view of maybe thousands of people.

He simply couldn't believe or understand it. What was even more incomprehensible was that as he looked round the busy interior of the control tower, no one else appeared to have seen or picked up on what had happened.

'Shit!' he shouted out loud and some heads turned in his direction disapprovingly. The binoculars were again raised. Declan was down on one knee, facing the retired

Chapter Twenty Eight – The Escape

British military intelligence officer and some sort of conversation was taking place. It was a short one. The Englishman picked up his two bags and moved quickly to his aeroplane. He didn't look back.

Bags were thrown in ahead of him as he clambered aboard, slamming the door shut and starting the engine. The little aircraft looked absolutely tiny from the height of the observation tower as it swung round and literally raced across the apron, past a still stationary Paddy Doherty and in the direction of the main taxiway. By now, Gresham was at the elevator again, pressing the button and willing the lift cage to rise quickly. The first call in to the tower for Hotel Yankee was being answered as the elevator doors closed behind him.

The ride down was interrupted twice as four more individuals took up space in the cramped confines of the elevator cage. A normally calm and collected Colonel Gresham was perspiring with frustration in the gently scented, air-conditioned atmosphere. As the doors opened on the ground floor he pushed rudely forward raising a comment from one of the manhandled occupants.

His mind was not on the derogatory remarks echoing from the elevator, or the busy 'Met' room as he continued to push a way through the several aircrews crowding the front counter. His mind was on the situation playing out on the broad expanse tarmac on the General Aviation apron some hundred or so metres away.

He burst through the Met Office door on to the aircraft ramp area. The heat hit him unexpectedly. He paused, looking round calmly, getting his bearings and turning toward the concrete pathway between the two apron areas. Through the opaque, floating heat haze he could just make out the body on the ground. The standing figure was now moving toward the body. Gresham had no weapon on him. What would the slightly eccentric British Ex-Colonel do if approached?

The gun was probably still in his pocket and although with only an effective range of about fifty or so metres, Paddy was a good shot. He had just proved it. Gresham knew he was wasting valuable seconds thinking about it as the distant figure now appeared to be stopped and bending over the shadowy corpse of the obviously deceased suicide bomber. He set off at a run.

The flash from the explosion literally blinded him. Milliseconds later the noise created by the pressure wave deafened him. As the radiating shock wave travelled over his flailing body, it threw him to the granite hard concrete pathway with such force that literally every bone in his body was broken.

Then came the heat!

There was no feeling of pain as the two thousand degree fireball swept over him, wrenching every last dying breath of air from collapsed lungs before leaving

Chapter Twenty Eight – The Escape

his body a black cindered outline on a scorched limestone grey background. The final conscious, reluctant and dying thoughts rattling through Colonel Gresham's mind were shrouded in the last words he would ever hear from Mohsen Raza, head of the Army of the Guards of the Islamic Revolution…

'Leave him … leave Doyle alone … he is mine!'

~~~~~~~~~
~~~~

Epilogue

The events of November fourth, nineteen eighty seven, in the straits between Geneveh town and Kharg Island, combined with the world financial crisis triggered on Black Monday, October nineteenth, would create a set of circumstances that had the capacity to change the shape of the world forever. In less than a year, the Iran Iraq war would come to a diplomatically stumbling end as a result of UN Security Council resolution 598. This resolution led to a ceasefire on August twentieth, 1988. Iran was being strangled economically with increasingly limited means of exporting crude oil or refined product in sufficient volumes to finance a cash hungry war that was going nowhere. Ayatollah Khomeini died on June third, 1988, creating enough political space for the Iranian clerics to come to terms with a crumbling financial and social system within Iran, allowing them to find a way to agree to resolution 598 without losing that most important of Middle Eastern qualities - face.

Casualties on both sides were horrific although difficult to confirm. The best estimates are that more than one and a half million people were either killed or severely injured as a result of the prolonged campaign in which the superpowers stood by for more than seven years and did nothing. They had their own agenda. The war had driven oil prices down and that was good for

Epilogue

their economic health. However, this happy situation masked a deep seated problem with the overall state of the western capitalist economies when the world's financial securities systems collapsed on that fateful day, entered into the annals of economic history as Black Monday.

This was a severe and unexpected wakeup call. The US Dollar had been declining against other major currencies since 1985. Oil prices after the crash continued to fall, despite OPEC quota agreements, as certain major producers in the Gulf pumped more and more. The Gulf Arab War needed a resolution and with a certain level of reluctance, the Americans, the Russians and to some extent the Chinese political machines began to exert pressure on the two warring parties.

After hostilities were officially declared over, the infighting began. The Iranians, having literally no one to borrow money from during the previous eight years, were financially decimated but now had a chance to rebuild a badly bruised economy. With the Ayatollah dead, there were few political egos to satisfy, so they simply got on with it. Iraq however, was a much more complex matter. Saddam Hussein had been sucked up to by the Americans who had provided covert military assistance to the Iraqi's during the war as well as carrying out actual military operations against the Iranians. He had borrowed money to finance a war that did not give him the territory or the resources he had planned and that many western governments had told him he could have. All he had to do was to beat the Iranians. He was pompous and arrogant and as the Americans were to find out to their displeasure, very difficult to deal with after the fighting ended.

The Kuwaitis, who had lent Saddam more than eighty billion dollars to finance his war machine and had over produced oil during the conflict, thereby keeping Iraq's revenues down, now wanted their money back. As far as he was concerned, he had won the war although no territory was finally gained by Iran or Iraq, as the UN resolution required both sides to return back to pre-war borders. As far as Saddam was concerned, he was the glorious victor and would accept no other recording of the outcome.

He now had a massive war machine at his disposal, well trained and battle hardened. As a result, he advised the Kuwaiti's that he would not be paying back any 'loans' that they felt were due to them as he regarded such funds as a straightforward gift to a brother, Muslim neighbour, a neighbour in deed and a neighbour in need.

The Kuwaiti's were furious and insistent, but the answer to the problem would turn out to be amazingly simple for the territory hungry megalomaniac Saddam Hussein. So, on August second, nineteen ninety, he invaded Kuwait and made it the nineteenth province of

Epilogue

Iraq. The reason provided to the impotent super powers was that Kuwait was illegally slant drilling for oil in Iraqi oil fields and literally stealing the liquid black gold from under Saddam's very feet.

This was to be the first world changing event as a result of the Gulf Arab War and the way it was ended. It would also be the trigger for other horrific events that would be recorded in their detail on the headstones of a new age of peacemakers.

THE END

The Doksany Legacy

The sequel to The Geneveh Project is now available in paperback and E-Book entitled 'The Doksany Legacy'. This story tracks Declan's progress through Asia, on to Europe and back once again to the Middle East, in search of a new fortune to save his business, complete the contract at Geneveh and therefore save his life!

www.quentincope.co.uk

Printed in Great Britain
by Amazon